Deathlinks

E. M. Duesel

outskirtspress

DENVER, COLORADO

Outskirts Press, Inc.
http://www.outskirtspress.com

ISBN: 978-1-4787-6024-5

Outskirts Press and the "OP" logo are trademarks belonging to Outskirts Press, Inc.

PRINTED IN THE UNITED STATES OF AMERICA

To Tina, Bill, Stephanie and Jim
for having faith in me when I had none

"*After Jesus rose from death early on Sunday,
he appeared first to Mary Magdalene from whom
he had driven out seven demons. She went and told
his companions. They were mourning and crying;
and when they heard her say that Jesus was alive
and that she had seen him, they did not believe her.*

*After this, Jesus appeared in a different manner
to two of them while they were on their way to
the country. They returned and told the others,
but these would not believe.*

*Last of all, Jesus appeared to the eleven disciples
as they were eating. He scolded them, because they
did not have faith and because they were too stubborn
to believe those who had seen him alive.*"

Mark 16: 9-1

Chapter One

Fletch, Call Me!

Fletcher slammed his pen down on the desk. Why for God's sake didn't he just say it? When you lose faith that's it, by God, that's it! You lose, no more chances, game's over. Fletcher Hodges could not write another word of this bullshit sermon. He couldn't even understand the mystery of life himself, much less try and explain it to others. He lost faith. The faith that sustained him through so many hardships, so many times of personal sorrow just "flew the coop" as his grandfather use to put it. *Get it together, man. Write the damn sermon.*

Life goes on with its seasons and unexpected changes, its grand, majestic miracles, and specifically its unavoidable disenchantments, and every once in a while one cannot help wondering why? Why do we exist and is our existence just a test to see how much we can endure?

He could take what the world dished out to him. After all, he didn't have such a bad upbringing. He had a mom and dad who loved him, a corny, fun-loving sister who idolized him, and the best text-book big brother any guy could ask for. Like that day he was blinded in one eye from a misguided fly ball at the ball diamond, he turned to his faith in God and the people who loved him to get him through. His experience became a metaphysical miracle where something or some-one lifted him out of despair, and it didn't even come as a surprise to him. *Yeah, use that.* Fletch continued to write.

Humans bear the most unbearable hardships and constantly confront the confusion of cross-purposed relationships. Indeed, people are the hardiest of God's creatures.

It was about this time at age thirteen that God started working in

Fletch's life. He had big plans for this high-spirited child, and it would not be long before Fletcher Hodges would become one of God's soldiers. His desire to serve God increased steadily as he possessed an uncanny ability to show others how important faith was in their lives. As Fletch remembered his calling and all of the important milestones of faith he experienced in his life, a cement wall built up in his soul separating him from his faith. He now lived in the thick of sin and passive acceptance of human degradation, poverty, and misery. Fletch's soul simmered with discontent and he continued writing fueled with passion.

But there are those whose feelings are too dear to take all of the injustice in the world and that insurmountable heap of judgments, labeling and misunderstanding. There are those who break under the weight of the cruelty inflicted by others and who then bury the hurt deep within, causing them mental and physical illness. Some can no longer go on because life simply chose to randomly rearrange their lives.

As an inner-city minister, he was very involved in community affairs. He was on boards for homeless shelters, orphanages, and shelters for domestic violence. The weekly trip to the domestic violence shelter was always his most fulfilling ministry. Working with the children, he saw every child as a new beginning whose very presence affects the current dynamic of the universe. They are the reminiscence of innocence—those days when everything and everyone is so simple.

Today, the day that would change his life forever, a new child was brought into the shelter. Fletcher could not believe what he saw. Annie was two years old. Her face was bloodied and beaten and her head was still bleeding through the bandages wrapped around her little head. She had been thrown against a wall and stomped on. After all of this, she endured the rape of her infant body. This sweet innocent child didn't look at him. He wasn't sure whether she couldn't or she just didn't care. At any rate, that poor baby was victim to the theft of her being; her very essence. Annie's haunting eyes provoked a dismal nausea in Fletch's gut, but he fought to find meaning.

But, my friends, it takes many personalities to make up the world; person-alities which are crafted and molded by our experiences. Our personalities are gifts from God. We are born into the universe as a package of flesh and bones and a bit of that breath acknowledged as the soul. That light is what separates the knowing from the unknowing conscience. This is the part of us that is also a part of God. It is reflected through the eyes of every individual who walks and only a tiny number of the population truly understands its power—a power that can affect the very course of a life and the lives of many others. Combined, these souls, good and evil, have dubious results; some where their owners know full well what they are doing, but some who just plod along on their path, liv-ing in faith . . . bla,bla-bla,bla-bla.

Fletcher was so lost in his own painful thoughts and resolve to fin-ish his sermon that he didn't hear the footsteps of his best friend.

"Fletcher, are you almost ready to leave?" Sister Kathy rounded the archway of the rectory library where Fletcher was working. She stood there in her blue jeans, sweatshirt, and a baseball hat. The changes the Roman Catholic Church made post Vatican II sure created the birth of some strange clericals. Sister Kathy was one of the most vivacious persons he had ever known and her zeal in combating the evils of the world was hard to match. He really admired her and considered her one of his best friends.

"Oh, hi, Kath. I didn't hear you come in."

"Mrs. Schmitz let me in. Hey, are you still coming to the anti-abortion rally tonight? We really wanted representation from all of the churches in town, and your presence is powerful with the teens; maybe not with me so much, but you know, the kids kind of like you." Kathy grinned from ear to ear, snapping her gum and nudging Fletch with her elbow.

"Kathy, after seeing Annie at the shelter, my faith in what we are rallying against is a little shaken. Did we ever find out more about who did this to her?"

"As a matter of fact, one of the policemen who transported Annie from the hospital to the shelter went in to see how she was doing. He told me they arrested her seventeen-year-old father for the assault."

"What? The child's father did this? Why would . . . how could a child's own father do such despicable things?"

"Fletcher, when children have children, all they can do is what they know. Sadly, the father was raised in the same dreadful environment. He probably has a history of abuse himself. I've been around this depressed part of the city for five years now. Sometimes it feels like it's been twenty. Without wanting to, you find yourself getting desensitized to most of these situations, but then out of nowhere, bam! One will twist the guts right out of you." Kathy put a comforting hand on her friend's shoulder and sighed, "I can't tell whether they gradually build up or what, but it just takes one to test a person's faith. I tell you, Fletch, faith is the only weapon we have to get us through. Faith that somehow, some way, God has a reason for allowing all of these things to happen."

"Kathy, this incident did that to me. How could a loving, omnipotent God allow such terrifying acts? How could He watch from His comfortable heaven and sanction this violence? This isn't war where soldiers are fighting for some damnedable cause that a greedy government cooked up . . ."

"But Fletch, this is a war and we are fighting it. We are fighting it for God."

"But we're talking about children carrying guns and knives and not thinking twice about using them. We're talking about the cold, ruthless beatings of innocent children for no other reason than they got on someone's nerves, or they were crying from hunger and the parent had no food to give them, so they just beat them out of their own helpless frustration. Who am I to think there is something that I can do to help these people, these souls with no faith, or worse yet, no desire to know God." Fletcher's hands were shaking. He still had not recuperated from his recent reverie and his vocal chords ached, and his voice crack as he spoke. Passion waned as scenes continued flashing through his mind; inconceivable scenes he witnessed over the last year in the inner-city slums. He saw things that made his stomach weak. His body trembled a little and he just couldn't let anyone see him like this. "Look, Kathy, I'm going to take a walk. You better go to the protest without me. I'll catch you later."

Fletcher skimmed past his astonished friend. Hands and forehead sweating, he made his way out the front door and onto the street with Kathy calling after him. After running a block or so, he found rest against a street lamp. He took a deep breath to cleanse his spirit of everything he just remembered.

As he continued to walk, better memories surfaced like the first time he met Kathy. It was crazy. The inner-city churches decided to come together and develop an ecumenical committee in order to strengthen the fight against drug abuse and violence. Kathy came strolling into the meeting with that jazzy walk of hers, dressed in her jeans and sweatshirt. Since the meeting was meant mostly for clergy, he went over to her and kindly suggested she leave because, ". . . this meeting was intended for the leaders and lay ministers of certain designated churches and perhaps you would feel more comfortable waiting for the follow-up meeting aimed at parishioners." He could not forget her broad smile and the snapping gum inside that smile as she proceeded to lay him out flat.

"Never fear, my man. Don't let the threads fool you. I am Sister Mary Kathleen from St. Charles Parish and I am the chair of this committee. Why don't you just have a seat there, so we can get this party started?"

It was then he realized God chose people from all walks of life and backgrounds to achieve His purpose. Kathy was as charismatic as she was unusual. They became very close friends and if it weren't for her vow of celibacy, they might have dated. He cherished the moments they shared heartfelt challenges and was honored she counted him in her circle of confidants. Her lack of conformity only made her arguments stronger and more acceptable to the people who lived in the area. She was filled with light when she spoke and her eyes reflected the love of the Holy Spirit, no matter how mischievous her smile. He really hated leaving her in a bind, but this faith crisis of his was getting out of control and he had to find a way to pacify it.

What was his life about and did he really trust a God who permitted such contemptible things to happen in His world? His doubts diluted his desire to represent God's love to people when he didn't believe in it.

Searching for answers, Fletcher walked all over the city through the night until his legs ached. Morning neared and he took time to stop into his church to pray a little. He resumed his walk past decrepit apartment buildings that smelled of urine and vomit, and were representative of the corruption of slum landlords. He walked past schools in disrepair and parks with makeshift playground equipment. He listened to the sounds of a discontented, suffering community; a community with no hope or faith left to heal the daily wounds inflicted upon it. He walked until it was daybreak.

Fletch tracked his way back to the parsonage, and the nearer he came the more certain he felt something wasn't right. Lights were still on in the house and cars were parked in the driveway and on the street. In the kitchen he discovered three members of the anti-abortion group huddled around the table staring into coffee mugs. His housekeeper, Mrs. Schmitz, was crying into her apron. When she spotted Fletcher, she ran into the other room sobbing.

Jonah King, one of Fletcher's parishioners, gazed up at him with sorrow and their eyes locked. His large black frame arose anguished out of his chair and walked over to Fletch, and his great strong hands held onto the minister's shoulders to stabilize him. "Fletcher, we don't know how to tell you this. Yesterday, at the rally, several pro-choice people got pushy. Well, you know Sister Kathy. She . . . well, she . . ."

"Jonah, what are you trying to say?" The blood in Fletcher's body ran cold.

"There was a riot last evening. It started out as a scuffle over a woman who had just come out of the clinic. Somehow, one of Sister's teens from the youth group got caught between two adults, one from each side. Sister Kathy pushed her way through the crowd trying to get to the kid. Well, you know how teenagers are. They have big mouths that let it all come out using no discretion. The teen yelled . . ." Jonah smothered tears as he tried to continue, "baby killer . . . and out from the crowd came this gunfire and . . . "

"Gunfire! For God's sake, Jonah! What happened? Where is Kathy?"

In smothered sobs, Jonah choked out, "She threw herself in front of the teen and . . . she's dead, Fletch! She's dead!"

Fletcher's knees hit the floor. Jonah tried to comfort him, but all Fletcher wanted to do was run again. He shook Jonah off and ran out the door into the morning sunshine. As Fletch ran, he wondered, *what good was a beautiful day when the inner spirit of mankind sucked. This is just cosmetics, Lord. Your world is like the beautiful actress who has all kinds of plastic surgery to enhance her looks, but inside she is a bogus bitch.* He ran past a young mother walking her child. He almost ran into a kid on a bike. Every scene seemed so senseless to him. Who would be next?

Fletcher ran until he couldn't draw another breath without wheezing in pain. Debilitated, he staggered and finally collapsed to find himself on the lawn of Kathy's parish church, St. Charles or "St. Chuck's" as she called it. Still wheezing and breathless, he was compelled to enter. It was dark and peaceful. He walked toward the altar, and the painful reality of what happened to his righteous friend came charging back. He stood there and carefully examined the cross with Jesus hanging on it. Iconic and unaccepted in his Presbyterian doctrine, it held a painful representation. There was his Lord, crowned with thorns, side lanced and bleeding from the nails in His feet and hands.

Fletch lost it. "Why did you die? Why did you go through all of that torture and pain? We still have the same bastards on earth as you did centuries ago! She's dead. One of your brave and beautiful soldiers is gone from this world and you did nothing to stop it. Some devil made them shoot her, is that it? Well, I don't buy it and I don't want to be one of your chosen anymore. Innocent people are being sacrificed, and for what?"

By this time, tears streamed down his face. Grief overwhelmed him as he sobbed. He crumpled to his knees, his eye patch flipped up, and he buried his head in his hands. Fletch's heart was broken. He lost his faith, he lost his friend, but most importantly, he lost his passion to love God.

Out of the darkness came stillness and a peculiar tranquility; the kind a baby experiences after crying long and hard before falling into a peaceful slumber on his mother's lap. A gentle hand rested on Fletch's shoulder causing him to look up. He fell backward in total astonishment. Kathy stood before him and a strange man stood beside her.

"Fix your eye patch, Buddy."

Flipping his eye patch down, he stood up. "Kathy! What the . . . are you still alive?"

"Nope. My body is as dead as those science projects you have stowed away in your frig. Fletch, whether you can believe it or not, God is omniscient and He does have a reason for all of these things. The big war has begun and my death had a purpose. God is with us and with you and has commissioned us to save souls—souls that would otherwise be lost because of bad judgment, not evil hearts. There will be many soldiers working on His side, but the souls we are charged with are considered kind of, well, recycled. The realm of evil knows of God's plan and is out to gather up and destroy as many of these unlucky souls as possible. Satan has already been dealing out his dirty work. This is Michael. In his life on earth his name was Michael Harrison. It is important you remember that, because you are to contact a very powerful woman. This woman knew Michael at the time when God chose her to be one of the go-betweens from our spiritual warriors and the, well, fleshy ones. Only by knowing his name will she believe you are sent by God."

"Wait, wait, how am I supposed to believe this? I could be hallucinating for all I know. You could be a delusion or, wow, shades of Ebenezer Scrooge."

"Fletcher," Michael moved forward. Fletcher jumped back as he gazed at the apparition in disbelief. "I was a minister. I understand what you are feeling. A person tends to look at only the visible picture and fails to encompass God's entire universe. Life is more than the life we have on earth. It is our total existence now and after our body dies. When our body dies, all we shed is a vessel. God has allowed evil to exist to separate the good and courageous hearts from the evil ones. He only wants goodness in the kingdom He has planned for us. God is leading us to the end of all physical bodies, the end of the world—Armageddon. He is granting a few of His most trusted, beloved children the honor of defending those souls that couldn't quite make it; couldn't quite withstand the weight of the world on their own. I have been sent to you because you, like me, are a minister of God's Word. God is granting you the honor of joining His holy troops."

Fletcher stood frozen in doubt. "How am I to rely on this? Holy troops? Are you kidding? What if this is just a mental collapse?"

"Oh, you big baby. You will go through much more than this before it's all over." Kathy just grinned in her impish way.

"Kathy, how do you explain the horrors God allows to go on every day? You've seen them as much, if not more, than I have. What about poor little Annie and her ignorant teenage father? How does God explain that?"

"There is a lot of suffering in the world, but listen, God has a reason for everything that happens, and you can't discount man's free will. Free will is a gift from God, and each of us decides whether to follow the right path or to follow a selfish, unloving one. Everyone has a spiritual path of learning, and situations occur in every life in order to purify the soul. Annie's father has now been given the chance to follow the right path for himself and his daughter. He is getting the counseling he needs and it will be up to him to change. He will be judged on what he does from now on. Meanwhile, there are those evil entities out there that want to disrupt these kinds of changes and they will work very hard against the light to keep souls in darkness."

Fletcher felt stupid. The answer was right there in front of him. Of course it's free will. Even though his Presbyterian upbringing may look at it from a different perspective, free will is free will. Were the dark spirits clouding his thinking? He was an ordained minister, for crying out loud. How could he have not seen such a simple answer? The realization clinched his resolve.

"What do I do now?"

"That-a-boy. I knew you just had a memory lapse. You will need to contact a Mrs. Emily Walker. She lives in Branchford, Alabama. All you have to do is mention Michael's name. She will fill you in on the rest."

As Michael and Kathy began to fade away, Fletcher couldn't move. He didn't want them to leave; yet, he really did. He shook his head, made a kind of garbling noise, and when he opened his eyes, Michael and Kathy were gone.

"Can I help you with something?" Fletcher, still paralyzed from the recent vision, choked back a snort. There in front of him was Sister Kathy's "Father Okeydoke." Kathy told him that when this man gave absolution after her confessions, he would pat her on the head and say, "Okeydokey, now. Go in peace."

After everything Fletch just experienced, seeing this darling man tickled him into laughing hysterics. He managed to mutter, "No, thank you" and rushed past the befuddled priest.

Once outside, Fletcher walked back to the parsonage feeling blessed and thoughtful. He no longer was confused; he was at peace.

He had to seek out this Emily Walker. His spirit confirmed there was truth in his recent encounter, and he shuddered at the thought of tackling devils. Yet, there was no place for fear. There was only enough room for faith and courage. Yeah . . . let's not forget courage.

Chapter Two
Timing Is Everything

She sat on the white porch swing, rocking back and forth while taking a break from the heavy responsibility she bore. The May breezes brushed past her face. Spring air whispered a song to her while caressing and embracing her now thin, salt-and-pepper hair. Emily Walker knew she was living in the End Times. She rejoiced, knowing the time had come to engage and defeat the evil in the world; and they were ready. Her band of Deathlinks and few compadres had been preparing for years. She was starting to worry, though. God gave her dreams and visions of a young minister who was supposed to join them. His spiritual demeanor seemed unstable and moody and she hadn't seen or heard anything from him. She feared the old brat, Satch, found a way to deter him, or worse, to defeat him, but certainly God would have allowed her to know that. Still, she sensed this young man was naive and this war had no place for naiveté.

She looked out on her Uncle Zeb's farm and realized this journey of hers started so long ago, even though it seemed like yesterday. She relaxed to the swaying lull of her beloved swing and allowed the beauty and freshness of the day to sweep and enfold her. Memories flooded her mind; her total conversion, her hard but necessary lessons in faith, and finally the spiritual battles that brought her to acknowledge God's will for her. All of the events that took place in the past were crucial occurrences in the definitive and final plan ordained by divine providence.

It was a hot September day where perspiration formed under

Emily's lightweight cotton dress and she felt the roughness of her uncle's freshly harvested crop beneath her bare feet. She decided to lie down in the field where stillness surrounded her. Even the bees found it too hot to move. Her dreams that day were of a handsome young man she met at a church social. Her uncle introduced them and their meeting was quite brief, yet she felt drawn to him. In her heart she knew he was going to be something special in her life. He was a tall, six-foot, three-inch blonde with curly hair and the biggest blue eyes she had ever seen. Emily was not usually attracted so easily to young men. She was labeled aloof and tom-boyish growing up, and the locals loved to tease her about those characteristics every now and then. But, she was easy to love because of her kind nature and loving, cheerful disposition. So no harm was ever done.

Michael was his name, Michael Harrison. What a splendid name. What a marvelous name for the strong and sensitive being she just had the pleasure to meet. She was sure he seemed interested in her as well. Who could she ask, though, to make certain? As if he wasn't handsome enough, he played the guitar and sang so as to make a girl's stomach flip flop and heart pound. Like St. Michael, the defender of God's children, her Michael . . .

"Well, hello Miss Treece. What are you doing out here all by yourself?"

Emily was startled by the voice, and couldn't make out the face for the bright afternoon sun, but the voice . . . something in the voice. Jumping up like a jack-in-the-box, she stood face to face with none other than her beautiful Michael and some woman. Who was this woman? She hadn't noticed her at the social. Who was she?

"Emily, I would like to introduce you to my fiancée, Miss Claire Overmeyer. Claire, this is Miss Emily Treece. We met earlier at the church social while you were visiting your aunt."

"A pleasure to meet you, Miss Treece. I'm not from around here. Actually, my family is from the East, but my mother's sister, perhaps you know her, Mary Tuggle, has lived in Branchford for years."

"How . . . how do you do? You . . . you startled me. I guess I was day dreaming a little." *A little, you were darned near knocked out into another universe, you silly girl.*

"We are on our way to meet with your aunt and uncle. Your aunt has offered to help me get started organizing the church's first youth choir. I understand that you are quite the singer yourself."

"Yes, I mean, I guess. That's what people tell me. Anyway, I like to sing. Do you sing, Miss Overmeyer?" Emily asked because secretly she wanted to know just how much of this newcomer she was going to have to tolerate.

"Lord, no! I couldn't hold a tune if my life depended upon it. It's really a curse, you know. Michael has such a gift and I'm afraid I truly shame him, truly."

Michael had his arm around Claire and he gave her a slight squeeze. Emily thought she would simply vomit right there on the spot, but guessed this would *truly* ruin any good impression she managed to make up to this point . . . *truly*.

The very awkward threesome walked the quarter of a mile to Emily's house. There her Aunt Jenny and Uncle Zeb were on the porch; their usual place on a sunny Sunday afternoon.

"Well, Reverend Harrison, what a splendid surprise," greeted Emily's Aunt Jenny.

"What brings you out this way, son, and who is this delightful creature you have beside you?" Emily wanted to sock her uncle for the unsolicited flattery he decided to throw that woman's way. *I mean, let's not bring it all to Michael's attention all over again.*

Emily felt very young and unsophisticated next to Claire. Claire was built like a china doll. She had impeccable taste in clothing and seemed to have an innate ability to know when to speak, laugh, giggle, and flirtatiously roll her eyes. On the other hand, there was Emily, with her underdeveloped seventeen-year-old body and her absolute inability to do anything the least bit enticing at any given time, much less know how to do it. So, there she was, leaning over the porch railing, wondering just when this nightmare was going to end. A piece of her auburn hair fell down in front of her face. She started to watch it swing back and forth in a hypnotic fashion and as she started to get caught up in the rhythm of the whole thing, she heard her Aunt Jenny say, "Isn't that right, Emily?"

"What . . . Aunt Jenny, Oh, I'm sorry, I . . . I mean what were you saying?"

"Honestly, Emily, I was just telling Michael and Claire how you sing like an angel. She really does. She brings tears to your eyes. I can't wait for you to hear her."

"Aunt Jenny, please don't go on so. I'll be so embarrassed if he doesn't, I mean, they don't think so. Oh, you know what I mean. Does anyone want any lemonade?"

The afternoon wore on. Plans were made regarding the new youth choir. Emily's aunt and uncle filled Michael in on all the local residents; how long they had lived in Branchford, whether they had past relatives who fought for the Confederacy, and who most likely would be *good* parishioners. Finally, rehearsal times were set and Emily was volunteered to make sure all participating youth were advised.

Emily was filled with the anticipation of working with Michael in the choir. He mentioned that perhaps they might sing a duet together, and she couldn't believe it. She felt she had died and gone to heaven. Tryouts were scheduled to begin the following evening, but the time from now until then was going to be agonizing.

The next morning, Emily got dressed, gulped down her breakfast and all but ran to school. In her mind the faster she went, the faster the day would go. She hustled down the old familiar path, through the woods and was almost to the clearing where the old schoolhouse stood when her books were popped out of her arms. She lost her balance and fell to the ground. Looking around to determine who did this, and as she was picking up her scattered papers and books, the figure of Bentley Madison loomed over her. She never could understand why this boy always unsettled her. He picked on her relentlessly. It's not as if Bentley were huge. He only stood about five feet seven, and had a husky build. He just was overbearing and mean. Bentley's face could have been considered handsome, if he lost that sour expression he carried around with him all the time. "Hey, sweet Baby Goodnight, how's your sweet, good lookin' self doin' today?"

"Bentley, please stop pestering me."

While Emily got up brushing herself off, Bentley grabbed her by the shoulders. His icy blue eyes shot through her, paralyzing her. She tried to tug away from the grip he had on her, but she barely budged.

"Listen Emily, you know how I feel for you. I lay awake nights thinkin' about you, your body, and your sweetness. I want you, girl. I want you and you mark my words, I'm goin' to have you, one way or the other."

A shiver made its way down Emily's back. She froze under his power. He always frightened her, and there was something sinister about him; some eerie aura that followed him around and he always found ways to get her attention. Usually they were cruel and unthinking, but he never before said things like this. She looked into his cold and riveting eyes. He pulled her nearer to him and before she knew what was happening he had his lips on hers. The kiss was hot and unlike anything she ever experienced. It was wild and fearsome and filled with passion. Her senses were rattled. No sooner was the kiss planted than Bentley released her with a jerk and ran ahead, laughing in a crazed high-pitched laugh on to the schoolhouse.

Emily gasped trying to catch her breath and evaluate what just happened. Her heart thumped. She wanted to cry, but she was so shocked she couldn't. Bentley was gone, but the evil remained. She tried to shrug off that aura of insanity as she picked up her books from the ground, and in a dutiful daze, walked to school.

Inside her schoolroom, everyone was talking about the choir. He's a tenor, and she's an alto, and the other one was a soprano. Emily was still so stunned she didn't even take part in a conversation that genuinely spiked her interest. She felt cold and shaken. She looked over at Bentley, who stared at her with a half-smile plastered on his face and an expression of quintessential evil.

The school day passed. Emily tried to ignore the feeling that she was in unexplained danger. She just wanted to get through the day. As she was leaving, Sally Traverse stopped her at the door. "Em, what's up with you? You feeling sick or something? Boy, I hope not. We have auditions tonight, and you are sure to get some kind of solo to work on. You have got the best voice . . ."

"Sally, please walk home with me. Please . . . walk slowly and walk all the way to my house. I need to tell you something. I don't know what to do."

"Sure, Em. What's going on? Talk to me, friend."

Emily and Sally stepped out into the bright, September afternoon. The sun lit up the beautiful autumn sky and a gentle breeze blew through the clearing, which made things seem almost normal.

Sally was Emily's best friend since the second grade. They were inseparable. The townsfolk used to tease them, calling them Siamese twins, "practically joined at the hip." Emily told Sally about the morning incident.

"Oh, Emily! I think that, well it's, well it's devilishly romantic!"

"Are you out of your mind? Sally, it wasn't like that! It was as if Bentley were telling me he and only he had power over me; that he could do whatever he wanted to me, whenever he wanted! It felt dirty. It was the most frightening thing I have ever experienced!"

Sally soon was affected by the story. "Em, what are you going to do?"

"I don't know. I guess I'll just pretend this never happened and maybe he'll stay away."

Emily and Sally decided to try to stay together. They would walk back and forth to school together. Maybe this would deter any further situations. They hoped, anyway.

Chapter Three
Life's Decision

Everyone and that means everyone who could sing or who thought they could sing, was present for the auditions for the youth choir. Emily looked around. She saw many of her classmates and even friends that were out of school already. It was evident by the turn out poor old Branchford just didn't have that many exciting things going on. She began to warm-up when she spotted Bentley. It was unbelievable that he was going to audition for the youth choir. Her body quivered. *Shake it off, Emily. Maybe he really likes to sing.*

Michael Harrison took his place at the front of the church. "Attention! Attention everyone! I want to thank you all for coming tonight. I must say I didn't expect this great of a turn out. I'm pleasantly surprised. I'm going to take the auditions in the order that your name shows up on the sign-in sheet. Now, let's see here. Okay. Here we go, Miss Emily Treece." Excitement filled the air as everyone prepared to hear one of the best voices in town. "Emily, would you please come up to the front of the church. Go ahead and situate yourself by the piano. What is it you plan to sing?"

"Well, I thought I would audition with 'Oh Promise Me' if that's all right?"

"Of course. You may try out with anything you feel comfortable singing."

Emily began to sing. Her soprano voice was clear and vibrant. Michael's face was in awe of the beauty that filled the room. Melodic intonations, power with gentle overtones enchanted the hearts of the people present. When she finished, the room fell silent. Michael just stood in place for a moment. His face was flushed and Emily could tell a new admiration had developed within him. He was moved as was everybody. Emily, breathless, and Michael captivated were locked in a mutual appreciation of each other's talent. For a brief moment, their souls united. A loud applause and whoops and hollers filled the church and the moment ended. Emily looked around only to discover that Bentley was also in tune with Michael and Emily's *mutual admiration society*. He glared at Michael and then at Emily. Hatred oozed from him. Michael was a threat. Not only because Bentley saw that Emily had a fondness for him, but because Michael was a man of God and Bentley hated religion. It all was so hypocritical and he was going to do something about this and soon. Fate began to dance its terrible dance in Emily's life. She knew it, Bentley knew it, and she was terrified.

The church filled with vocalists soon narrowed itself down to the real talent in the community. Out of forty youths who auditioned for the choir, only twenty were chosen. Luckily enough, Sally's rich alto voice captured the interest of Reverend Harrison, so Emily felt at least she had her friend to protect her. Bentley Madison, however, did not make it into the choir; a decision that made Bentley furious. He left the church agitated.

Emily and Sally were getting ready to go home when Michael stopped them. "Emily, you possess a remarkable talent. Your Aunt Jenny was right. I had no idea your voice was so beautiful. I just assumed it was parental pride. Would you honor me by performing that duet you and I talked about earlier?"

"Michael, you flatter me. I . . . yes, I will do the duet. Thank you!"

The happy girls left the church. They couldn't talk about anything else on the way home. Sally walked Emily to her house. Still dizzy with excitement from the evening, Em wasn't paying attention to what was around her as she made her way to the back of the farmhouse humming her audition tune.

"Hey, Baby Angel!" Bentley stepped out of the shadows where he was waiting for her. She tried to run back to the front of the house, but he grabbed her. He pulled her close to him. His strong chest pressed against hers. Backing her up to the house, Bentley's face got so close to hers, and she saw a different face before her. It was fiendish. It was evil, and it left her immobile and helpless. Bentley's grinding pelvis pinned her entire body against the house. With every breath that he took he rubbed up against her. "Emmy, girl. I told you this morning that I love you. I really hope you and that Reverend choirmaster don't plan on having anything goin'. If you would just tell me you love me, I can make you feel real good." He unbuttoned the top button of Emily's dress. She squirmed in protest. He kissed her, only this time his mouth was open and a forced tongue salivated into hers. Engulfed in his foul alcoholic breath, she choked. Every beat of his heart, every pulsating movement was angry and tormented. He unbuttoned the second button and slipped his hand down her dress. She was powerless. Bentley wanted more, but a door slammed and the spell was broken.

Uncle Zeb called, "Emily! Em, are you out here?"

Bentley put his hand over Emily's mouth. "Baby, don't say anything. He'll go away and if he doesn't, you just tell him that you are with a friend talkin'. You hear me? Do you hear me?" Emily was shocked at how terrifying a vulgar whisper could be. She nodded. Uncle Zeb was not giving up.

"Emily Marie Treece, you better answer your uncle or there's gonna be hell to pay."

"I'm here, Uncle Zeb. Bentley walked me home from choir practice and we are just talking. Is that okay with you?"

"Okay, darlin'. But you come in soon, an' make er' quick!"

Bentley let up on Emily. He buttoned the buttons on her dress and gently kissed her on the mouth. "You see how wonderful I can be, Baby Angel? I love you and nobody is going to love you but me." He left Emily shaking. She knew she had to get a hold of herself before going into the house. How could she tell her aunt and uncle? In this town, everyone thinks when something like this happens, the girl is to blame.

The girl led the boy on. *Oh, my God! What am I going to do?* Dread filled her soul. Emily knew in the traces of her heart the inevitability of what was to come. She didn't know how it was going to happen and she didn't know what she could do to stop it.

Chapter Four

The Surrender

Emily walked up the lonely flight of stairs to her bedroom and got ready for bed. The night was cold and empty. Fear encompassed every fiber of her body. Unable to sleep, she shook through the night with her thoughts racing. How could she possibly escape this obvious plight? She knew what was happening and what Bentley was planning. She wondered if it could be avoided. Her only recourse was to tell her aunt and uncle what was going on. They always seemed to be supportive, so they would certainly believe her. That thought and that thought alone comforted her. Slumber welcomed her with the affirmation all would be well in the morning.

A dream-like state held her captive. The textures of her room shifted and changed. A menacing demon approached her bringing with it many other screeching and tortured souls. She lay screaming in her head; paralyzed with fear. Unable to move, she observed an array of sickening scenes paraded before her. She was tortured with unthinkable abominations. Each creature was more depraved than the last; each sinful act frightened the pure soul who never witnessed or experienced turpitude before. At long last her prayerful soul broke the charm and she continued to pray for these pitiful, morally abandoned wretches. They vanished. Clammy and with sweat dripping down her hairline, Emily sat straight up in her bed. *Dear Lord, what was that all about?* She didn't know, and still trembling from fear, it took a minute for her to realize it was over.

The next morning, Emily got dressed and went down to breakfast. She found her aunt at the stove and her uncle sitting at the table drinking his morning coffee. "Aunt Jenny, do you think maybe I could talk to you alone?"

"Well, I can see when I'm not wanted. A little girl-talk, eh, Em? I know that boy Bentley's father. Met him a couple a weeks ago at the lumber yard. He's a very decent fellow, if ya'ask me." Zeb left them to their talk.

"Well, well, Miss Emily. Are ya finally interested in a young man? I can tell you that it's about time!"

"No, Aunt Jenny, you don't understand. There is only one way to put this. I need help. Bentley is making unwanted advances. I don't know what to do!" Emily wasn't sure, but by the look on her face, Aunt Jenny was not clear about the meaning of "unwanted advances."

"Emily, dear. Of course, a young man is makin' advances toward you. You are young and pretty. You mustn't be too coy though or you'll discourage him. I have waited so long for you to finally notice boys. Lord knows, you are almost a woman. It wouldn't be totally out of the question for you to marry soon, you know. Your Uncle Zeb and I were married at your age."

"Aunt Jenny, you don't understand. I don't really like Bentley. He's forceful and . . ."

"Emily, you want a man to be forceful. You want him to be strong. How else can he be the head of his household?"

"I don't want . . ."

"Emily, you better get off to school. And don't worry about this gentleman, Bentley. He sounds like he is takin' care of business just fine."

Oh, yeah. Gentleman Bentley certainly did know just how to take care of business. Emily didn't know what she was going to do. Hopelessness overwhelmed her. Her family was her last resort. Disappointed, she made her way to the end of the walkway and saw Sally coming to join her.

"Emily, aren't you positively excited about the choir? Michael Harrison is the most handsome man I have ever seen. You are so lucky to be able to sing with him."

"Sally, listen to me! It happened again. Only this time it was worse. He unbuttoned my dress and was touching me. On top of all that, I had a horror filled night with the most god awful apparitions. I think that I'm losing my mind."

"When . . . where did this happen? Oh, my gosh, Emily! I'm so sorry. What can I do to help? Listen, you're not losing your mind, you're just frightened, that's all. I'll be a better friend. I'll be here for you no matter what."

"No one can help me, Sally. I even tried to tell my aunt and uncle. They dismissed it as a wonderful boy showing interest in their late-blooming niece. I'm just going to try to avoid him and hope for the best. I feel so desperate. Is this how it is supposed to be? A man can just choose whomever he wants and take them by force?"

"I think that there are those men out there who are civilized and caring. Some of them are even gentlemen. Maybe it's just luck and who knows which of us are going to be the lucky ones." Sally walked a little ahead of Emily and seemed suddenly despondent at the prospect of depending solely on luck for her future romantic happiness.

The girls had a regular day at school. Bentley wasn't there, much to Emily's relief. A choir rehearsal was scheduled for that night and Emily was looking forward to it. Singing, above all, took her mind off her troubles, although she could not help but wonder where Bentley was and what he was planning to do next.

The rest of the day passed. Sally ate dinner with Emily and her aunt and uncle so they could walk to the rehearsal together. Twilight shepherded the girls as they skipped together down the road to the little church.

Concealed by a thick hibiscus bush, Bentley watched an excited Sally and Emily enter the big, white doors to rehearsal. Something wild possessed him every time he saw Emily; her slender frame, her eyes, her sweetness. He lay awake at night pretending to have her. *She wants me, too. I know it. I'm sure of it.* During his private, passionate moments of self-gratification, he had trouble distinguishing between reality and the sheer lust built up in his body. It was welling up inside him again. Just thinking about her made him feverish. He couldn't stop the thoughts of all the things he wanted to do to her. Even more provoking was the need to own her. He needed to control her. Aside from the animal in him that wanted her, the essential drive to manipulate his victim came from deep within his spirit. He didn't know from where this uncontrollable passion and need for domination came, but he had to have her and he knew just how he was going to get her.

In the church, rehearsal started. "All right, ladies and gentlemen, listen up. We have a lot of music to learn. I would really like to have a couple pieces prepared for next week's services. I want to show you off. I think we really have a fine group here." Michael began the rehearsal unaware of the lingering malevolence.

A calculated and destructive plot threatened just outside the church walls. Bentley's hands shook while he lit the first handful of hay. He placed them all around the edge of the brittle church foundation. It was a quiet and effective way to flush everyone out. What a great diversion this would be. The little white place of worship was far enough removed from the rest of the community that it made Bentley's plan so easy to execute.

At first, nighttime breezes blew the flames from the gasoline soaked hay around, playing with Bentley's mind - demonic flames sure to engulf the church in white hot fire. Soon the church lit up with raging blazes that crackled and moaned, and terrorized the innocent victims within. It brought about the desired effect when choir members came darting and shrieking out of the church. No one was looking where anyone else was going. They only wanted to escape the fire.

Emily ran out the back of the church. She lost track of Sally and could scarcely believe what was happening. Backing up in disbelief, she watched the church grow into hell's inferno. As she turned to escape the fire further she ran right into Bentley.

"Hello, my baby angel. You must be coming around. You ran right into my arms. Am I to take this as a yes?" Bentley, put his hand over her mouth and dragged Emily into the woods behind the church. Pinning her back to a tree he said, "Now, can we continue our discussion from last night?"

"That was no discussion, Bentley. Why are you doing this? Can't you see I don't like you?"

Bentley grabbed Emily's face and squeezed her lips together. "Darlin', don't ever say that again. By the time this night is over, you will be madly in love with me. I'm gonna see to it. You were told this was going to happen." Emily's eyes filled with questions. "Last night the demons came to you, don't you remember?" Bentley was wild with frustration and agitated beyond all reasoning. He dragged a shrieking Emily in an uncontrollable frenzy, stopping to tear at her dress and suckle her exposed breast while pulling her farther away from the screaming people. He carried her, kicking and screaming, to an abandoned barn. Inside the barn, he threw her onto a pile of hay. Emily didn't know what to do. She froze in bewilderment and confusion. This was the dreaded moment she knew was coming. Her mind raced as she struggled to remember what she had told herself to do.

It all happened so quickly, she didn't have time to get away. Straddling his victim, Bentley unbuttoned his pants. Before Emily knew it he was on top of her. She felt him pull her dress up around her waist. His breath was hot, his face was feverish and she was helpless and panicked. His mouth covered hers and he forced his tongue almost smothering her. It was foul and frightening. She struggled to push him away, but he was so forceful . . . so strong. Despite his small stature his body was immoveable. He ripped and pulled at her underwear until it was torn off. His legs pried her legs apart. Bentley's savage desires were being fulfilled. Emily's heart pounded out of her chest. *Oh, God, what did I tell myself to do? I can't . . . I don't want to but I must . . . I can't push him off . . . I can't move . . . if I don't let him he will kill me!* Emily tried, hoping with the strength of one great movement to administer a final blow. Bentley blocked her fist with his arm and pressed his forearm into her throat. Powerless and defeated, Emily gasped for air. After what seemed forever, he must have realized he was choking her. He released his arm. Emily coughed and gagged and tried in desperation to gasp in air. She tried to speak but couldn't. Despite her choking and gagging sobs, she tried to beg for reprieve. Eyes glazed over and feral, Bentley kept pushing his way into her. Emily's mind kept searching. Screams would not come. *There must be a way out . . . this isn't me . . . it is just a body. God! But it is my body . . . what can I do. God! Help me, please help me. What can I do?* She knew that the only way out was surrender. At that moment the poor helpless girl fell limp with exhaustion, and her screams in pain and fear heightened Bentley's desires as he penetrated her defenseless body again and again until his lust and need for control were satisfied.

She lay in the hay listless. There was no justification for this horror. *I tried to ask for help, I didn't lead him on. Did I? I don't know anymore. What now? Where is he?* She was afraid to look for him. She was afraid to move for fear he would violate her again. *God, I didn't ask for this. Why did you let this happen to me? I have always been a good person. This was not supposed to happen in my life! Not in my life. Please, God. Make it go away. Make it so it didn't happen. Let it be this morning, again.* Emily buried her head in the hay and sobbed.

Bentley's presence provoked nausea. He sat down beside her and gently stroked her hair. Stiffened with fear, Emily's skin crawled at his touch. He drew back shocked at her reaction. As she cried, he took her into his arms and rocked her – rocked her like a baby. "Shhh, baby angel. I'm here. Nothing is going to hurt you. I love you, Emily. I love you." Emily's stomach wrenched. She felt the sense of upchucking swell in her throat and as she threw up, Bentley released her and started to cry. He held her hair back from her face and he cried with her as if to actually mourn the violation and death of her virginity with her. Emily didn't know what to think. He was a different person. He was treating her with gentleness and care and remorse filled his tearful, red eyes.

How do I react to this? The monster who just raped me is reduced to sobbing over me as if he were sorry. "Bentley! Why are you crying?"

"Emily, I love you. I never wanted to hurt you. You understand, don't you? The devil took me. He makes me feel like I have to take what I want. I knew that if I didn't take you, I never would have you. You would never let me have you. This isn't how I dreamed about this." The expression on Bentley's face changed again. It was distorted and cruel. He screamed at her. "I wanted to rape you, you bitch! You walk around town without a care in the world. You may not believe this, but I have dreamed day in and day out of making you scream with pain as I raped you!" Then the twisted contorted face changed as it softened again and he gently said, "I never wanted this to be mad and mean like. I never thought it would be like this. Let me help you. Can I get you anything? Now, you will never, ever love me. I've made you hate me! God, forgive me!"

Yes, indeed! God forgive him! God forgive me for the emptiness and hate that I feel! Even though Emily was frightened and confused by his inconsistent personality, she was enraged and the rage empowered her. "I want to go home, Bentley. I want to go home now, and I never want to see you again. Ever!"

She kept thinking about what he stole from her. He stole the one thing that made a woman decent. He stole the remainder of her girlhood. He stole her self-respect. She would never again be that funny girl everyone loved. Selfish desire and violence pushed her into womanhood without her consent. That decision was made for her and was just another one of the many things that had been taken from her and remained out of her control. Her soul, frayed and scorched from a vicious attack, remained sick and depleted and all but removed from a body aching as a result of cruel abuse. She wanted to go home, but the anger toward her aunt and uncle subdued her. *Why didn't they listen? I was abandoned by them. I am just a girl. I want my mommy and daddy. God, why did you take them away from me? If they were still here, this wouldn't have happened. Would it?* Her aunt and uncle believed that girls didn't understand the ways of the world. They are to be protected by men. *Really? Well, what man protected me from this man?*

Bentley, in his own emotional stupor, helped Emily to her feet. Revolted by his touch, she pushed him away. He began to cry again. Emily joined him with great, painful sobs as she tried to cope with this nightmare. Home was where she had to be and as she ran away, she screamed, "Bentley, stay away from me. I hate you. Do you hear me? I hate you more than I've ever hated anyone."

Bentley watched his victim flee. He turned and bolted into the night, whaling and screeching like a madman and wasn't seen in Branchford for weeks following the rape.

Chapter Five
God's People

Life is filled with encounters. We are exposed to every kind of person in our families, in our churches, in our social surroundings and in areas of our life we have no control over, such as our schools and places of employment. No one can say why we are meant to meet and interact with the people placed in our lives. If one believed in predestination, one might believe that these people were brought to us in order for us to grow and become the kinds of human beings God had ordained for us to be. That kind of thinking takes a faith not only in the omnipotent God, but also a healthy reliability on philosophy.

That beautiful autumn morning, Michael Harrison was preparing the first sermon he was to preach after the fire destroyed his church. He, personally, believed in predestination. How could he not? His own life was placed in the hands of the loving Savior of the world. His responsibility was to bring God's word to whatever people were brought to him. Words in the Bible were easy enough to teach. After all, as an accountant tallies columns of numbers, the Bible lays out the way, a map so to speak, on how to live. Now the philosophy, however, was an entirely different matter. People weren't so easily swayed by the ramblings of Thomas Aquinas or Augustine, especially in this rural community. Not that the members of Branchford were rubes, but they were fundamentalist, to be sure. To complicate his spiritual life, Michael wasn't convinced the Presbyterian doctrines he was entrusted to teach were altogether genuine. He trusted his heart, and sometimes the doctrines of the church and his heart did not agree.

Since the fire, Michael was plagued with many concerns about the new people in his life. Emily Treece became very distant and quiet.

Her singing lacked something. He couldn't put his finger on it, but it was soulless. Then there was the matter of the Madison boy. He simply disappeared. No one knew where he went. His mother was worried out of her mind. His father, on the other hand, was as cold and as discomforting as any man Michael had ever seen. When Michael visited the Madison home in an attempt to offer solace, Mr. Madison demanded any concern be dismissed. He didn't allow Mrs. Madison to cry or Bentley's sisters to express sorrow of any kind. Michael felt that fear dominated that household and it had a firm grip on everyone belonging to it. The family was to remain emotionless, as if nothing had changed. He also noticed Mrs. Madison bore bruising on her fore-arms and hands. The intensity of cold repression was so great, Michael dared not ask about them. Yes, indeed, there was some incredible mys-tery going on, but Michael didn't have the first clue.

Then, there was Sally Traverse. Usually, Sally was bouncing around, driving everyone crazy with her giggles, incessant talking, and ques-tions. Since the night of the fire, she just huddled around Emily like a mother hen tending her chick. Odd, very odd and he had to find out what was going on.

"Michael, I mean, Reverend Harrison?" Michael turned. Praise God. In walked one of the pieces to this puzzle. Emily made her way around the furniture Michael strategically placed in the rectory to make it look like he was preaching to a congregation.

"Why, Emily, how nice it is to see you. Is everything all right?"

"Well, I, you see, no . . . everything is definitely not all right! Oh God, Michael, I hope you can help me!" Emily broke down with such intensity Michael hardly knew what to do. She collapsed into a chair exposing a sort of raw despair. He had never seen such desperation and anxiety in someone so young.

"Emily, my God, what is wrong, what has happened? Is something wrong with your aunt and uncle? "

"Michael, I need your help. I have nowhere else to turn. My aunt and uncle would never understand and I need your promise that what I am about to tell you will be kept in complete confidence."

"Of course." Michael had no idea what fate was going to present to him. He had no idea he would be calling on the angels in heaven to help guide this child through the most traumatic time in her young life. Nor, that what he was about to be told would be the difference in making Emily's life a strong and incredible influence in the lives of so many other human beings. In the present, in the here and now, he did not realize the link he was going to play in bringing peace and comfort to the dead that this girl would come in contact with throughout the rest of her life.

Emily described the terrible scene the night of the church fire. She spilled out her pain and mistrust in any kind of God, much less Jesus the Savior, who she was taught was always there to keep her from evil. She told Michael that everything that she held dear was taken from her. Her parents were killed in an automobile accident when she was only ten. Her hopes to become a beautiful and decent woman were dashed. Her innocence was stolen away just because someone physically stronger wanted it. How could she honor, adore or love a God who allowed these things to happen to her? She asked, no she screamed for His help, and He didn't help her. What could He possibly want from her?

Michael was taken aback by the child's pain. He didn't know what to tell her. How could he explain the workings of the omnipotent God in her life without making her feel used and bitter? This was a seventeen year old girl. It would not be easy for her to understand that God sometimes lets things happen to us in order to help us grow in his love.

Michael held Emily. He held her with tender attention, but firm enough to let her know there were men in this world who could distinguish the difference between gentle strength and brutish vulgarity. He silently prayed for help from whatever sources God wanted to provide. This child was in need of everything sacred and wonderful to be revealed to her now, right this very minute, and she only had the prayers of a small town Reverend to rely on - and don't you know? Miracles do happen. Sometimes they come in very paradoxical packages. The ability to recognize them highlights the wonder of His omnipotence in our universe.

"Hey, you! I saw this house and I thought maybe you could help my mommy!" A boy, not more than four years of age, was standing in the foyer of the rectory. He was dirty and it appeared he wasn't afraid of anything. However, his appearance displayed want.

"What is the trouble, son?"

"My mommy is having a baby. She is outside in the woods across the road."

Michael rolled his eyes to heaven as if to ask God what He thought He was doing; first, the trauma of Emily's situation and now this.

Emily and Michael rushed outside. They heard the screams of a woman in labor. Propped up against an oak tree across the road they found her. The little boy followed behind them saying, "I been takin' care of her all by myself. She's been real sick. Please, help my mommy! I can't stop her from hurtin'"

Emily ran into town to get the doctor. Michael helped the woman to the rectory and within minutes the doctor was there.

Away from the sounds of childbirth, Emily took the little boy into the living room. While snuggled on her lap she found out that his name was Aaron and as far as Emily could understand, he hadn't eaten for two days and neither had his mother. Emily listened as Aaron ate an apple and told her how everything was fine until his daddy left them. He and his mommy had to leave the room they lived in and his mommy had to find a place to work. She found lots of places to work, so they moved around a lot. The child talked himself to sleep. Emily couldn't help but feel pity for this little fellow and his mother. She guessed that everyone had dragons. It's just that some dragons breathed fire and others were just there to torment. Emily, not in a very charitable state regarding men, believed the woman's husband to be worthless and irresponsible. What a tragedy. Little did Emily know the unfortunate soul that lay misused and abandoned in the other room would become a guiding light and her salvation from a life of despondency.

Chapter Six
Spiritual What?

What a day this had been. Emily looked out her bedroom window into the cool darkness of the night. This was the first night since the rape where she felt normal. Fatigue draped a heavy cloak over her and that was good. Maybe tonight she would be able to sleep. Recently, her sleep was interrupted with night sweats and dreams of Bentley attacking her again. She wondered where he was and if she would ever be able to trust a man again. One of her most precious desires, as with most young girls, was for the day she would fall deeply in love with someone and live the rest of her life in love with him. Now, she wondered if Bentley hadn't stolen that from her, too.

"Emily, the Reverend is here to see you. Are you asleep?" Emily's Aunt Jenny called upstairs demonstrating a little concern. She noticed a change in her niece and wondered what she had missed.

"Tell him I'll be right down."

Emily straightened her hair and made a tired attempt to fix her crumpled dress. Down the steep decent of the stairs to the dining room she went where she spotted Michael sitting at the table. He stood up respectfully as she entered the room.

"Hi, long time no see." Emily decided to make light of the fact she just left the rectory an hour before.

"Emily, I realized I forgot to work out our rehearsal schedule. Do you think we might have a few moments alone to sort that out?"

"Sure, let's go out on the porch." Emily knew that Michael wanted, no, needed to continue their earlier discussion. After all, he was her pastor and that was his duty, right? They walked out the front door and sat down on the porch swing. It was so odd that one incident could alter how she felt about the handsome man before her. Now, she could care less whether he found her attractive. He was amiable enough, but she just felt numb. There was nothing to feel.

"Emily, I'm so sorry we were interrupted. That sure was strange, don't you think? Anyway, I'm glad. It has given me time to pray and search my feelings. Really, how can I ever hope to offer you any kind of solid consolation? First, I'm a man." *Yes he was a man wasn't he?* Emily wondered if all men were capable of that same animal lust that besieged Bentley. Could she ever believe in one of them again? "Secondly," Michael went on, "unless someone experiences the exact same thing, I don't think that they can honestly say they understand. However, I can tell you that I feel nothing but the greatest empathy for you and you may think this is crazy, but I also envy you."

Emily's mouth dropped open. What on earth was Michael saying? What a colossal joke. His desire was to experience rape. Infuriated by his comment, she opened her mouth to give him a piece of her mind when he gently squeezed her arm.

"I know it sounds ludicrous, but hear me out. I pray about everything that happens in my life and in the lives of people close to me. This is my way of communicating with God and He communicates with me. Today, in prayer, He assured me the events that have taken place in your young life are important to your growth as one of His chosen ones. He told me the more pain a person experiences in their lives, given the right direction, of course, the closer they become to understanding their purpose here on earth. Emily, He has great plans for you. I don't know the specifics, and that will be up to you to determine. All I know is the events in your life are directly linked to the direction and salvation of many others. I also felt He will give you a sense of direction very soon. You must work on centering yourself. You will be given what some consider a sixth sense. I prefer to think of it as an awareness and sensitivity to God's universe. Do you think you can accept all of this? I didn't know how to approach you. I'm used to living on this level of spirituality, but many others find it strange and a little kooky so I don't talk about it very much."

Emily didn't move. Awkward silence took a seat between them. She simply didn't know what to think. This is how God chooses people to follow Him? Confusion replaced the anger and contempt she was feeling earlier.

"So, let me get this straight. God allows all of these bad things to happen to people in order to bring them closer to Him? Brother, this sure puts an edge on love. Anyway, I thought using a sixth sense and seeing and communing with the dead is a sin." Emily was so very tired and this kind of reasoning from the only man she thought she could trust simply unnerved her more. "I don't know if I can accept this, Michael. I respect you, and I don't think that you are kooky, but this is just too hard to believe, and I'm tired."

"What is so hard to believe, Emily?" God loved His Son, Jesus, didn't He? Look what happened to Him. All of the most abhorrent things happened to God's own Son."

"Yes, but that was His destiny. Jesus knew those things were going to happen, didn't He?"

"Did He? I think He knew what His work was on earth, but I really don't think He knew the extent of His own humanity. He felt pain, both physical and emotional. He had relationships and interactions with others just as we do. I'm sure those human feelings got in the way of His divine expectations. Besides, don't you think we all have a destiny? As far as the blessing of a sixth sense, it is just like being blessed with your physical five senses. Sometimes you can trust them and sometimes you can't, but that doesn't make it a sin to see or hear or taste."

"Oh, Michael, I am just so confused. I think I need some time alone." Emily just wanted him to leave. She didn't want to tell him that if all of these things were true she might just give God the old heave ho. "Thank you for stopping by and I promise, I'll pray about this, too."

Michael Harrison left. He hoped he delivered the message to this child in the way God intended. Sometimes he felt a huge burden, this living in God's spiritual realm.

Emily watched Michael walk down the dirt road heading back towards the direction of the parsonage. Her eyes burned with tears. Her chest ached over a suggestion that her God might have not only allowed her to be raped but sanctioned it. She was bewildered. Weary, she sauntered back into the house and up the stairs to her room. The starched white nightgown felt good against her skin as she slipped into it. The gown flipped up revealing the now yellowing bruises left from the rape on her inner thighs. The sight of them threw her into a bitter sobbing spree. Stifling her tears because she didn't want her aunt and uncle to hear, the sadness and the distress quelled deep within her. She fell to her knees beside her bed and began to pray. "Dear Heavenly Father! If what Michael says is true, please help me find peace and acceptance."

At the moment of her deepest grief, a light flashed in her soul and peace took the place of all of the anxiety. An inner voice, one that dwelled in the recesses of her heart, spoke to her. *Forgiveness.* Serenity was her gift and she awoke the following morning feeling a harmony and thrill in greeting the new day. She couldn't understand why, but she wasn't going to question the perception.

Outside the old farmhouse, Emily met up with Sally and they traveled along the road to school. They were chatting and enjoying the crisp morning air when Emily thought she saw a shadow in the thicket of trees along the side of the road. Fear grabbed her. *Bentley! Oh, my dear God, Bentley is back.* She kept a watch out for him, but she didn't see anything. She decided it must have been her imagination and she wasn't going to let this ruin what was starting to be a perfectly beautiful day.

Her school day was wonderful. She did not have a day like this in it seemed like forever. Laughter bubbled out of her and she felt peace in all of her friendships. She excelled in her school work and even Sally relaxed. Her dearest friend shared the pain of the rape. Besides Michael, Sally was the only other living person whom Emily told.

Sally couldn't walk home with Emily after school because she had a doctor's appointment. It didn't even matter because Emily felt so good and was relishing her new found happiness. The late October sun cast warmth upon her face and her spirit seemed to fly with the excitement of her perfect day. Her feet danced their way home. It was so long since she felt so light.

As she reached the clearing, fear gripped her. She started to run. In her haste, she dropped one of her books. *Darn!* She turned around to pick up the book, but Bentley was already handing it to her. Frozen, she could hardly breathe.

"Emily, please can we talk?"

"I can't even imagine what we might have to talk about." Emily stood paralyzed.

"Emily, I have been wanderin' all over trying to bring this awful thing into something that I can understand. I've been drunk most of the time. I'm haunted by sick, ugly demons. They come to me in my dreams at night. They trouble and muddle my thinkin' when I am awake. Please, Emily, I know that I can never replace what I took from you, but as God is my witness, I don't know what came over me. I need your prayers, but most of all I need your forgiveness. Can you forgive me?"

There it was. *Forgiveness. Isn't that what God wants me to do? Is this the price I need to pay for such a glorious day; perhaps a glorious life? Am I to believe that just by forgiving him this one time he wouldn't do it again?* As she thought this through, she was trembling. Bentley fell down on his knees. She guessed it wasn't her responsibility if he would or wouldn't do it again to somebody else. Just as long as he didn't come near her again. Her responsibility was in the forgiving, and she knew that she would never be forgetting.

"Bentley, you . . . you repulse me. I hope you know just what you have done to me . . . the agony, the loss and the fear." Emily's voice quivered. Tears filled her eyes. "Yes, I suppose . . . I forgive you." She broke down and sobbed, "I forgive you because God wants this from me and I love Him, and because I love Him I must forgive you. I forgive you, but don't ever come near me again." With that Bentley got up and disappeared into the woods.

It's not easy loving God and doing His will. The responsibility of it all is harsh and sometimes overwhelming, but the dawn of a new soul and an exquisite being was reflected in God's eyes that day. For her obedience and her love and respect for Him, He blessed her with a light that would guide her into the souls of men. He would strengthen her with wisdom and a divine knowledge of humanity. She would help Him. Even though she was a bit rough, she would maneuver her way through the pitfalls of evil and raise the less spiritual to a place above what they could not acquire for themselves. Yes, He loved her and counted her among His very special faithful.

Chapter Seven
God's Medium Is Born

What a horrible dream! Oh, dear Lord, did that dream seem real! Emily awakened; her sheets wet with cold sweat. She lay there struggling to remember everything. An angel appeared to her, and what a strange angel. This angel was ruddy looking, with dark hair and no wings. She knew this was an angel, though, and a messenger from God. He pulled her into a deep sleep and she began to see and feel everything that little Aaron's mother was feeling; the abandonment, the despair, the feeling of being used. Emily's heart pounded as she remembered how easily people took advantage of a mother's vulnerability. They knew she was desperate and would take any work that was offered to her. She was hired but paid meagerly for long hours doing tedious work that required, oftentimes, physical strength. Emily felt her exhaustion at the day's end. She saw little Aaron being abused by caregivers, who took most of his mother's earnings. Finally, she suffered this woman's anguish at the impossible prospect of having to provide for two children all alone. She walked with this lady into a barn or a shed of some kind and watched her reach for a rope. The rough texture and the twine-like prickle traveled through her fingers as the woman made a hangman's noose. In horror, Emily sensed the rope being placed around her neck and an elevation as the woman stepped onto an unstable wooden crate. Her stomach was sick with fear and her heart hurt and her throat choked and strained through tears. Finally, she heard and experienced the crack of her neck as the box was flung out from under her only after an intense thought of absolute resolve.

Emily jerked from sleep. The dream was so real. She felt an urgency to get to the parsonage. She had to see that Aaron's mother was all right.

Emily got dressed and ran down the stairs as fast as she could. Her aunt and uncle barely got the chance to say good morning and she was out the door. Perplexed, they watched their niece tear down the dirt road that led to the outskirts of town. Emily pounded on the parsonage door.

"Emily, hey what's the matter?" Michael answered.

"Where is Aaron's mother?"

"Well, I don't know, I guess she . . ."

"Don't guess, remember! Please, this is so important!" Emily saw the questioning look on his face.

"I saw her walking toward the old woodshed not ten minutes ago." said Claire.

"Emily, what is this about?" Michael was keenly aware that something metaphysical was afoot.

"Ten minutes. Oh, my God. I hope it's not too late!" Emily bolted out the door of the parsonage with Michael and Claire behind her.

"What's her name?" Emily demanded.

"Uh, Grace . . . Emily, what is going on?" Michael also sensed that something was not right.

"Grace, Grace, don't do it, Grace!"

As they reached the entrance of the shed, Emily heard something like wood falling and a muffled, guttural gasp. It was too late. Time has its own meaning and those who threaten to alter it only tend to hasten its purpose. Grace was hanging and swinging. Through their screams, Emily helped Michael grab Grace's body and lifted it to lessen the cruel clutch of the rope while Claire climbed up on a pile of wood to loosen the rope from the beam. Together, they laid Grace down on the ground.

"Oh, God. She's gone!" Michael was in shock. He kept pressing the side of Grace's neck hoping to find a pulse. Nothing.

Emily fell to her knees. "No! This isn't right! This wasn't supposed to happen. I was supposed to stop this, wasn't I?" Emily rambled in disbelief. Why did God give her that dream if He didn't want her to stop this tragedy? She just stared at Grace's body. Michael helped Emily to her feet, while he motioned to Claire and they both guided Emily out of the shed. Walking back to the parsonage where Aaron was sitting on a step of the porch, he looked like he possessed the wisdom of the ages. Emily broke away from Michael and Claire to hug the quiet little boy.

"My mommy came to see me, Emily. She said she was goin' to be with the angels. Claire, where do the angels live and why is she goin' away without me? Don't the angels like little kids? Why can't my brother and me go, too?" Michael and Claire just stood before Aaron in disbelief.

As Emily cradled the little boy in her lap she said, "Oh, Aaron! When did your mommy say these things to you?" Emily assumed Grace prepared Aaron this morning sometime after she made her decision to take her own life. *How could she have done such a thing? Someone would have surely helped her. I would have helped her through this. What was Grace thinking?* As her mind carried on, she was distracted by Aaron waving at someone.

"Who are you waving at, Aaron?"

"Mommy, Emily. Can't you see her over there by that big tree? She's been standing there for a long time."

Emily looked only to see what she thought to be a shadow. "Aaron just when did your mommy talk to you?"

"Right before y'all came running up and scared her away. She still loves me doesn't she, Emily?"

Poor little fellow. What would happen to him now and did he really see his mother standing by that tree? A sense of deep sorrow burrowed its way into her heart. Emily also was an orphan and she was well acquainted with the feelings of abandonment and loneliness. She ached for Aaron, but in the deep recesses of her soul was the constant source of intuition which reminded her of something she heard once. *Because of loneliness, I can find the strength in my aloneness.* Unaware of it, she was on the precipice of her own aloneness that would be with her for most of her life.

It was evening. Emily rocked with a steady rhythm on the porch swing and remembered the first time she sat on it. Her aunt and uncle brought her back with them after her parents' funeral. The need to be by herself made her sneak out of the house to the porch and perch herself on the swing with her little legs dangling. There she found comfort. From then on, Emily found herself sitting on that swing whenever she needed security. It was as if she felt the presence of everyone who had passed on before her. She believed that the angels frequented this place too, for how else could she feel such peace?

The nights were warm in Alabama through the end of October. As she rocked, she sensed uneasiness. A chill passed by her and a breeze blew through her hair making her feel strange and unsettled. She stopped the swing and sat straight up. A filmy, noiseless melody moved her spirit. Leaves rustling from the soft breezes brought her to her feet and drew her to the porch railing. The melody intensified and was more compelling. There was a presence. Someone was behind her. She quickly turned to see Grace perched demurely on the swing.

"Whoa . . . Grace, how can, how . . ." Emily was speechless.

"I reflect the light. The brighter I am, the more light I reflect to chase away the darkness." Grace just sat on the swing and gently rocked back and forth.

Emily felt no fear and sat down next to her. This was too much. *Maybe because of all of these things happening, the rape, Grace's suicide . . .*

"Emily, I am here now until my lesson is done. I stopped myself from learning and now the light has sent me back until I help someone else complete my lesson. You must help me become a mirror for the truth. I must be a Deathlink for another or I will never live in the eternal light."

"Am I really talking with you, Grace?"

"You are my guide, I am to follow you."

Emily blinked. *What? I am to be a guide for this poor dead soul? Well, she really isn't dead, now, is she? Is this what Michael meant when he told me that God was going to work through me?*

"Grace. God sent you to me?"

Grace just sat there gazing off into the darkness. Emily realized the extent of her communication with Grace would be cryptic to say the least. Her mind started to race at the prospect of what was supposed to be her calling and just how she was going to understand her part in God's plan. She would also have to depend on the spiritual communication of prayer for a while, until she got this thing down. This must be what Michael was referring to when he told her about God's love for her. God had started the refining of her soul and she realized she better hang on tight. Things were taking shape and she was only a pawn. It was awesome and she was humbled, but also exhausted. Grace was fading away. She was very faint now and Emily felt weary. All energy was sucked out of her body and this was so much to take in at one time. Drowsy, she rested her head on her arm. *I will be prepared and eager for the adventure . . .* Emily's heart was talking to her again, but she couldn't hear it. She was asleep.

Chapter Eight
Bentley, You Devil You

Now, during the heavenly appointment of Emily as a spiritual guide for the unfortunate souls of God, Satan also prepared his army; all of them selfish, greedy and loveless creatures. They were offered the chance to change their lives for the better, but just couldn't gather enough faith in their fellow human beings and trust in the almighty God to try.

Bentley Madison sat in the deep, dark, blackness of the night. The place he visited most of his life for protection was now his prison of demons. The damp, hard walls of the cave felt good against his back, but he sensed no help, no salvation from what he just did. It was bad enough he raped the girl of his dreams last fall, but this was incomprehensible. Those demons, those sons of Satan, they were the ones that drove him to this last despicable act. He shuddered in disgust at what transpired. The image of his fourteen year old sister, lying on the floor in shock and fear would never be erased from his mind. How could he have taken her? He should have changed when he had the chance. Emily forgave him, but he didn't seize the opportunity to change.

That day, after Emily trembling with fear forgave Bentley, he felt renewed; almost saved. But there was something about the thrill he got as he recalled the look of terror in her eyes. He felt powerful and in control. He had to stop himself from finding her and doing it to her all over again. Control was something he never was allowed to feel at home. His father made sure of that. Everyone, including his mother, walked on egg shells around his father. He was like a time bomb *ticking, ticking, ticking*. The family never knew what to expect from him. Then, this morning, Bentley was home alone with his sister. He watched her intensely and he felt the need to torment her, so he jumped out from behind a door. She screamed so loud. It was such a fix that he wanted to hear it again. It made him feel powerful and he didn't want that feeling to go away. So, he seized her, threw her on the floor and there it was; the horror reflected in her eyes. That was the adrenaline rush he needed. Satisfaction filled him as he proceeded to terrorize her. He lost control and everything else was a blur until he saw her frightened, half-clothed body, cowering on the floor.

Now, it was too late. It wasn't him, he really didn't do it. He was a pawn, wasn't he? He could rationalize raping Emily, because he convinced himself that he was so in love he couldn't control himself, but this, this . . .

"Bentley, Beeentley, *Bentley!*" the demon's voice that interrupted his thoughts was deep, raspy and as cold as a snake's belly. "Bentley, you have done my bidding. Why so depressed? Don't you think she liked it? Or is it you didn't think you were good enough?" The demon laughed wickedly.

"Go away! Go away! Why me? Why do you make me do these things! I, I . . . don't want to do them. You bring these ideas into my head and then you force me to do them. I'm done. I can't do these, these favors for you anymore!" Bentley was engulfed with fear and sickened by the evil that overpowered him.

"You are my servant! You were spawned from my loins. Don't you know you have no choice in this matter? You are mine, forever. To live in the lowest level of the earth, to eat vomit, and sleep in stench will be your greatest happiness, because you are doing it for me! Do you understand, Bentley? You are the lowest form of animal, and you belong to me." The demon loomed over Bentley speaking despicable words using them as a tool to sooth his own spirit. Its presence was terrifying and the extent of Bentley's oppression was limitless.

Continuous streams of evil in the form of demons filled the cave.

The idea was to torment and trap their brother into yet another revolting act of violence. This time they wanted blood. They wanted to see red and Bentley knew it.

"Mom, Mommy, I want my mother! Help me, someone help me!"

"Your mother? Your mother can't help you. She lives with one of mine. He dominates her every movement. Why do you think you are so easy? He helped make you! He is from me, Bentley!" Jeers, vile spits and growling surrounded Bentley until he thought he would lose his mind. The demons encircled him, around and around making him dizzy and nauseous. Profanity filled the air and he felt faint consumed in deep depression while the gravest of sufferings were shown to him. With a sudden jolt, Bentley was jerked to his feet and held against the cave wall. A scene of terror played out before him. A little boy and his infant brother were stolen from their beds. They were to be drowned in the river and the man doing the deed was him. As the scene evolved, a band of angels appeared and leading the group was Emily. A battle engaged and Bentley knew it was for more than just the rescue of the two children. It was for salvation. A savage scream escaped his lips while tearing himself away from the fierce grip of the devils. Falling to the ground he scoured the cave's floor for his knap sack. His hand fumbled around inside until he found the clump of cold steel he thought would become his savior. He pulled it out, placed it to his head and squeezed. In a sudden jerk of blasting pain, his spirit separated itself from the midst of splattering blood and pieces of what used to be his brain. Shocked and horrified, Bentley floated above his mutilated, bloody corpse and realized what he thought would be his salvation was his condemnation. His body died and his soul now lived in sin and fear. He didn't want it, nor did he expect it, but his purpose was fulfilled. He was now one of Lucifer's soldiers. Faith and trust in the goodness of the world faded away; so far away that all that remained for him was evil. He looked up to see the light that was the energy of God. It was so beautiful and peaceful. He could have been forgiven, if he just asked, but the comfort and serenity belonging to the force before him was no longer attainable. The demons wasted no time in sweeping his essence into their pack. He yielded to evil and hell was upon him.

Chapter Nine
Home, James!

"Well, well, well, my Miss Emily. To think we finally are gettin' you married off." Emily's Aunt Jenny was beside herself with happiness and what Emily surmised was relief. After four years at the University, Emily finally landed her B.A. in Music Performance and now this afternoon, her M.R.S. with a certain James Andrew Walker. James was a stocky young man possessing rugged good looks. She loved the way his eyes sparkled when he got excited during stimulating conversation. He was quick and intelligent and easy to talk to about anything. They both loved to read and he seemed to be very interested in the arts. During her college career, Emily learned to love the theater, the ballet, and of course, the opera. James took her to performances every chance he could, given the time and especially the money. More importantly, his sense of humor had depth and thought and was always a delightful challenge to Emily. There were only a few things that bothered her, and she didn't dwell on them, yet they did bother her. Monetary gain seemed to be ranked very high on James's list of important goals and the other was a quick temper followed by long, moody depressions. Emily thought maybe the first was due to his upbringing. James had to take a job when he was only twelve to help support his mother and sisters. His father became ill and bedridden for many years, leaving James with much of the financial responsibility of the family. She felt the moody depressions were just youthful antagonisms which he would outgrow. At any rate, they were deliriously happy and in love and that was all that mattered.

"I swear, Aunt Jenny! Have I been that much of a burden?" Emily teased. She was gone from her aunt and uncle since she was eighteen.

Her aunt looked at her twenty-two year old niece with respect and affection.

"You, my sweet darlin', have been the light of our lives and you know it. Your Uncle Zeb and I are just so happy for you. We missed you while you were away at college and really wanted you to come back here to live for a spell, but honey, when love beckons what are you goin' to do, eh?" Aunt Jenny squeezed Emily so tight she thought her eyes would pop.

Even though Emily still harbored a little resentment, she loved her aunt and uncle. She heard that Bentley committed suicide after raping his own sister. What a tragedy. God wanted her to forgive him and she did, but she couldn't help but wonder what good it did. "Did you get that sash ironed? You know the one that goes on the back of my wedding gown?"

"Yes, child. Are you startin' to get some pre-weddin' jitters? You know, Emily, Michael is so proud to be the one to marry you and James. Since he and Claire adopted the boys, he hasn't had much time to come around and talk to us. So when we asked him to do the honors, he was quite thrilled."

After Grace's death, Michael and Claire could not stand the thought of those little boys growing up without a family. So since they were getting married in December of that year anyway, they proceeded with the adoptions. They made such a sweet family. Aaron was eight now and Jacob would soon be five. Divine providence certainly led Grace to Branchford, of that Emily was certain. Grace was her constant companion. A quiet one, but always present just the same.

"Em! Emily, are you here?" A voice from Emily's past came floating in through the screen door.

"Sally, gosh, oh, gosh it's so good to see you. Does the bridesmaid's dress fit you? I know I sent it kind of late, but our decision to be married was so fast." Emily looked into the eyes of her very closest and dearest friend. How she loved Sally. How she missed seeing her friend's clear green eyes cheerfully dancing in front of her. "Sally, it's so good to see you, I missed you so."

"Emily, you squirrel. I missed you, too. Who would have thought your homecoming from college would also be your wedding day."

"I know, I know. I've already heard that litany from Uncle Zeb."

"Are you one of the lucky ones, Em? Is he caring and is he a gentleman?"

Emily remembered this conversation from a long time ago. It made such an impression on Sally that she even remembered the exact words. Emily shook it off. "You silly girl, you bet he is!"

"Well then, let the festivities begin!" Sally grabbed Emily by the hand and pulled her up the stairs to her bedroom. There Emily's wedding apparel was all laid out and they proceeded to get ready.

Evening was setting in and the mood for the wedding grew more and more exciting. All of the people from Branchford were invited. The new, bright white, little church filled up with well-wishers. As her uncle's buggy rounded the bend, Emily could see James and his mother and sisters waiting outside the church. James caught sight of the buggy and walked over to greet Emily and her family. His look was stern. Emily tried to joke him out of his obvious irritability, but that only resulted in anger towards her. She hated when he fell into these slumps. He never had a reason for them and today of all days was supposed to be one of celebration. *What, exactly, was his problem?*

James ushered Emily into the church. His hold on her arm reminded her of a more threatening individual. After everyone walked ahead of them, James spun Emily around to face him. "After today, you know that you are mine."

Emily, in an attempt to be understanding and loving said, "James, of course I will. I'll be your wife, silly."

"And don't you ever forget that, Emmy!"

After the day and the night, Emily worried just what kind of mistake she made. James put on a pleasant face for the wedding guests, but when it came time for them to leave on their honeymoon, his black mood came right back. What was supposed to be the most romantic night of their lives turned into a night of gloom. James's demeanor was sullen and scary. Emily never told him about the rape, but because of her traumatic experience with Bentley, she really needed her groom to be loving and gentle. Shockingly, James showed no interest in her at all. Their marriage was not even consummated for three days. Emily's self-worth was so low that when they finally made love, her soul was barren and her love making void of any emotion. This infuriated James and the rest of their honeymoon was spent tiptoeing around each other's moods.

Sally's question regarding James's status as a gentleman always hung over Emily. *Why didn't God stop this marriage?* As the years passed, she decided it wasn't the marriage for which she had hoped. There were moments of kindness between them, but there seemed to be more moments of depression for James and loneliness for Emily. The worst was the occasional physical abuse that she hid from her family and friends. Emily came to believe the reason God allowed her marriage to James was for them to have Andrew, their son. Andrew Walker would become mighty in faith and blessed with great fortitude. He would be a much needed leader in the final battles, and Emily told Andrew he was important to God every chance she got. Emily suspected God's plan would always be more important than her desires. This was such a hard pill to swallow. She prayed and prayed for God to make her marriage more tolerable and more loving. But James never softened and as he grew older, he was more and more obsessed with money. Emily had a beautiful home and almost every luxury a woman could want. What she never received was the kindness and gentleness in love she so desired. But, she believed her destiny was ordained. This kind of suffering must have a reason and who was she to challenge the plans of the Being who made the heavens and the earth and possessed all of the kindness, gentleness and love in the universe. Emily knew this to be true because she witnessed these things daily in other people's lives. Her life would be one of constant hope for those gifts to somehow find their way to her; from her heart to God's ears.

Chapter Ten
About James

Well, this was it. James did it, but now he was wondering what possessed him to get married. Sure, Emily was beautiful and talented, but hadn't he had enough responsibility all of his life? Love blinded him. What an incredible experience it was to be in love. Emily would do anything for him, but he just couldn't find that kind of devotion within himself. He really could not trust that if he gave all of his love to her, she would not just end up hurting him. Something was bound to happen and when it did, he was not going to be the one hurt. He experienced enough of that in his life, and he wanted none of it now. It was simply better to let Emily be the romancer.

As a child, James watched his father's health decline. His mother took in laundry and cleaned other people's houses in order to help meet the bills, but it was never enough. Finally, James went to work at a warehouse after school when he was twelve. The men there were gruff and treated him badly. Bullying James became a common sport for them. One day a kindly supervisor, Oliver Tully, took James's side. He put a stop to the abuse and befriended him, and James felt he was given a guardian he could talk to about things and depend on for direction and advice. Tully would have James over for dinner and they talked about school, his father's health, and the general state of the family.

About two months went by, and James began to feel less stress and actually happy again. Tully asked James to come over for dinner and asked if he would spend the night because he needed help painting one of the rooms in the house and it would be quite late by the time they finished. Painting and talking proved to be a great time, and they even got into a paint fight. James believed Tully was the father his father could not be. The two got cleaned up and Tully ushered James to a bedroom next to his. James fell asleep instantly, but in the middle of the night woke to someone in bed next to him. It was Tully and he was fondling him and whispering that if he played along with him, he would make his family life easier and even make sure there were extra benefits in it for James. James pulled away from him and put on his clothes to leave. Tully blocked the door to the bedroom.

"Listen, James. I can do all kinds of things for your family. I have no one to give my money to, and you mean so much to me."

"I don't care! I'm not like that! Not only am I leaving, but I'm going to report you to the boss." James was livid. He was betrayed and he thought that Tully truly liked him for himself and not for some perverse desire.

"Oh, no you won't! If you do I'll just tell them that you were the one who stole the money from the office last month. I will no longer defend you from those thugs and it won't take much to tell everyone that *you* are the pervert."

"That's not going to happen. No one is going to believe you."

"You don't think so? Who do you think they are going to believe, a sniveling little twelve year old brat or a supervisor that has worked for them for ten years? Listen Jimmy, I don't want this kind of friction between us. There is so much I can offer you. You want a college education, don't you? Well, be this kind of friend to me and I will make sure you go to college and your family never goes hungry. Besides, you really don't have much of a choice. Go to your parents with this and all it will do is cause them more grief and problems they can't and don't have the resources to handle. On the other hand, you can make everyone's life easier if you just cooperate."

James was furious. He left Tully's house thinking he would never be back again. He felt betrayed. He was indignant. He depended on Tully's companionship; something he missed with his own father. James was hurt to the core.

The next day at work, three warehouse men jumped him and beat him. All they said was he needed to listen to orders more and every time he stepped out of line, they had the boss's permission to handle it any way they saw fit. They walked away laughing and flexing their muscles as if they had something to be proud of instead of recognizing their obvious bankruptcy in the brain department. Bloody and in pain, James's mind was reeling. *How hard is it to beat up a twelve year old kid?*

James started to get up. Tully pushed him back down, wiped his wounds with a wet towel and then invited him to his house for dinner that night. He was trapped. If he didn't go along with Tully, he might even be killed and where would that leave his family? James submitted against his will as he lay in Tulley's bed that night with his eyes closed. He tried to ignore what was happening to him, and every time thereafter, always leaving Tully's house sick to his stomach, occasionally throwing up his dinner into the bushes. If James thought of stopping the arrangement, or would not show up when he said he would, the warehouse thugs would find him and beat him.

After James turned seventeen, Tully had a heart attack and died. Whatever Tully was, he was at least true to his word. Not only was James free from his abuser, but Tully left him a large inheritance and a college trust fund. James was released from physical bondage, but his emotional and mental health would forever be wounded and those wounds, without the proper help, never went away. Unfortunately, James was a big believer in self-help, and the sickening memory of what he had to endure in order to survive and become something in life stayed with him every hour of every day.

Sometimes, especially during the Christmas season, Emily persuaded James to contribute generously to some charity. He agreed to do this and at first, he was extremely proud and happy he was able to give such a large amount. But then, as the reality set in, he turned on Emily. He took it out on her with his fists. Afterward, she looked at him with deep sadness and an inquisitive expression peered out of a tear stained face. Quietly retreating to the guest room to hide her physical and emotional wounds from her son, she escaped the unexplained wrath of her attacker. James never seemed to care that he hurt her. Really, he didn't even remember those times of intense rage. He only knew he would never be so poor that anyone could take advantage of him or his family again. But Tully took more than James's innocence. He stole his ability to trust and fully give love.

Emily was never told about this part of James's past and James tried to bury it, but the pain manifested itself in so many other ways and Emily was the one who bore the brunt of it. Because she loved him unconditionally, she was an easy target. She suffered his pain without the knowledge of its source. She took it upon herself and never asked why. James never knew of Emily's rape; Emily never knew of the theft of his body, mind and soul, and this was the tragedy of their union.

Chapter Eleven
Batter Up!

Lucifer was hanging out at the little league diamond, wearing a baseball hat, chewing gum and looking altogether too excited about his next scheme. Recently, a young kid by the name of Fletcher was called to become a minister of God. The best time for Satan to turn the destiny of one so inclined was when their hearts were fertile and unsure of the world. On top of that, it would not be too long that this kid's mother was going to become seriously ill, and Fletcher would have to watch her suffer for a long time before losing her. Events that could be used by evil to plant the seeds of doubt in God, and the rush of selfishness because of emotional hurt were tools used to cultivate faithlessness in a boy's life. But, Lucifer was not satisfied these things would be enough to curtail the kid's calling, so he was there to perform one more act of suffering as an insurance policy.

Fletch was out in right field when a fierce swing of the bat and a major connection with the ball split its seam and sent it sailing with incredible velocity through the air. By a wave of Lucifer's hand, the ball hit its target and punctured Fletch's eye. The crowd went crazy as the young man fell to the ground in excruciating pain while blood ran down his face. His brother, who was watching the game from the stands, bolted to his side. The umpire screamed for someone to call an ambulance and the game came to an abrupt and unsettling halt.

"Lukas, help me! It hurts so bad! Luke, are you there?"

"Don't worry, Champ. I'm right here and I'm not going anywhere, I promise. We're getting you help. Try to stay calm, okay? Crimany, Fletch, do you have to go after every ball the batter hits?"

"Yeah, pretty stupid, huh?" Fletch rolled on the ground in pain, but insisted on setting the record straight. "I really didn't go for . . . "

"Quiet! Just stay quiet until the ambulance gets here."

The ambulance drivers hurried Fletch to the hospital where he was taken into surgery immediately. Luke called their parents and their sister, Olivia, and then sat down anxiously to wait. He needed to find some kind of reasonable answers to what happened to his brother. One minute he was sitting there watching the game and the next his kid brother's eye was bleeding profusely after being gouged by a ball that looked like it had a mind of its own.

Joined by his family and after hours of pacing and imagined fears, the unimaginable happened. Doctors came into the waiting room and explained to the distressed family that the fly ball had punctured Fletcher's eye too deeply and there was nothing that could be done. Fletch would be blind in his right eye for the rest of his life.

Luke and Olivia were in shock. They let their parents go into the recovery room alone, while they huddled together to try and figure out how they were going to help their little brother through this awful time.

"Why him, Liv? He is such a great kid. He didn't do anything to deserve this, and what are we going to say to him when he wakes up?"

"I don't know, I guess just pray for answers. Pray for him as hard as we can."

Fletcher was out of it. He was still under the influence of the anesthesia, but he felt at peace. He saw angels standing in front of him, and as they parted he saw a beautiful young woman, holding a young teen and rocking him. Tears flowed down the pretty face as if her heart was broken into pieces. Somehow, he knew this woman was a part of him, but he didn't know how. Then the woman and child faded away and one of the angels stepped aside where he saw a man with a patch over one eye and this man was confident and strong. Fletch identified with him.

"Son, wake up. Fletcher, wake up." A doctor was trying to arouse

Fletcher from his deep sleep, but Fletch wanted to hang on to one last feeling of peace. He saw the woman again, but this time the man with the eye patch held her as she grieved. Brilliant light surrounded them.

"Fletcher! Come on, son, wake up, now." Fletch tried to open his eyes, but only one would open. The other, the one that was hit by the fly ball, was patched up. He woke up at last, and through the blur saw his mother and father.

"Mom, Dad, where is Luke? He said he would stay here with me."

"He's right outside, Fletch. I'll get him." This was a convenient excuse for his mother to leave the room in order to hide her tears. Fletch's dad was close behind. As she escaped through the door, her eldest son was there to embrace her.

"It's going to be alright, Mom. You'll see. Nothing is going to stop him. He is special and besides, we will all be around to help him."

"He doesn't know yet, Luke, and I don't think your father or I have the heart to tell him."

"It's okay. Liv and I have worked it out. Liv?"

Olivia and Luke walked hesitantly through the hospital room door and stood on either side of Fletch's bed. There they each took a hand and squeezed.

"Hey, Champ! How's my buddy?" Luke tried to cover his quivering voice.

"Fletcher, you could have waited for me to be there at one of your games before pulling the biggest spectacle in Springfield Little League history." Olivia's face was stressed, but there was a forced smile through her moist eyes.

"Listen, Champ, Liv and I want to talk to you about something. Who is your biggest hero ever?"

"Well, I guess Uncle Matt."

"Why?"

"Cause he lost his arm in Vietnam and when he came home, he didn't let it stop him."

"Right! He is an example of a guy, who could have given up because of something bad happening to him, but he went right on chasing his dreams and now he is one of the most important construction contractors in Springfield, right?"

"Yeah, but what's Uncle Matt got to do with anything?"

"Look, Fletch. Luke and I need to tell you something. But before we do, we want you to know we are here for you and we know that, just like Uncle Matt, nothing can stop a Hodges from accomplishing everything they set out to do."

"Fletch," Luke's voice was gentle but hurt. When the ball was hit by the bat, the seam broke open and when it hit your eye, it . . . it, well it punctured your eye."

"Buddy, you have lost the sight in that eye." While Olivia squeaked out the news, Luke squeezed Fletch's hand. Fletcher appeared almost in a daze. They thought perhaps they lost him to shock, when a look of awareness covered his face.

"That was me! That was me in that dream. But who was the woman? Hey, Luke, how do you think I would look with a black eye patch?"

Chapter Twelve
How Bad are the Bad Lands?

The walk was hot and dusty. Trails of rocks were strewn out ahead of him, making his hike up the mountain like walking on rolling marbles beneath his feet, but Andrew Walker was determined to explore the possibility that his dreams were valid messages from the Creator or this Wankan Tanka. A great chief came to him during times of unconsciousness after Andrew was shot in Vietnam. His mother didn't know that he was shot while under attack at Khe Sanh, and he was never going to tell her. His purple heart remained hidden in a trunk. Emily Walker raised her son to believe that God was always with him, but during those torturous days of the war he believed her to be delusional. Andrew watched his comrades die. He watched them blow up under a barrage of grenade fire. He witnessed flying limbs from the bodies of his friends after encountering buried explosives. In and out of consciousness for three days, Andrew was visited by an Indian spirit dressed in a wondrous headdress of white and black feathers. He called himself Feather on the Wind and led him to a threshold of luminous white light several times, but Wankan Tanka refused to accept Andrew's entrance over the great divide. Angels stood at the entrance and told him that he was to be a warrior for the Creator and he needed to return to the land of the living to begin grooming himself for this most important role.

So, now, after years of wandering across America looking for avenues of godliness where his hands were God's hands ministering to those with no homes, or food or clothing - where he needed these actions to cleanse his mind of memories of war and restore a belief in his mother's God, Andrew finally went in search of Feather on the

Wind. Here in the Bad Lands he hoped to find proof of the existence of a Creator of the universe. This position of warrior for the Creator was still ill-defined in Andrew's heart. Existence of God remained unsubstantiated for him, but perhaps if he found new life in Native American spiritualism a link would form between Andrew's lack of faith and Feather on the Wind's constant presence in his dreams.

Another continued toward Andrew whose black soul was in pursuit of the destruction of the pure yet formidable man forging a path up Castle Trail to the most sacred grounds of the Lakota. There Andrew hoped to commune with the spirits of the past. The evil hid waiting for the right moment to strike. Its tail rattled as its body streamed closer toward the target. Deep in thought, Andrew pounded the trail looking down at his feet as he climbed the sometimes narrow corridor where anticipation of answers fogged his sense of reality. Slithering and rattling, walking and contemplation shared a rhythm as each got closer to the other. A howl from the mountains startled Andrew from his meditative stupor. A quick lunge and the snake sunk its fangs deep into Andrew's leg. It hung on, dangling for a moment assuring a full deposit of venomous fluid. The snake dropped away as Andrew shook his leg in furious panic. It slinked away triumphantly and as it slithered it dissipated into a cloud of black smoke.

Andrew lost his balance and fell to the ground. He found his pocket knife and tried to lance the bite, but too much venom was already surging through his bloodstream. Even when the sun was setting, it still streamed endless heat upon the Bad Lands. Andrew was hot and now growing feverish. He struggled to stay conscious, but fell into oblivion as dusk turned into the blackest of nights.

Darkness in the Bad Lands is void of light from cities or highways and the barren landscape is filled only by sounds of the coyote prowling for food. Andrew awakened to a billowing fire before him. A young Indian warrior knelt and chanted before the warm, dancing flames. He turned to see Andrew trying to stand and rushed over to assist.

"Who are you?" Andrew wasn't sure if this man was a vision or actual.

"I am the Son of Wankan Tanka as all humans are the Sons of Mother Earth and the Creator. I am here to assist you on your life quest."

Andrew looked deep into the young man's eyes. They were gentle and loving. "Do you know Feather on the Wind?"

"Ah, Feather on the Wind is your spirit guide and you will depend on his wisdom throughout your quest, but I am here to teach you."

"Teach me? Teach me what?"

"The ways of life . . . the ways of death . . . the ways of a great warrior."

"Why?"

"Because it is your path to fight for the Creator. Purity should be the only thought in the minds of man, but man, presented with many wonderful choices, has chosen to think only upon evil – this has given evil power. Now, man must defeat evil. I am here to give you the tools to do this."

Andrew, feeling sick and faint, was not in the mood to argue. "Please, fill me in."

The Son of Wankan Tanka sat down next to Andrew. "Nothing stands between you and Wankan Tanka. His presence is immediate and personal, and the blessings of Wankan Tanka will flow over you like rain from the sky. Wankan Tanka is not apart from you and is ever seeking to crush evil forces. He does not punish the animals and the birds, and he does not punish man. He is not a punishing god. The Indian knows that there was never a question as to the supremacy of the power of purity over and above the power of evil. There is but one ruling power, and that is purity and goodness."

Andrew listened intently to the Son of Wankan Tanka. "But, what does Wankan Tanka think of death? What does he think of killing our fellow humans and how does he react to the injustice and hate in the world? These are the things that disgust me and discount any faith in the benevolence of a Creator."

"A man must live his life free from fear of death. This is done by honoring everyone's religion and respecting their views. You must demand respect for your beliefs. You must learn to love your life, perfect your life and see the beauty in all things in your life. Make your life long by being of service to people. Greet your fellow man with respect, but grovel to no one. Give thanks for your food and the joy of living. Stay away from alcohol and drugs because they cheat your spirit of vision. When it comes time for you to die, be not filled with fear, but sing your death song and die a hero to yourself and your people. Seek power through purity. Your example of love will balance injustice and hate."

"Yeah, well, just how am I to do all of this? I am no longer connected to any church, and if I am to respect all religions, how can I become rooted in just one?"

The Son of Wankan Tanka smiled with understanding and moved closer to Andrew. "It is because you are no longer connected to one church that makes you so valuable to the Creator. You have touched many lives in your search for inner peace. Even with all of your heartache you have managed to love your fellow man. This is purity in its finest form. This is what shoots fear into the evil of the fallen angel. He tried to kill you with his poison, but the Father sent me to you and chose this time to lay out His plan to you."

"There was a snake wasn't there – almost forgot. He was a big guy - god, how I hate snakes. Okay, if I decide to believe you, where would I start? I mean, this is really weird. You know, it is weird and I could be in like a coma or something. I could . . ." The Son of Wankan Tanka punched Andrew in the arm. "Ouch, why'd you do that?"

"Can you feel pain in a coma?"

"Yeah, I guess, I don't know." The Son of Wankan Tanka hit him again.

"Yeah, okay, okay, I get it. Can't feel pain in a coma. Well then, where does this journey start?"

"In the arms of the woman that began your life's journey with you. Go home, Andrew Walker. Go home to your mother."

Chapter Thirteen
What Do You Want From Me?

The day broke like any other, and she was tired of constantly intercepting thoughts from a metaphysical realm. For the last twenty-six years God placed Emily in a hospital atmosphere, where she was able to counsel people before they died. Some of the souls put in her charge were able to make sense of their situation and develop a faith that allowed them to die in the grace of God. Some were filled with hate and regret and never seemed to grasp the idea of their spirituality. Emily prayed for their souls and they died without the graces provided through forgiveness and love.

It was very clear what God wanted from her, however, deep in her heart, she still wanted desperately to be loved. Now, a widow with a grown son, her spirit yearned for honest love between a man and a woman. When she married James, she believed him to be the love of her life. That might have been true, but no one informed James. Marriage, in his mind, was just another means to attain his monetary and, what Emily considered, worthless goals. Her life with him was one of necessity not one of love and respect, and her marriage vows were made before God, so she stayed with him until he died of a heart attack, but it was simply obligation, nothing more.

James abused her mentally and sometimes physically. He used her for what she could give him, but never gave anything in return, unless there was a hidden benefit in it for him. He then magnified the deed or the gift so family and friends would certainly pat him on the back and congratulate him for being such a wonderful husband. Every gesture was used to make him appear wonderful. Emily wanted to believe someone who loved her was truly wonderful, but that experience just seemed to elude her.

Because she adored being in a city with such history and availability to the arts, she moved to Boston, Massachusetts. It also moved her away from many bad memories. Then, of course, there was the spiritual push which she could never deny. It had become such a part of her. God made it very clear to her in dreams and meditation that Boston was the place she needed to live. This in itself was unsettling because when God made her do something like this, the number of Deathlinks grew and they worried her. She wondered whether she would be able to fulfill her responsibility to them. During her marriage to James, there were very few times when she could meditate, but during those times God found a way to bring her a lost soul or two. She accumulated as constant companions, besides Grace, a boy of sixteen named Jason, and a middle-aged mother named Marie. Emily was still at a loss as to how God's plan was going to play out, but she trusted He had everything under control.

That day, a fluttery feeling in her stomach kept coming and going. She couldn't help but feel something incredible and important was going to happen. She was going to meet someone. This wouldn't be like the others; this person was flesh and blood. It sounded funny to her that most of her real friends were her deceased students of the universe. No doubt this sounded equally as crazy to someone else, even though Emily never divulged her spiritual experiences to others. She could hardly grasp the significance of them herself, so how could she expect anyone else to comprehend them?

The daydreams continued. She referred to him as her soul mate. Everyone has a soul mate, but not all soul mates are meant to live out their lives together. Sometimes, they are only meant to brush into each other on earth, but that special moment keeps a person on their spiritual path. Downhearted, she wondered if this is what was going to happen to her. She prayed so hard all of her life for this. All she wanted was someone to blend into her life. She was living her life for God in this weird manner ordained for her, so why was this so unattainable? It was unfair. Adam was given the gift of Eve. Emily had learned though, that if God did not want something to be, it would not be, and fighting was futile. It is akin to slamming into a brick wall, again and again, until awareness is learned.

During the day, Emily's stomach flip-flopped. This only happened when the carpenter who lived across the street came and went from his house. She liked him. They met at a block party and his manner was so calm and he seemed to be so gentle and kind. Considering her past experiences with men, gentle and kind were very attractive characteristics. *Is this the man in my dreams? He doesn't look like him, but appearances don't mean anything.* Learned through many painstaking spiritual encounters, Emily knew how a person was pictured in another's psyche did not always reflect the physical realities of their existence. Sometimes their spirit resembles an identity from another life.

God created such a vast universe. In doing so, he left humans without a manual to navigate the unknown territories of their existence. Life could be so exasperating. Emily decided to just throw these unsettling feelings into the universe and if God meant for her to meet this man again she would, otherwise it was not meant to be.

Three weeks went by. The idea that the carpenter across the street was the man in her fantasy faded, even though she was still experiencing the dreams and the spiritual sensations. It was driving her insane. *What could possibly be the use of these feelings? I haven't met anyone new, nor have I had the time to worry about it.* Even if this were true, Emily consistently suffered the breathless intensity that drained her of any other kind of spiritual energy.

In prayer one evening, she sunk into deep meditation. A little girl came to her. Although very distant, she wanted something from Emily. Emily never before sensed this child near her and her spirit exuded grave concern and sadness. This must be the reason for the deep emotions stirring within her recently. No sooner did the child make herself known, than she faded away. Abruptly, there was a knock on the door shaking Emily out of her meditative state. As she opened the door, who should be there but the carpenter?

"Hello, Emily." Joseph Cercione stood at her door with a bag of tomatoes in tow. Emily was so taken by surprise she could hardly speak.

"Joseph, please come in. What on earth do you have there?"

"Well, along with carpentry, I love my garden. It's in the back of my house so you probably didn't know I had one. I just thought maybe you would enjoy these tomatoes."

"Oh, thank you. You know, I make a mean beans and rice dish. Would you be interested in joining me some evening for dinner?" Emily's heart was beating out of her chest. She wondered if Joseph could hear it every time she opened her mouth. Emily was mesmerized. He was so tall, possessing brown eyes that struck her with truth and innocence, yet they were rooted in a dense sadness. She wanted desperately to find out all about him.

"Wow, sure, I mean, yeah I would love to. When do you think we could do this?"

Joseph's smile was unsure but whimsical and so impish. How Emily loved impish. This trait in a man always stole her heart. Her son, Andrew, had that certain air about him. He could always melt her heart with just a look and a smile.

"Well, we could set a date for tomorrow evening, say around 7:00?" Emily tried to remember a coquettish smile. It had been so long since she used one.

"Seven it is. Thank you, I'm looking forward to it." Joseph turned and walked back across the street to his house.

"It's him, I know it! It's him. Thank you, God, thank you, thank you, thank you!" Emily danced around the living room like a teenager. She was alive again.

The brilliance of the next morning gave way to thoughts of events to come, and cooking reigned supreme in between voice lessons. The house filled with the rich smell of southern cooking. It had been a very long time since Emily had any inclination to cook like this. Normally, she loved to cook, but when there was no one there to appreciate it, it seemed unfulfilling and pointless.

After her last voice student left, she retired to relax in a luxurious bath. Emily considered baths to be the essence of sheer rejuvenation and she needed this for this evening's date. She picked out the sweetest flowered dress and with one last look in the mirror, the doorbell rang. Running to answer the door, the sensations pulsated within her. Something was coming and it didn't have anything to do with Joseph.

"Hello, I hope I didn't keep you waiting too long." Emily tilted her head and smiled.

"No, not at all." Joseph looked perfectly wonderful. Emily loved the way he wore his hair. It was salt and pepper, and he wore it longer than most, but not long enough to make him look shaggy.

"Please, come in. Make yourself at home. Dinner will be ready shortly."

"I, ah, brought some wine. I hope you don't mind. I didn't know if you even drank wine, but in my family, you don't go to anyone's home for dinner without it."

"Certainly. How very thoughtful of you. If I get some glasses, would you do the honors?" Emily loved having a man around who actually knew how to experience the niceties of life. James always frowned on anything that was remotely comforting. It made him uneasy to experience normal familial pleasures.

Joseph poured the wine into the glasses and sat down next to Emily on the couch. Contentment and rich conversation filled the room. Emily's lust for this kind of companionship was insatiable. She didn't want the evening to end. If Joseph wasn't her soul mate then God must have someone so incredible it boggled her mind.

"So, Joseph," Emily began,

"Call me Joey, that's what my family calls me and I would like you to call me that, too."

"So, Joey, if you don't mind me asking, how long have you lived alone?" Emily winced when she saw the smile fade from Joey's face.

"Oh, I guess it's been five years in August. My wife died a while back in childbirth. My baby, Angela, died five years ago. She had bad kidneys. There wasn't anything the doctors could do. I'll tell you, Emily, outside of losing my wife, losing my little girl was the most devastating time of my life. Angie was only seven years old. How could God take someone so sweet and kind from me like that? You know? She was all I had. The pain doesn't go away; it just dulls a little every day. I tell you, I remember the smell of her hair, the feel of her little hand in mine, the way she used to make me laugh when I gave her heck. She was the best thing I ever did. I've lost faith because of it. I don't mean to say that I don't believe in God anymore, but I've lost faith, you know I've lost touch and I can't seem to find the desire to care about God. I just don't care."

Emily knew this was not the time to try to resell Joey on God. Her heart hurt for him. She knew how hard it was to lose people who were close. You do wonder why God puts people in your life, makes you love them and then takes them away. However, there was the more philosophical viewpoint, and she hoped she would remember it if she needed to. Everyone comes into the world by themselves and they leave by themselves. If your path crosses with another and love is exchanged, it is up to the individual to seek the lesson to be learned, no matter what the outcome. That is the struggle in living in perfect, absolute faith. Poor Joey; what consolation could she offer him? She opted for silence.

Chapter Fourteen

I Don't Get It!

The next day, Emily was sure she would see Joey. The thought of waving to him from across the street excited her. Finally, a new relationship with someone so worth loving and Joseph Cercione deserved love. He deserved respect and the deep caring of another individual. He saturated all of her thoughts. The desire to take care of him and nurture a relationship with him was her destiny, and this surely was God's gift to her for being such an obedient child.

She saw Joey come out of his house. The postman was making his rounds, so it was an opportune time to go out onto the stoop and say hello to her new friend. Emily walked out of her house and as she caught Joey's eye, she raised her hand to say hello. He avoided her glance. He turned away and went back into his house. She couldn't believe it. *What did I do? Did I delve too far into his personal life too soon? Didn't we have a terrific time?* His mood returned to normal before he left for the evening. After they had dinner they even talked about normal humdrum types of subjects.

That afternoon, Emily had some free time to pray and meditate. Falling into her frequented state of prayer, the little girl who had crept into her awareness earlier returned. This time, the little girl was crying. Emily saw angels comforting the little one and the presence of Jesus was very close at hand. He too, comforted the child and with His arm around her He turned and pointed to Emily. The girl turned her face in Emily's direction. This had to be Angela. Who else could it be? Angela communicated a depth of concern and sorrow. Emily tried to mentally speak with her. She could discern helplessness for someone that Angela loved deeply. *Pray for him, please. Reach him for me.* The pain that Emily felt for Joey and Angela was depressing. She prayed for Joey, she prayed for Angela and she prayed for strength.

Six weeks came and went. Emily did not see or hear from Joey. The odd sensations remained whenever the relationship came up in prayer. She prayed very hard for Joey and actually saw Angela more and more during meditation. Nothing was happening in the physical realm. She sensed the attraction Joey had for her, but she also sensed the rejection. Joey had no intention of pursuing a relationship with Emily, of that, Emily was certain. Prayer on his behalf was blind, but Angela's request took precedence for who was Emily to deny the request of a spirit already living in the presence of God?

That afternoon, Emily saw Joey in front of his house. Unable to stand it any longer, she left her house and wondered how to introduce such a sensitive topic. *Joey, I like you, do you like me* seemed a little juvenile. Perhaps if she approached him with finesse she could get the job done. "Brother, what a pain in the neck, this male/female babble can be." Emily turned to look at her roses and was so preoccupied with her situation she didn't realize she was talking out loud.

"Yeah, Emily. It is a pain in the neck. Especially when I like someone as nice as you and I don't want a relationship." There, standing behind her was Joey; all six feet plus of him. Her heart stopped and then twisted with the disappointment of hearing those words.

"You do, I mean you don't, I mean. Oh, darn, I don't know what I mean. Joey, why don't you want a relationship? Everything was going so well. It clicked didn't it?" Emily was disappointed and she was horrified at the way she was handling the situation.

"Yes, it did. I didn't expect it to click as well as it did. I thought by acting as if we just shared a friendly evening, it would be easier to forget you. I was able to do it for a while, but lately you just keep coming up in my mind. I shouldn't be telling you these things. Emily, I don't want this. It can't happen, and I'm not going to let it. Please try to understand, and forgive me." With that said, Joey walked briskly back to his house.

Emily was sick with grief over the loss of something so new and beautiful, but now could never happen. *God, why are you doing this to me? You can't tell me you can't just wave your hand and allow something to happen. You're God. You can do anything.* Emily had to take a moment to recover. She was never to have the one thing in this life she prayed to experience. It was inconceivable that the God she served so steadily all of her life was now going to deny her this one request. If He had some-one else in mind, why did she experience the truths of Angela's exis-tence? Was she just to pray for Joey and was the metaphysical shakeup just Angela's way of getting her attention? Emily was exhausted. She looked up just in time to see Rosemary, one of her more promising students getting off the bus. A half-hearted wave flew from her hand and she went inside to prepare for her next lesson.

In their future, Emily and Joey were to become the best of friends, but stayed away from talking about feelings. He was there for her whenever she needed a good neighbor and she helped him with any neighborhood gatherings, but the subject of romantic love was aban-doned. Emily did not understand why Joey was brought to her, but she did not deny him friendship. Life simply continued.

Chapter Fifteen
Oh, My Rosemary

Good girls did not do what Rosemary did with Gabe. They knew each other for ten years. She could still remember the first day she met him. Both of their families were Catholic so it would stand to reason the children were sent to parochial school. St. Peter's was the best. The children always remembered the sisters and the priests with great fondness. Rosemary's personal favorite was Sister Mary Stanislaus. She was so alive and happy all of the time, and played jump rope with the girls. Sister's habit flew all over and her rosary bounced up and down as she attempted to keep up with the swinging rope. Then things sped up with the implementation of some salt and pepper. Sister worked hard to keep up, but usually the rope would get the best of her.

Gabriel de la Rosa was always a rebel. Rosemary believed his propensity for insurrection was the reason why she liked him so well. Their first grade teacher seated them in alphabetical order, and since her full name was Rosemary Catherine O'Reilly, she was supposed to be seated next to Peter Michael O'Toole, but Gabe slid right into that seat. An argument ensued as Rosemary told him he didn't belong there. Gabe insisted that he did belong there, and from then on they were great friends. It must have been fate, because Sister never did move him out of that seat.

When they got to high school, their friendship turned into a romance. Their parents were not sure they cared for this. Gabe was a first generation American whose family came from Cuba and Rosemary was first generation Irish American. The families relented since at least the children were both Roman Catholic, but they still had many reservations regarding the differences in culture. Rosemary secretly thought the name Rosemary de la Rosa had kind of a silly ring to it, and had no intention of getting married to her high school sweetheart anyway.

Pondering these things, she hopped on the bus to go to her voice lesson with Mrs. Walker. Rosemary loved her voice teacher. Mrs. Walker's voice never weakened with age. Since she was fourteen, Rosemary sang her way into Emily's heart. What a life Mrs. Walker had. She married right out of college and gave up a promising career for her very demanding husband. Mrs. Walker never went into it, but Rosemary got the impression there was unresolved pain from the marriage. After her husband died, Mrs. Walker moved to Boston. Rosemary always suspected her to have disturbing ties to the spiritual world, too. You could see wisdom and sensitivity in her eyes and when she sang her world existed only for the music.

However, Rosemary had more to think about than Mrs. Walker. Her period was late and she didn't know what she was going to do. *I'm only seventeen years old. My parents are going to be so ashamed and Gabe's parents will blame me.* Her best bet was to try to keep up with her normal routine. If only her period would start. Everything would be back to normal and she would never have sex with Gabriel de la Rosa again.

During Mass that morning and communion, she prayed as hard as she could. "Please God, don't let me be pregnant. If I'm not, I will always be faithful to you and follow your commandments."

Rosemary, in retrospect, thought this was such a stupid bargain to make with God. *I'll always be faithful to Him and I'll always follow His commandments, although, I sure messed up the sixth one.* If you look at the whole situation, God had everyone over a barrel - everyone who was truly a Christian, anyway. As a Christian, your life is given over to God, no matter what kinds of sins are committed. She couldn't think about these things right now. She just had to keep going as if everything were normal.

The bus stopped in front of Mrs. Walker's house. Rosemary waved to Emily as she got off the bus. Petulance and remorse spread through-out her demeanor as she rang her teacher's doorbell.

"Hello, my dear Miss Rosemary. And how are we today?" asked Mrs. Walker.

"All right, I guess." Rosemary choked back tears.

"Well, dear, you don't sound as if you feel all right. Is there something bothering you? Can I help or at least listen?" Mrs. Walker was a wonderful listener. Rosemary confided so many things to her voice teacher. One time, when she got into some mischief with some other girls, she told Mrs. Walker first, even before her parents. She found her to be someone with remarkable insight and appreciation for life's problems. But, this she couldn't confide. This was just too terrible and she couldn't bear losing the respect of her teacher. Besides, it could be a false alarm and why let Mrs. Walker know everything if it wasn't necessary?

"I just don't feel very well, Ma'am."

"Is your lesson prepared?" Emily looked into her student's eyes. There was something more going on. She would have to do some serious meditating with the angels tonight. Something about Rosemary disturbed Emily, but she couldn't put her finger on it.

"Yes, Ma'am."

"Let's get started then." Emily kept a close eye on her student as she performed her lesson. Rosemary had a remarkable range. She could give her practice pieces with differences of three to four octaves. She had a harder time with the lower notes, but still, the girl was an extraordinary talent. Warm-ups today seemed decidedly better than usual. Rosemary was not the kind of student who liked the mundane but necessary ritual. However, today, it served a purpose. After warm-ups, Rosemary started singing Schubert's "Ave Maria" and Emily found it hard to keep tears from surfacing. Rosemary's voice was filled with such deep feeling and purpose; the song was now a prayer in every sense of the word. As she reached the pinnacle of the crescendo, her voice wavered, and out of nowhere Rosemary fell apart.

"Mrs. Walker, I . . . have . . . to go. Please, forgive me." Rosemary fled Emily's home in tears.

Emily watched Rosemary run down the street. She didn't even wait at the bus stop. Yes, something was terribly wrong, and Mrs. Emily Walker knew in her heart that something big was coming her way. *Could the problem be so horrible that Rosemary would do something drastic? Rosemary was so level headed. She could never be overwhelmed, so insane that she would be driven to well . . . no!* Rosemary was a dedicated Roman Catholic. Suicide, because suicide meant damnation of the spirit, would never be entertained. Emily had to meditate. Rosemary was in trouble.

Walking the entire two miles back home, Rosemary saw Gabe waiting for her on her front porch. He was pacing and looked as bad as she felt.

"Rose, thank God you're home. How are you feeling? Are you still sick in the morning? Have you found out anything more?" Gabe was frantic. The pressure was getting to him.

"Terrible! Yes! And how in the world could I find out anything? If I go to the doctor, my parents will know right away."

"I've been thinking about that. Rosemary, my cousin Billy knows of a doctor who can do a test for us. He will do it and not tell anyone. What do you say? Will you go with me?"

"When would this be? Tonight, tomorrow, when?" Rosemary was agitated. She remembered when they decided to become intimate. She trusted Gabe with every fiber of her being. He told her everything would be fine, but here they were, and everything was awful. On top of that, she felt Gabriel was getting cold feet. If they did find out she was pregnant, she wasn't quite sure he would stand by her.

"We could go tonight. Just tell your parents that we have a date. I'll pick you up like I usually do and no one will be the wiser."

Rosemary's world was crashing down around her. Her soul was on the verge of complete moral collapse and she shuddered at the thought of finding out what she already knew in her heart to be true.

"Okay. What time?"

"I have it set up for 7:00 p.m. Rosemary, this guy, uh, this guy also does, well, you know, he can take care of the problem, you know?" Gabe looked at her half hoping and half ashamed at the suggestion.

"Oh, my god, Gabe! You can't be serious. You can't mean that we should kill our child?" Rosemary was horrified at the possibility Gabe could be serious. She thought she knew him, but now, god, how could she have been so wrong?

"Rosie, honey, this is the only way. Your father will kill me. My parents will disown me. My whole future, all of my plans will be gone, forever. If you don't do this, I will be forced to deny everything."

"You slimy, contemptible . . . how dare you use me like this and then toss me aside as if I meant nothing to you." Rosemary's Irish temper was flaring and a bit of her mother's Irish brogue slipped into her speech. "You could defile our Catholic upbringing by murdering our own child? You could spit in the face of our Church and our families by sanctioning this outrage?"

"Yes, I'm sorry, but I have no other choice." Gabe looked at her with determination.

"I'll go tonight, but by myself. I won't be seen with a murderer. Tell me where to go, and then you go straight to hell where you belong." Rosemary wasn't sure whether she could continue. Her anger was great and her heart so wounded.

Gabe handed her a piece of paper with an address written on it. Then he walked away and that would be the last time she would ever see him.

Chapter Sixteen
Come On Down!

Prayer and meditation engulfed Emily as she looked out her kitchen window. The room was dark except for the candles she lit for companionship. The embrace of all of the spirits entrusted to her surrounded her. Sorrow crept into her prayers for she knew she was soon to be joined by yet another lost soul. Her heart beat knowing full well. She knew, although, she did not want to believe. *Why does God not tell me about these situations before they get so out of hand?* Emily prayed hard about this. If correct, this would be the hardest of circumstances. *The territory of spiritual warriors is the soul; their weapons are the word and love and understanding of God.*

Rosemary found her way to this "doctor's" office. The front door looked like a store front. As a matter of fact, the sign above it read *Stan's Drugstore*. What a dilemma. She had no other choice and needed to find out for sure.

There were several young women seated in a waiting area. *This makes me sick to my stomach. I know why they are here. Oh, don't overreact, Rosemary. Maybe they are just here to pick up medicine.* Rosemary continued to admonish herself as she made her way to an empty chair. The office smelled like a drugstore. It was clean enough, yet she just felt so uncomfortable. The surrounding mood was dreary and uncertain.

"Rosemary O'Reilly?" Stan the Man with glasses and a nervous smile came out of another room.

"Yes, that's me." Rosemary jumped up, startled at hearing her name out loud as if Stan were announcing to the whole waiting room that she had sinned . . . grievously sinned.

"Come this way, please." Rosemary followed the man into the next room. There was an examination table and all sorts of doctor's equipment. She felt very strange and frightened. "Now, let me understand. You only want to know if you are pregnant."

"Yes, I certainly don't want to do anything else." Rosemary was so angry Gabe left her to do this by herself.

"Then let's get right to it. I'm going to take some blood and I think I can give you a definitive answer tonight if you let me give you a physical exam." The little man was serious and abrupt. He scared her, but she really had no other alternative. She needed to know as soon as possible.

Rosemary tried not to shiver as she lay on the examination table. It was so cold. Her eyes felt like they were bulging out of their sockets. *This is July isn't it? Why does it feel like the middle of February?* The man's hands were cold and clinical. That was probably good, but she just was so terrified and felt all of this was so dirty. Finally, the exam was over and she was allowed to put her clothes back on.

"Well, Miss O'Reilly. You are definitely pregnant. From the looks of it, I would guess about seven or eight weeks. Is this all that I can do for you, or do you need anything else?" The man gave her what to Rosemary seemed like a demonic look. She hated him and what he did. The more she looked at him the more demonic he became. Perhaps this was due to her overactive, girlish imagination, but if she didn't know better, she believed he was transforming into a devil right before her eyes. She couldn't get away from him fast enough.

Rosemary ran out the door of the examination room, through the midst of all of those other women and out the front door. The July heat felt so good. Still shivering from the ordeal, her worst fears were confirmed. *I can't go home. What will my parents do?* As she walked down the narrow dirty street, she saw a sign advertising a hotel. Maybe she could get a room for the night. Away from everyone, she could sift through the turmoil going on inside. She got a room on the top floor. This would get her far away from everyone and high enough in the air to . . . well, she might think about that later.

Meditation brought deep serenity and it was satisfying. Perhaps Emily's previous notion was just that, a notion, a guess. She could accept that. Her eyes closed as she took a deep cleansing breath and gagged. A putrid smell filled the air, and shocked back to physical reality, she opened her eyes to a demon glowering inches from her face. Emily shot up and said a quick prayer. The demon laughed maniacally, dancing and hissing. His iniquitous troops appeared one at a time. Sick, deformed, evil little spirits filled the room with a ghastly odor. Emily prayed and the battle began.

"Come to me, little ones of God. Bring your weapons of faith and love. Unite with me and bring with you the Holy Spirit!" First Grace appeared, then the others. "Through Jesus, I invoke all of the warrior angels to come to my aid!" The room was crammed with angels and the demons shrieked and moaned. Profanity and prayer resonated throughout the little kitchen. A contest of profound noise grew producing utter chaos. Grace quoted the Bible, Emily raised her voice in song, and the others prayed prayers into the faces of the demons.

Rosemary lay on the bed in the humid, hot hotel room where she tried to rationalize her circumstances. It was no use. There was no rationalization here. Her parents would lose all love and respect for her. Gabriel's parents would look upon her as a filthy tramp for trying to implicate their son in her problem and she would be disgraced in the eyes of her family and in the eyes of her Church. She could go to Father Moscow and he would probably place her in a home for unwed mothers. This was too terrible. Gabe was right. How lucky he was to be a man. He could just deny all responsibility where a woman is stuck with the tell-tale signs of motherhood. *What a coward he is. I could never, ever take the life of my child. I could never live with myself knowing that I had done such a thing, yet . . .* She looked at the open window before her. *I could die with my child. No one would know why I did it; no one except for that contemptible Gabriel de la Rosa. Let him live with that for the rest of his life.*

Her emotions churned. *How high is this window from the ground?* She certainly wanted it to be over quickly. Rosemary stroked her abdomen. Poor little soul didn't even have a chance to live. She stepped up onto the ledge of the window, tears flowing down her cheeks. Grief and fear filled her broken heart. *Can I really do this?* She balanced in the open window as she looked down at the pavement. A case of vertigo and hiccupping sobs handicapped her breathing and hindered her balance. Tears blurred her vision and her legs shook as she thought of her innocent baby. *I don't know. Maybe being a single mother won't be so bad, or I could give the baby up for adoption.* Rosemary's breathing was more even now. She changed her mind and decided to face the music. *Be careful. Climb down from this window and . . . what the . . .* The heel of her shoe caught on a piece of cracked wood in the window frame. Giving it a quick tug . . . screams permeated the air. Rosemary tumbled out of the window and crashed onto the pavement below. Her head split with a sudden, intense pain and blood gushed from her broken skull.

Two spirits emerged. Rosemary floated above to see her mangled body, and a diminutive light, similar to the size and elegance of a butterfly drifted away from her abdomen. A blinding white light led it upward. Deep remorse surrounded Rosemary. This was her child leaving her for a better place.

Rosemary's spirit was not permitted to linger and was violently sucked into a vacuum and spewed into a room filled with demons, and spirits and angels all engaged in a horrible battle, and . . . *for heaven's sake, there is my own Mrs. Walker.*

Unexpectedly, the clatter stopped. Everything disappeared and only the first demon remained. Emily recognized that face. It was the face of the demon that terrorized her; it was the face of the demon reflected in Bentley's eyes as he raped her so long ago. Looking into her soul it hissed, "We have just begun. Prepare for the long road to hell!" And as he prepared to leave he pointed to the corner of the room and said, ". . . and I'm taking her with me!"

Of course Rosemary was going to hell. She killed herself didn't she? She turned her back on everything she believed in because of her anger at Gabe and her fear of the responsibility that was rightfully hers.

"God spare me!" She shrieked.

The demon lunged at her and his dark cloud besieged her. Rosemary felt inundated in evil. Emily prayed as loud as she could, but her soldiers were nowhere to be found.

Out of the evil smog and rancid smells a voice commanded, "Stop, in the name of the Creator, Wankan Tanka."

Everything ceased. Emily turned to see her own son, Andrew Walker and beside him stood two warrior angels and an Indian Chieftain. The demon shrank in terror and then dissipated, and the angels bowed humbly to Emily and left, and the Chief faded away. Emily ran to Andrew. Her son returned to her, and he was transformed. Emily hardly recognized him. No longer was he just her son, but a great warrior in the army of God.

Emily carefully beckoned to Rosemary. "It's all right, child. You are with us. Rest easy in the love of God." Two other Deathlinks appeared and escorted Rosemary to the nebula where they were granted sanctuary from the demons of hell.

Clearly, Emily and Andrew had their work cut out for them. In prayer, they were shown the army that Lucifer was gathering. The army was just like him; depraved, selfish, and sheer evil. Their destruction came from all over the world and in every nook and crevasse veils of darkness infiltrated communities with pods of sin against mankind. Emily and Andrew needed the armor of faith and courage, and they needed it now.

Chapter Seventeen
Infected, Infectious Fiend

Evil encircled this officer of the court. Geoffrey Myers Downing, Esquire, was taking one last gander at his office, his desk, and all of the possessions that made his depravity possible. The brandy he sipped was one of the finest as was everything he owned. He loved owning, eating, drinking and wearing the best. He had unimaginable wealth even beyond what he thought possible. Knowledge of the law was the way he manipulated his colleagues, his clients and friends, few as they were. He had the talent to be an outstanding lawyer, one with integrity and real grit. Instead, he chose an easier, less demanding route to abundance. His last win permitted one of the wealthiest corporations in the world to continue to secure more properties and air space in order to command and devour the smaller less successful companies. Many people lost their jobs and the smaller companies were destroyed.

Another company he represented needed to sell the pesticides that it produced, but the company realized if their workers were exposed to the product, men were likely to become sterile and/or get testicular cancer. Geoffrey found a way around disclosing this important information to the company's employees legally, and made a huge profit for his client at the expense of their workers, many of whom became sick and died. This tragedy increased exponentially until the company was forced to divulge records; however, all of the legal documents had pertinent passages expunged and redacted.

Geoffrey had the chance to change. Before he sold his soul to you-know-who, he was in love. Barbara was a beautiful woman, but beyond physical beauty she possessed a beautiful soul. She was a good influence on Geoff for a while, but he just could not function without making the amount of money he wanted as fast as he wanted to make it. He was as greedy for lust as he was for possessions. Barbara found him in bed with her roommate and the relationship ended. She wasted no time in ridding herself of a man who did not deserve her - smart woman that Barbara.

Unfortunately, Geoffrey blamed everything and everyone but himself for losing her. He tried to convince himself she had fallen for another man and that was the reason for their breakup. He sunk into a deep depression, and this is where Monsieur Diable picked him up. He created a demon worse than even he ever envisaged.

Geoffrey was behind hundreds of underhanded, unethical and sinister deeds. No one, except for one, knew of his black secret. All of Geoff's cunning was sold to him. It was sold to him for a solitary payment - his soul. Now, the law he had abused so adeptly, caught up with him. He was caught with his hands into a speck of organized crime, a little teen-age prostitution and just a bit of money laundering, followed by a smidgeon of foreign female slave trade. His time was up. Too soon as far as Geoff was concerned, but this was a matter of contract interpretation and it was slippery and ironclad. Attorney Downing was very familiar with contracts, but this time he was debunked, outsmarted, snookered. Fear entrapped him. His skin crawled and his stomach was making some rather frightful noises because he knew that, well, this was it. The contract specifically stated that payment was due upon death or at such time he could no longer deliver the corruption he had promised. His fate was locked in. Just as his wealth was assured, so was his damnation.

"Counselor!" The room filled with the foul pungency of Geoffrey's master. He didn't just look like all of the pictures you see growing up. Whatever you like to call him; Beelzebub, Satch, Satan - he was terrifying. The horror was not so much in his appearance, but in his aura. Amoral thoughts oozed into the atmosphere in his presence. Murder, lust, deceit, profanity walked with him, and every movement mandated fear.

"Master!" Geoffrey fell to his knees.

"Your time has come to join me." The demon encircled him, smothering him with his putrid smell and carnivorous thoughts.

"Yes, Master."

"Come now, Geoffrey. You are afraid, but all of that will pass with your passing." The demon chortled at his little witticism. "When you die, I will take command of your spirit and you will become powerful! I need you. You see there is this woman, this wench that has been groomed by the righteous . . . " As he tried to reference God, the demon writhed in pain, letting out a great groan. Geoffrey quaked with dread. The thought of asking for forgiveness entered his mind, so the demon wasted no time in squelching any thought of vindication for his new soldier. "Not a possibility, my dear, Mr. Downing. Your soul is mine, remember?"

Geoffrey pulled himself to his feet. Mournful, he walked to his desk drawer where he kept a small pistol. As he checked it for ammunition, the evil spirit lorded over him, keeping him in a state of choking nausea. Barren music hovered around him, first engulfing his soul and then lifting his mind to a state of bewilderment. He drew the pistol into his mouth, licking the barrel. The taste excited him. He stroked his face with it. His shaking body pressed the insanity on to another level of degradation. Intimacy with the gun became more and more intense until, Geoffrey pushed it so far into his mouth he gagged and was compelled to pull the trigger. The contract was executed. The deed was done. The explosion blew Geoff's brains away, and as his body lay dead in a puddle of blood, his soul was immediately injected with the infected stream of sins and wickedness with which he led his life. His master was only too glad to collect the debt and make plans for an even more abhorrent period where he wanted, no, he needed Geoff's depravity to prevail. This war was getting trickier and perversion was the only path to victory.

Chapter Eighteen

The Formation Begins

The world was introduced to many new inventions, new philosophies, and new medical procedures. Good men in politics were proven to be not so good men before God. Children preached "make love not war" and did it. Governments sent men to fight for their own power and greed and passed it off as a just war to end oppression. Emily's own son Andrew had to fight in Vietnam in 1965. Andrew saw many abominations while he was there and hesitated to talk to Emily about them, yet she knew, somehow, just as she knew when he was drafted into the army that God had a reason for him to go. Andrew was trained in the killing fields. It was God's boot camp for all of the frightful things awaiting Andrew and Emily's army. Other Vietnam Vets were being called to fight in God's Great War and didn't even know it; the war that would finally combine heaven and earth and totally annihilate hell. Lord knows the boys who fought in Vietnam experienced hell. Lucifer was given carte blanche in that place and blanketed it with fear, murder, rape and every kind of mortal carnage. Andrew came home from the war, much to Emily's surprise, devastated and without hope. He roamed from state to state trying to find himself. VA hospitals, halfway houses, and the streets where the homeless took up residence were his places of employment as he hoped to regain his faith. This is where he met Anelise. She changed him and forced him to feel again. They were inseparable, yet Andrew could not bring himself to trust her or himself in a permanent relationship. After years of waiting, Anelise stopped the relationship, leaving him without a word.

"For God's sake, Mother, what are you doing?" Andrew came rushing into the kitchen. Smoke billowed from the stove.

"Oh, my Lord, I was so deep in my own thoughts, I forgot about the dinner that I had on the stove." Emily grabbed the burning skillet and threw it into the sink.

"Geez, Mom, I just love it when you make me one of your best home-cooked meals." Andrew winked at her and grinned.

"All right, all right, wise guy, you know you missed this. We can go out for dinner. Emily breathed a deep sigh. "You know, we need to summon all of our Deathlinks together."

"Yes, let's do it tonight!" Andrew said this with such fierce single-mindedness, it made Emily uneasy. The thought of him mixing it up with the king of evil was terrifying.

"Honey, how great is your faith in the power of prayer?"

"Oh please, you can't be serious, Mother. I prayed, hour by hour, minute by minute in Nam. You are right, though. I did question His existence until recently when I took a trip to the Bad Lands. God is real in many ways and has as many personas as there are differences in the men He created." Andrew was obviously very agitated by his mother's assumptions, but understood her concern.

"Andrew, I'm sorry. I didn't mean to infer that you aren't in touch with God. But we are talking about a very intense and volatile issue here. These spiritual warriors, these Deathlinks are not flesh and blood. They are hurt, recycled souls. They rely on the unwavering strength of their faith, because they know that if they fail they will die and there will be no eternity."

"Mother, I am aware of this and I am ready. I want to do this tonight. God saved me so many times in the war. It took me a long time to finally get to this point. I've been knocking around the country for too many years now, and I am ready to serve Him. He has chosen me and He deserves this from me."

Emily didn't feel connected somehow, but she learned early on working for God meant what she felt sometimes just didn't matter. Under her breathe she sighed, "All right, Lord. Please, let us know what we are doing."

After they dined on take out, Emily lit the candles all around the kitchen. She and Andrew sat down at the kitchen table and began to pray. For Andrew, this was an eerie but fascinating sight. Slowly, one by one, the souls appeared; first Grace, then Rosemary, and Michael Harrison who had recently joined them after dying a natural death in his sleep the year before. God sent him to assist. Others, Andrew did not know, slowly entered the room. They all looked so lost and frightened.

With Andrew came his own entourage. He was unaware that they were attached to him, but leading the group was Feather on the Wind. The rest were people whose lives Andrew touched before they passed over and now came back to fight evil alongside him. Andrew and Emily were dizzy with the reality of each presence and the task set out before them.

Hidden behind Grace was Angela. Emily wasn't sure why Angela would be here at this particular gathering, but she wasn't going to question God. The mood was solemn and tense. She could tell Andrew felt it too. Abruptly, a loud thump interrupted the intensity. Before Emily could stop him, Andrew was out of his chair and on top of a huge man sprawled face down on the floor. He had the man's arm bent behind his back and was choking him with his other arm.

"Stop it! Andrew! He's a friend."

Andrew released him shaking off the fear. "Don't you know better than to sneak up on a guy who served two tours in the most evil place on earth?"

"Please Sir, don't hurt my daddy." Angela, unruffled by the skirmish, calmly bent over Andrew.

"Angela, my Angela! Where did you ever come from?" Andrew looked upon her in total amazement and Joseph Cercione, in disbelief, gazed at his little daughter. Over the years, Joey stayed friends with Emily and would come over to visit. He had come over to do just that and tripped, as he so often did, when coming through the back door.

"Daddy, I'm here to give you a message from God. He wants you to listen to Emily. He wants you to help her in her work."

"Angela, how is this possible?"

"I am with God and Mommy. There is to be the last war between good and evil. Emily is one of God's chosen and she needs your help. You will help God won't you, Daddy? He asked me to make this message mean something to you. He has been trying so long to make you hear him when he speaks to your heart, but you closed it all up after I left you. Promise me that you will help. Please Daddy, please?" With that the little girl's image began to fade.

"Angela, my baby, yes, of course I will help God. Angela, don't go, come back." The grief Joey had been holding in came forth. Angels comforted him. Emily, Andrew, and company prayed in silence. This meeting of God's faithful was over. His purpose was served and Joseph Cercione would prove to be one of the Creator's most courageous warriors and eventually, the man of Emily's dreams.

Later that evening, after Andrew and Emily soothed Joey's broken heart and sent him home to quiet himself, they began to talk. Andrew had never seen Emily's spirits. He needed to know more about each of them.

"Who was that really young boy standing next to Rosemary?"

"That would be Jason. He was sixteen years old when he and his friends were playing a game of Russian roulette. His heart was so heavy when he came to me. He really never thought he would be killed. It was so senseless. Okay, I'm next. Who is the Indian fellow and the others? Andrew, are you a medium?"

"To be honest, this is the first time I saw Feather on the Wind outside of my dreams, and as for the others . . . they were, or are people I helped pass on. What about that middle-aged lady? She looks like she is in perpetual mourning." Andrew's heart hurt when he pictured all of them in his mind. He knew why they were there. None of the

Deathlinks had wanted to live and for most of them their problems in life were so insurmountable they willed to end their existence.

"Her name is Marie. She found out her husband of twenty years was having an affair. She took sleeping pills to help her sleep and one night she took too many with too many chasers of Jack Daniels. Unfortunately, three very distressed and angry teenagers were left behind."

"Mom, we need to organize them and send them out into the world again. When I was in Nam, Feather on the Wind visited me in my dreams. I didn't understand it all then, but now, after seeing these broken souls, it all makes sense. These souls who have been entrusted to us have unfinished spiritual concerns. Along with them being soldiers to fight against the evil in the last days, they also have to link up with someone who is about to do what they did and stop them. The people our Deathlinks save will finish their earthly missions. Until the Deathlinks complete their task, they can't join our troops for the final days. Our job is to pray and listen for guidance as to where to find these mortal beings that need the help of our Deathlinks. This doesn't give us very long to do all of the things God wants us to do."

Emily sighed. She already knew what Andrew said was true, but was glad he understood the severity of their dilemma. The question was how? She added, "All of them have got to find and help their mortal counterparts soon, or we will lose them to the other side, and you can bet old Lucifer has rallied his troops together to help stop them. On top of that, I fear God is sending more lost souls to us, only some of them have not passed on. These times have created much despair."

Andrew and Emily shared heavy hearts. They realized the righteousness of the world was relying partly on the success of their assignments. The Almighty had others working on His behalf, but none of them knew of each other's existence; not yet anyway. God gave these human beings a massive task with the salvation of so many souls resting on their shoulders. Sometimes, it was just easy to question faith. How was now the constant question.

The two ended this meditative session with prayer. Their eyes closed in reverence, a vision of a young man clothed in rags and preaching came into sight. This spectacle could have been on any street corner of a major metropolitan city anywhere in the world. But he spoke with a British accent, "All of you who proclaim yourselves to be better people than your neighbor because you spew words from the New Testament then turn around and are hypocrites in the eyes of the Creator are yourselves the anti-Christ. You who allow scripture to roll off your tongues simply to make yourselves feel superior to others are the anti-Christ. You who condemn your fellow man because they do not practice your personal sanctimonious religion are worshipping the fallen angel because you practice his way of conceit and you are summoning him by all of your deeds to challenge the Creator."

A policeman tried to remove the man, but a member of the crowd that had gathered asked, "Do you not believe that Jesus Christ is the Son of God?"

As the officer released his captive, the man replied, "Many religions believe in the Creator. Jesus is part of the Universal Trinity. In Polynesian religion the son of mother and father earth is Tane, Islam honors Jesus as a great prophet, along with Abraham. The Son of Man lives in all of us. "I Am, Who Am" and Yahweh lives in all of us. Not just Christians, or followers of Christ, but all of us who live by God's light. There is darkness, great darkness in all of us as there is vast wondrous light. It is ours to choose."

Around the young man angels hovered and there were souls bound to him. Andrew and Emily recognized them as this ragged prophet's Deathlinks.

The scene shifted to an Islamic teacher quoting the Qur'an "Do not turn away a poor man . . . even if all you can give is half a date. If you love the poor and bring them near you, God will bring you near Him on the Day of Resurrection." Around the man were angels and prophets and bound to him were Deathlinks.

In rapid succession similar scenes with men of God from various religious persuasions played out before Andrew and Emily. A rabbi was teaching a group of children. "Do not do to people what you do not want done to you. Always remember, God exists, God is one and unique, God is incorporeal, God is eternal, prayer is to be directed to God alone, the words of the prophets are true, Moses was the greatest prophet, and his prophecies are true, the Torah was given to Moses, there will be no other Torah, God knows the thoughts and deeds of men, God will reward the good and punish the wicked, the Messiah will come, the dead will be resurrected." As he spoke these last words he looked up at the Deathlinks bound to him and the rabbi bowed his head in silent prayer.

When peace finally came to Andrew and Emily the spell was broken. They did not speak, but they now understood that God was working through many, and other Deathlink mediums had been called from all over the world to follow His intricate plan.

Chapter Nineteen
A Trail of Ivy

"Yeah, bitch, well I don't have to listen to every goddamn thing that you say anymore! I'm eighteen fuckin' years old. If I don't want to come home until 5:00 a.m. then I guess that's my business, now isn't it?" Ivy Winston slammed the receiver of the pay phone down as hard as she could. That conversation with her mother was the last straw. *This is the seventies for Christ's sake. Mom is living in the past. Kids do what they want now. It isn't like it was in the fifties where everything was so goddamn provincial.* "Honor your father and mother? Screw that. What about them giving me a little honor." Ivy kept on talking out loud to herself as she walked. She thought that maybe by venting her anger out loud . . . no, it wasn't going to work. She was just damned depressed. Nothing was going right for her. Her grades were dropping. She was in danger of flunking chemistry and without that stupid grade, she wasn't going to graduate. If that happened, then she might as well start moving her things out of her parents' house right now. *I need a little something, you know, to like make me forget everything.* Recently, Ivy had become a frequent visitor to an apartment belonging to a friend. After his two tours in Vietnam he came home and brought his addiction with him and shared it with younger, impressionable people. He had things to sell to make Ivy feel better. She started going there about six months before, and that's when her problems began. First, a little pot and some booze. Next, came some uppers then some downers. She started to lose weight and sleep. But, the apartment is where everyone accepted her. Hell, she was a damn guru. Everyone thought she was *the* party girl. Yeah, that's where she'd go.

"Knock, knock!" Ivy opened the door to the apartment. It didn't seem like anyone was there.

"Ivy, baby, what's up?" Bill Benson slithered up behind her and put his arms around her. He started to kiss her neck.

"Billy-dilly, you have anything to make me happy?"

"I do girl, but do you have payment for the last two parties?" Billy-dilly traced his finger up and down Ivy's neck.

"Bill, look, I'm short on cash right now. My parents are giving . . ."

"Oh, Ivy, lady, we can work out arrangements. You know that. I'm feelin' kind of horny this morning. You think you could make me feel better? I know I could make you feel better, in more ways than one. A trade, you know?"

"Bill, look, I don't know. We did this before and I felt like shit after." Ivy tried her very best to pile on the sweet little girl act. "Can't you think of another way?"

"Bitch! You come to my place, take my drugs, drink my booze and then have the balls to tell me you felt like shit after I plugged you? Man, girl, you have got some kind of nerve. You should be lucky I didn't make you lay down for just anyone. I could you know. You owe me plenty. Now, how about you just come over here and be nice to me. You know you loved it last time. Besides, if you don't, you will with someone else, I promise. And I don't know who that someone will be. You get my drift, bitch?"

Ivy felt trapped. She really needed drugs. It was getting to the point where she needed drugs all of the time. *They just cost so damn much. So what if I give the guy sex. I'm on the pill. Who the hell cares anyway?*

"Okay. Billy-dilly. But I want payment up front."

"Ivy, honey, you drive a hard bargain, get it, hard? Ha! You know if you do right by me, I'll give you some of my primo. Something you have never done before."

"What's that?" Ivy undressed in anticipation of her new high.

"LSD, baby, that's what. You haven't lived until you've tripped on that stuff."

"Yeah?" Ivy slipped her naked body under the sheets next to Bill. "Well, come here, Billy, and let me earn my trip."

Mr. Lucifer was slithering around in that apartment, in that room, between the sheets and in that bed. He chose his primary soldier. This one, he was going to keep alive. She wasn't quite ready to join the ranks, but he was sure that Billy-dilly would be of enormous assistance. Between the drugs and the sex, how could he miss?

That night, Bill gave his usual Saturday night bash. Lots of new people were there. It seemed to Ivy this party was different from the others. There were older guys there. They all were really interested in the girls; too interested she thought. Earlier, Bill had slipped her a couple cubes. She took them and while she was dancing one of these new guys started to flirt with her. She felt antsy. She wanted to move. Dancing was a good thing. The guy danced with her and made his moves. He put his hand on her breast. She giggled. He giggled. It was so silly. They laughed hysterically. She never felt like this with any other drug. About forty-five minutes of pawing and sniggering went on, when Ivy saw her hand making a shadowy trace across her face. She looked around. *Who brought the black lights? No black lights. Huh.* She saw indistinct, filmy objects and felt a weird, macabre, and chilling presence. The party became a photo negative of events. The guy she was with made more serious moves and danced her into a bedroom where he shut the door behind them. Ivy felt very nervous and jumpy. She didn't want it, but the guy was really moving in on her. The buzz of the drug and the guy's face turned into something she couldn't believe. *This has got to be the bad trip everyone talks about.* His hands changed into talons, his smile was gruesome and hideous. Fangs, dripping with saliva, loomed over Ivy and the guy's ears turned into horns. The smell in the room was ghastly, as if a million people died and rotted there. She choked while dodging the dripping spit as the monster ripped off her clothes. She wanted to shriek from fear, but the odor filling the room stifled any attempt. The beast forced himself into her, brutally raping her again and again until he ejaculated, and then he let out a tremendous howl of triumph.

Satan had executed his goal. Pill or no pill, he had the power and he planted his devil's seed. Now he could watch it grow. The war would begin when his repulsive son came of age. A tangible essence living among those poor, unsuspecting people of his enemy God's earth would be born to help him dupe more souls. His army would become invincible, no matter who the man upstairs molded into veneration of Him and His promised kingdom. His son would be the ace in the hole. Lucifer looked up into the heavens, and making a small salute hissed, "Royal flush. Top that!"

Chapter Twenty
Ivy's Sentence

Ivy woke up in terror from what she thought to be a hideous dream. She could still smell death in the air. The vision of the beast lingered in her mind and her body ached from the recollection. She tried to climb to her feet, but her skin felt tight as if sunburned. Brushing her hand against her thigh, she winced. In panic, she discovered her body was covered with scratches and in some places her skin was torn wide open. She was naked from the waist down and her clothes were ripped. A terrible revelation occurred to her. Last night was not just a bad trip. Her life was such an enormous mess. She couldn't determine the difference between reality and what should have been a fantasy; a very horrible, terrorizing fantasy. She wrapped a sheet around her waist and fell to her knees. Growing up her parents made sure that Ivy attended church regularly. So being saved was not altogether a foreign proposition to her. She put her head in her hands and began to pray the simplest of prayers.

"Dear Lord, forgive . . ."

Ivy gagged. She ran to the restroom. Heaving into the toilet, a slimy, crawling sensation surrounded her feet. She looked back to see snakes slithering under and over her legs. Kicking them off, she scrambled to her feet, screeching with insane terror while stepping on the squirmy creatures. She finally managed to push them off. They hissed and lunged at her. Ivy's screams were continuous. She hated snakes. Of all God's creatures, she could never understand why He chose to create those slimy, shivering abominations. She jumped around trying to dodge them. *Where in the hell did they come from?* They rose up to surround her. Incessant fear-filled screams streamed from Ivy's mouth.

The bathroom darkened and the overwhelming smell of death and horror returned. She backed herself up against a wall in complete terror as a shadowy, black image appeared. It was the monster from the night before and the devil snakes slithered their way behind him as he walked slowly toward Ivy.

"You will never, ever call upon Him again for forgiveness. Is that clear?" As he said this he clasped Ivy's head between his giant hands and squeezed with rage. Fire shot from his eyes. His voice was gravely and hoarse.

"He does not love you, and will never love you again. You are going to be the mother of my son. How could He possibly love you, now?"

Ivy shuddered in disbelief. "No. That can't be!"

"Remember last night, my little acid cake? That was no trip you were on. That, my dear, was free gratis. That was me, the real thing and you are now carrying my son. Since we are family now, you may call me Lucifer, my. . . uh, well, God-given name." Lucifer bowed regally.

"This can't be true. Oh, my god, this can't be true."

"It is true, darling. You don't have to thank me. Just get used to it. You and I are going to rule the world and the son you carry is going to be even more evil than I; if that is at all possible. You see, there is a war coming, and our son is going to be the greatest doer of evil there has ever been."

Ivy crumbled to the ground. Lucifer crouched down beside her, embracing her. She shuddered at his touch. She was losing her mind and more than anything she wanted to go home to her nice, safe, bed, in her nice, safe, room, with her very boring and very nice, safe, parents. She was living a horrendous nightmare.

Lucifer once more grabbed her face with his cold hands and kissed her mouth. She wanted to heave again, but her dread stopped any bodily functions. He picked her up and carried her into the bedroom. There he raped her repeatedly, leaving her unconscious and traumatized. Her spirit which was polluted and torn by degradation and abuse, floated above her body. Below it, a scratched and torn body lay motionless and comatose as it pulsated in total shock and abandon. Her spirit had no home nor could it find rest. Ivy was nowhere but oblivion.

Chapter Twenty-one
Front and Center, Rosemary!

The humble little army huddled around Emily and Andrew as the meditation came to a close. What they just witnessed was bone-chilling.

"Well, there must be some reason why God wanted us to see that terrible scene." Emily was still shaken by the visions. She had repressed the feelings of her own rape so many years ago, but the rape they just witnessed was fraught with amoral repercussions. Satan had a reason. He planted his seed. Now, they knew the world was headed for more disasters, more inhumane misery, in short, more hell. What was this child going to grow up to be?

The room was quiet. The Deathlinks were stunned while pondering this new predicament placed at their feet.

"But, she was about to ask God for forgiveness. Maybe God wants us to find a way to save Ivy from her terrible hell. Even though the words didn't come out of her mouth, her heart had time to say them." Rosemary surprised everyone. She was the one who very rarely spoke out after meditation. Her spirit just soaked in the energies around it, and then she would serenely fade away.

"You're right!" Andrew said near tears. "During the war, when a man was dying, he would almost always ask God to forgive him. Sometimes they could barely get the words out before they died. I have always felt that strength of heart is more important than words. Vietnam was evil, but Ivy, and many of her contemporaries have been fighting their own war and Satan has taken advantage of this. God would never allow this."

"Oh, one of us has to help her. My daughters are about her age." Marie spoke up, still affected by the scene just played out before them.

Emily said solemnly, "Let's quiet ourselves again, and let us ask our Father to guide us towards an invincible strategy."

In the stillness, there was only one unmistakable sensation. Rosemary elevated above all in happy reverence to her God for having chosen her to fulfill this very dangerous and challenging task. Rosemary was Ivy's Deathlink. Ivy was her responsibility and her pathway to eternal life. All prayed in repose for divine direction.

"Well, wouldn't it just be a feather in the Deathlinks' caps if we were to save the mother of Satan's son from eternal damnation?" Joseph Cercione was relatively new in these meetings; however, since seeing Angela's apparition he became one of the most daring in the group.

"But how?" asked Andrew.

"By communicating to her spirit, that's how!" Rosemary was anxious, now.

"She's in a coma. Where is her spirit?" Jason knew he was with this army in order to save his own soul. But never before was he involved in the planning. He exuded naiveté' and they all looked to Emily.

Emily responded with the patience of the teacher she was. "When I counseled people who were dying, I always felt those in a coma had their spirit hovering around their body, waiting for new consciousness. Perhaps, Rosemary could make contact with her in that way? Joey, find out where they have taken Ivy. We must get to her before she awakens. Her mind and body will work against our efforts, if for no other reason than out of fear. Rosemary, this is one of our greatest tasks and will be one of our greatest achievements for God. Arm yourself with the Word. Know it and believe it before you make contact with Ivy. You can bet old Lucifer will be hanging around and there are others who only seek to obey his commands. Jason and Michael, I am sending you along with Rosemary. She needs back up. Remember, God only wants us to emulate His Son. The only force that can be used is by the power of God's Word and love of heart. Of course, God did bestow wit and cunning upon His people. Don't ever forget that. Stay holy and peaceful with the light of God."

Emily and Andrew had been collecting the stories of all of the spirits in their God ordained army. They knew God had a specific reason for picking each and every one of them, but all they had was their faith to guide them. God spoke to them in dreams and through signs. This, they thought, could be very dangerous. Nothing was ever specific. How did they know if what they perceived was truly what God wanted from them? They just worked and planned in faith, and prayed for confirmation.

In the case of Rosemary, God's plan unfolded before their eyes. How could they have ever doubted Him? In our lifetime, it seems some lessons are never fully learned. We need to experience His faithfulness again and again. How easy it is to forget. How much there is always to learn.

Chapter Twenty-two
Ethereal Chaos

Ivy's spiritual consciousness floated blindly in a foggy sphere filled with confusion and perceived danger. Her essence was preoccupied with the savage rape of her body and mind. Although she knew Lucifer was not here with her in this space, she did feel he was not too far away. Her spirit felt emptiness and the ruthless abandonment of everything decent and good, and it groaned with loneliness. Trapped in this haze her ability to see what was surrounding her was nil. She couldn't reach out beyond her own scope of terror, and panic devastated her. Her soul cried out for goodness in an effort to redeem itself. It lamented all of her wrong doings; her lack of respect for purity; her stubborn refusal to honor her parents. Suddenly, the foggy realm that once surrounded her was reshaping itself. She heard the flutter of wings. Her soul filled with peaceful revelations and she regained the ability to see what was around her. Beneath her floating spirit she saw her body lying on a bed in a hospital. Tubes were inserted in her arms and her mother and father were at her side. How lost they looked. How absolute was their despair. Why did she ever drift away from their perfect love?

Rosemary, Michael, and Jason stayed to the back of the hospital room. Their mission at this moment was to size up the situation. What, or more appropriately, who was occupying space in that vicinity? Ivy's spirit lingered above her bed. She was so defeated. All three of them wanted to rush to comfort her, but discretion was imperative. Slowly, the three of them split up, concentrating their prayers in the center of the room. Devotional energy filled the room, increasing its power as it filtered through the existing fear and loneliness.

The energy manifested itself into light and sound. Ivy's spirit turned to feel the impact and the warmth of God's forgiveness. It hit her like a gust of warm air right before a summer storm and the room filled with the smell of God's sum and substance. She smelled it before. It was a source of certain tranquility; the smell of a spring rain. It filled the room with strength and peace and her spirit was renewed.

The three Deathlinks were thrust into her space by an overwhelming power within them. Even they were taken aback by this sudden gift of integrity.

"What are you? Who are you? God, I can't take any more shocks today!" Ivy recoiled from the spirits shoved into her space.

"Ivy, we are here to help you." Rosemary moved closer to her.

"No one can help me. I'm damned to hell. The beast has taken me and claimed me for his own. My body is bearing his child."

Michael moved with care toward Ivy's spirit. "The child is not his unless you relinquish it to him. Every child is God's until its birth, even Satan's. Do you think that every child born of rape or incest becomes a devil? They are life. They are given the same gifts from God as His other children. Then they make their own way. You have the ability to dedicate your child's life to God just the way that Mary did Jesus."

An immense groan came from the corner of the room.

"Jesus, Jesus, damn the name of Jesus . . . it brings agony . . . such pain." The smell of death wafted through the air and then vanished. Ivy's spirit moved towards her body. The Deathlinks knew she was searching for a place to hide from the evil starting to engulf the room. They had to stop the retreat because she still needed to know so much. Michael placed himself between Ivy's body and her spirit.

"Let me pass, please let me pass. He is here. You don't know how horrible he is."

Michael, Jason, and Rosemary formed a ring around Ivy's spirit. Rosemary prayed aloud. "Put on all the armor that God gives you, so that you will be able to stand up against the Devil's evil tricks. For we are not fighting against human beings but against the wicked spiritual forces in the heavenly world, the rulers, authorities and cosmic powers of this dark age. So put on God's armor now! Then when the evil day comes, you will be able to resist the enemy's attacks; and after fighting to the end, you will still hold your ground."

Ivy's bed started to shake. The lights blinked off and on. Everything not bolted down blew around the room. Ivy's parents ran out screaming for a doctor and as the door to the hospital room slammed shut, Ivy's body started to levitate.

Rosemary shrieked with anger at the top of her lungs. "Purity is power, evil one. We claim this girl's body and spirit in the name of Jesus Christ. You no longer have a claim on her!"

Lucifer's immense dark shape emerged from the shadows. "Who do you think you are warring with you little bitch? You are no better than my whore. If I remember correctly, you also abdicated to lust. You are nothing to God. Come join me. I was given this evil power from God himself." His voice was chilling. The room was cold and damp.

Michael antagonized by Satan's deceit screamed, "You were given the power only to show how much greater is the authority of God. You can do nothing to us because we have faith in God to sustain us. We will not surrender her to you."

By this time, Ivy's parents and the hospital staff were pounding on the door. It was locked tight. The wind in the room grew even stronger. Lucifer joined by several others from his evil band, infiltrated the area with bloody shrieks. They slithered around the righteous threesome hissing and attempted to inflate their hearts with fear and discontent. The two inexperienced Deathlinks huddled even closer to Michael and the three together around Ivy's spirit.

With sudden repose, the wind stopped. The room, still, filled with the stench of rotting bodies. Lucifer eased himself towards them. "I don't want the whore. She is only a vessel to carry my son. If she has to die, so be it. Let me have reign over the spirit of my son and you may have her."

Jason, with all of his strength, lifted his spirit and in the most breathtaking prayer of self-sacrifice pleaded, "Lord, if you cannot take this trial from us, let the evil one take my spirit in place of Ivy and her child. Please, do not let him pour his evil into this unborn life!"

At that moment, a diminutive little light the size of a butterfly came down from above and landed on Ivy's body. It rested over her abdomen for a brief instant and then was absorbed into her body.

Rosemary stopped short. She knew this was her child - hers and Gabe's. This little soul as fragile and as small as anything she had ever seen was sent from God to protect the child within Ivy. This was the smallest Deathlink. Indeed, every life, born and unborn has purpose.

Enraged, Lucifer lunged at Ivy's body. It was too late. The little spirit made camp and was blessed with the strength of a thousand warrior angels. Lucifer withdrew in fear. He gathered his band of devils and retreated. "This is just the beginning. Tell your Mrs. Walker I know her and I know her fears. This little stunt will not be forgotten. You have brought the wrath of the greatest evil upon yourselves. If I don't have a son to assist me, I'll make my army out of already existing wretches, the likes you have never seen. Chaos is now upon you and you have only won a little battle. You have yet to see my real strength."

Everything was silent. The door opened and Ivy's parents fell into the room. Ivy's spirit drifted down to rejoin her body. The threesome, still in awe over the whole ordeal marveled at the authority of God and the power that came from simply having faith in Him. Rosemary hovered over Ivy's body and softly whispered, "Remember Ivy, purity is power. We will be back. You are now one of God's chosen."

The war was indeed beginning, but not in the way the Deathlink warriors had anticipated. Satan had revamped his strategy, and hell was going to be in the living.

Chapter Twenty-three
Graduate to the Pearlie Gate

What a huge rush! All of Fletcher's family was there for his graduation from seminary; all except the one who believed in him the most. This is something he had wanted for so long, albeit through some very tough times. Fletcher almost gave up when he lost his mom. Watching someone you love die such a painful and terrible death was hard to justify and he almost decided that Karl Marx was right when he said religion was the opiate of the masses. But, on what was thought to be one of her good days, Fletch's mother wanted to talk with him alone. In their discussion she helped him understand the difference between faith and religion.

"Come here, my good looking, wonderful son."

"Mom, you know that I look just like you."

"Yeah, I know, except for that dapper black patch, Mr. Debonair. But seriously, Fletcher, you have something more and that is the passion to make a difference in the world. Your faith will carry you to do whatever God would like for you to do. Please promise me when you graduate from college, you will go on to seminary. Promise me."

"Mom, I can't promise that. Not after watching you go through this. You are one of the most spiritual people I know. How could God allow you to suffer such pain?"

"Jesus suffered more than this and he was God's son."

"He was also divine. Besides, there are so many religions around, how do I know which one is the right one?"

"Fletch, faith is not about religion. Faith is belief that God wants you to follow your path and that means following your heart. Staying close to Him through prayer is the way you will recognize your path, and prayer is not just found in predetermined words. It's what is in your heart at any given time. It's conversation with the one who made you. Everyone's journey is different, just like their DNA. Every individual person has a reason to be here on earth and faith is the idea that a human being's spirit has a direct link of communication with their Creator." His mother was determined to relay this one last message. Her disease had left her so weak, but today she was filled with fortitude. God spoke to her heart and she knew her passion and the love she had for her son would bear the weight of the message which was profound and essential for him to hear.

"Mom, you are a marvel; a shining star in God's universe. I wish . . . I don't want to lose you." Fletcher's heart was breaking because he knew his mother had only a few more days. He turned away from her in order to hide his tears. Looking out the window of the hospital room, the sense of a swift wind blew past him. He turned around to speak once again, but she had passed. Just like that - gone. He could hardly believe it. It was sad and brusque, yet the circumstance of her death was a small miracle. The doctors told the family she would have a great deal of pain before slipping into a coma and then death. It did not matter. She said everything that needed to be said. She delivered God's message and He took her home. Fletcher would always remember her definition of faith. He did what she wanted him to do. He went to seminary and was now graduating. He was to become the disciple of God she knew he was destined to be.

Chapter Twenty-four
Grace's Quest

Patty Henderson sat at the edge of her bed in utter misery. She could not believe she was pregnant again. Already a single mother, she was sure she had taken precautions. Her two year old daughter was enough for her to handle and the funds were not there to take care of another child. Another responsibility was not something she needed. That's why she made the appointment with the abortion clinic. Stumbling around in her apartment, she tried to convince herself this was the right thing to do. After all, she didn't believe in abortion. That's why she had Amy. Her world without Amy in it would be nothing. So, what the hell was she doing, anyway? It didn't matter. She had no choice. They just could not survive with another mouth to feed.

Patty put on her coat and with great determination made her way to the clinic. There she was greeted by all those well-meaning pro-lifers. It was thirty years since the Supreme Court had handed down its ruling in *Roe vs. Wade* in 1973, but the pro-lifers and the pro-choice activists still hit the street. As Patty got out of her car, a sidewalk counselor rushed up to her. She hooked her arm through Patty's arm and stopped her from walking any further. "You know that abortion is murder. You are going in there to murder your own child. Do you need help? We can find you help. There are churches who can give you food and clothing."

"Leave me alone!" Patty shook the woman off her arm. *As if I want any part of a hand out. Why would I want to live in fear of not having enough to feed my children or enough money to buy them shoes for their growing feet?*

"Listen to me!" The pro-life woman was now in her face. She seemed crazed by the cause. "Do you want your soul to be damned to hell because you didn't have the guts to take responsibility for your own actions? If you are so cold blooded to kill your own baby, maybe you are cold enough to take the lives of others. Murderer! Murderer!" The woman was joined by more members of her movement. They were all chanting in Patty's face. Patty was rescued by a nurse as she got closer to the clinic door and they ran as fast as they could into the clinic.

The rest of the staff was waiting for her. They gave her time to recuperate, but then they prepared her for surgery. While she lay on the table, her legs in stirrups and feeling as vulnerable as a moth to a flame, she put her heart on hold and tried not to think about what was happening. Soon she was under. Her sleep was dreamless, but after she woke up from the anesthetic, she felt numb and nauseous. Attempting to gain consciousness, Patty felt remorse at what she thought was a necessary decision. A deep emptiness engulfed her.

"Do you think you can get up and walk around a little?" A nurse came into the recovery room.

Patty sat up and felt very dizzy. "I don't know. I'll give it a try."

"How are you doing emotionally? Do you think you will need to see a counselor? We can arrange that for you if you feel you need it." The nurse was kind but she only enhanced the reality of the abortion. Patty was feeling well enough now to appreciate what just took place. She, by her own will, destroyed another human being - not only another human being, but her own child. Patty Henderson, the girl who couldn't even stand to put a worm on a fish line for fear of hurting it, just killed her own child. Her knees buckled beneath her. "Whoa, girl . . . maybe you better lie down for a while longer. We've called the authorities about the protesters. They aren't supposed to get so close to the clients. I don't know where the police are. Don't worry. They should be subdued before you leave."

Patty didn't know how she was going to live with what she did. All she knew was she wanted to get out of there as fast as she could. She made herself get dressed and walked herself around the room until she felt that she could maneuver without falling on her face.

She left the clinic through the back door. Perhaps she could avoid the pro-lifers. She didn't get five yards from the clinic door and the pro-lifers were on her heels, but of course, so were the pro-choice activists. It was an insane battle between the two groups, with Patty in the middle. There were even teenagers with picket signs standing alongside her. She wasn't well enough for this. One of the pro-lifers yelled, "How does it feel, knowing that you're damned to hell!" Patty couldn't hold back the tears any longer. The pro-choice people were trying their best to shield her from the aggression, but she could still hear the chants.

"Murderer! Baby killer! What kind of mother kills her own child?"

After what seemed like an eternity, Patty made it to her car. It was dusk so she fumbled trying to see the keys but finally got in, and locked the doors. As she pulled out of the parking lot a pro-lifer jumped in front of her car holding a picket sign with a picture of an aborted fetus. It was shoved into the windshield of Patty's car. The picture sickened her. The car moved slowly forward, so as not to hurt the crazed woman that put herself in harm's way. The woman yelled, "See, now it's going to be easier for you to kill others. Do you want to kill me, too? Well, come on, I'm not that easy of a target!"

One of the teenagers and another adult joined in the chanting right next to her car. A pro-choice advocate gave the teen a push. Another woman in a baseball cap ran from the crowd and threw herself in front of the teen. Patty heard a loud thud as the woman fell into her car. Somebody yelled, "Gun!" Patty stopped the car. There was a pop and the woman slid down Patty's car window mouthing the words "I'm sorry" before falling to the ground. Then, everything went crazy.

Patty drove off, her entire body in shock. Never had she been through anything so dreadful in her whole life. Never had she expected this to be so despicable . . . and that poor woman. She needed a drink. It was dark by the time she arrived back at her apartment. Her mother had Amy for the night and Patty was all alone. She went to her cupboard to find the scotch she kept there for special occasions. This was not a special occasion, but it was needed just the same. Her hands trembled as she poured the liquor into a glass. Before she knew it, she had downed three glasses of scotch and was starting to feel it. The onset of a major drunken depression and crying jag was just a drink away.

By now, the old fiend Satch was watching this entire scene. He was patting himself on the back, for little did those self-righteous pro-lifers know he was using them to push his next victim into suicide. When were they ever going to get it? Anything unkind is from him not from *Him*. He found this very amusing. This was good. She was drinking now. That will make her nice and depressed. It was faint, but he felt another presence. *What the hell is this? Where did that essence come from? It isn't one of mine.* He sensed goodness and kindness.

Patty fell into a crying jag, and the vision of the aborted fetus kept intruding. She could not escape what she had done. Worse yet, she couldn't even talk to anyone about it. She had told no one. "I'm a murderer. Those people were right. I'm nothing but a cold blooded murderer."

Satch went to work. He sent in his slimiest imps to provoke the situation.

"You are so right, little girl. What kind of mother are you that you could take the life of your own child? You are loathsome. You are disgusting." The imp whispered.

Patty repeated, "I'm loathsome, I'm disgusting. I don't deserve to live!"

A light illuminated the darkness. Patty looked up to see a young woman. She appeared to be from another time. Her clothes were torn, but she could tell they were from the distant past. "Don't be afraid, Patty. I'm here to help you through this black time in your life. My name is Grace."

Satch was caught unaware. He swooped down into the room howling, and growling. He tried to get close to Grace to push her out, but as he grew close to her she began to speak.

"When the time came for me to show you favor, I heard you; when the day arrived for me to save you I helped you. This is the hour to receive God's favor, today is the day to be saved!"

The devil shrieked in pain. "She speaks the word of God! Who are you? You are nothing!"

Grace centered her spirit and remained calm. "Let us praise God for his glorious grace, for the free gift he gave us in his dear Son. For by the blood of Christ we are set free, that is, our sins are forgiven. How great is the grace of God which he gave to us in such large measure."

Grace was too strong. Her spirit aged in faith and grit with the passage of time. Once a weak and whipped young woman, she now was a lioness and a thorn in Lucifer's side. Her faith prevailed above everything and the protective force she had built between his intended victim and him was impenetrable. Realizing this Satan took his band of imps and fled.

Patty could not believe what she just witnessed. The day and the scotch took its toll on her emotions. She was now experiencing things she never knew existed. The one that called herself Grace was still there.

"They are gone now. Patty, I'm here on a special mission from God. Long ago, I found myself in a situation very much like yours. I had a little boy that was four years old and I had just given birth to another. I had no family and my husband left me with no money or support. I could hardly keep food in the mouth of my four year old and I didn't know how I was going to feed two children. Well, at that time, we didn't have legal abortion. I did the only thing left for me to do. I took my own life. I know that you are thinking about doing that right now. But, I'm here to let you know that everyone's life has a special meaning to the Creator. Without you here to complete the plan that

has been ordained for you, you become incomplete as an eternal being. All of our sins and all of our shortcomings are already known by
Him. Our lessons on earth are learned from the mistakes we make.
Some mistakes are worse than others, but that is why God gave us his
Son. All He asks is that we ask Him for forgiveness and that we place
our lives in His hands. If we do that, our hardest decisions will be
made easy. Our most despicable sins will be forgiven. You will not be
damned to hell if you give your life to God and ask His forgiveness.
Taking your own life only takes away the divine gift that God wants so
desperately to give you. God wants you to live, Patty. He wants you
to live your life in His presence so that He may guide you to happiness
here in this life and in the life after."

"I'm such a miserable wretch. I'm a murderer and a detestable
mother. How can He love me?"

"I know that He does, because He loved me enough to give me a
second chance even after death to redeem myself. In saving you, I save
my own eternal soul. God is good, Patty. He loves us above all of His
creatures."

Patty bowed her head in reverence to God. Grace's reprieve was
finally won. She lingered to watch her sister happily embrace the free-
dom of faith that was just bestowed on her and Grace's spirit reveled
in exhilaration because she knew she had just won a very important
battle. Grace was donning the apparel of a spiritual warrior. Time was
getting short now. Before long all mankind would meet its final judgment and endure earth's final days, and after Grace's intersession, God
was gaining strength; Satan was lagging behind.

Chapter Twenty-five

The Greatest Sin of All

There were many of God's children being seduced by Satan, but some have it innately in them to succumb to evil ways. Perhaps, because of the way they were raised. Parents sometimes do not realize the power they hold in their hands when they are raising another human being to adulthood. It is in this failure to exercise God's love for mankind that Lucifer found his greatest satisfaction.

One of his most pleasing followers was Winifred B. Thitch. Winifred had never declared or given her soul over to Lucifer. She just lived. By every word out of her mouth, every deceitful, selfish act she bound herself to him. One of her most award winning stunts was to blacken another person's name out of jealousy, or because that person stood in her way. She would smile and presume to be their friend, but at just the most appropriate times, twist a fact she knew about the person into something untrue, and very damaging. It was just enough to make others distrust the person, or just enough for that person to lose a special assignment or a potential lover. The scenario didn't matter. Wini just wanted it all. She wanted power over people. She wanted great sex. She wanted money, and Wini just didn't care what happened to someone else as long as she acquired her selfish desires. Lucifer loved this about his little disciple. She was becoming a masterpiece of horror. Everyone she touched was destroyed; even someone who should have been her greatest treasure.

Wini was the head of the women's clothing department in a prestigious store. She worked in this store for twenty-five years and to her dismay not quite close enough for retirement. She was now in her early fifties and losing her youthful good looks. Her black hair was getting gray, and because she was often discontent with her life she ate too much to fill whatever voids happened to be there at the time. She was gaining weight and looked altogether frumpy. This became a huge inconvenience for anyone younger and prettier who worked for her. Wini so wished that she were younger. In this day and age all of her angles and antics were considered acceptable. It was survival of the fittest and she just wasn't as fit any longer.

As Wini pondered her plight, the store livened with customers. She had to fill two positions today and this was a specific challenge for her. It was distressing to interview applicants who were younger, prettier, and better educated than herself. To top that, her assistant cut her off at the ankles, having learned all of Wini's tricks, and was promoted to assistant buyer.

Jana Blevett was her supervisor. Wini hated this woman. She was so sweetly-sweet that it made her teeth hurt just to listen to Jana talk. Jana was in her forties, but somehow had maintained a gorgeous figure. Her subordinates, all except for Wini, loved her and were extremely loyal. Yes, today was going to be a bitch. Not only did she have to interview new and exciting blood, but she had to do this with Jana.

"Hey, there, Wini, my girl!" Jana rounded the corner where the cash register stood. "Ready to fill those two very important positions?"

"Jesus, Jana. You scared the daylights out of me. Do you think you could tame it down just for today?" Wini wanted to lunge at her and scratch out her big blue eyes.

"Now, now, Winifred. Let's not use the Lord's name in vain. Besides, cheer up. By filling these positions you won't have to put in so much overtime. I see by your time card that you worked sixty hours last week. Very impressive." Little did Jana know that Wini had doctored her time card - a few hours one day, a few hours the next. The store trusted her. What they didn't know wouldn't hurt them. Besides, Jana was so damn gullible. Wini could pull anything over on her.

"You know, Wini, I was thinking. You have to fill your assistant's position. Have you considered Ivy Winston? "

Wini choked on her coffee. Jesus Christ, another goodie-two-shoes. Ivy was one of the most beautiful young women she had ever seen. To be around her all of the time would eat at Wini like a cancer. Ivy also had no problem displaying her faith. It made Wini's skin crawl whenever the subject of God came up. Ivy didn't talk much, but when she did she was powerful.

"No, Jana, actually I haven't. You do know that she is known for using drugs and that she has a child and has never been married?"

"Well, I knew that she is raising a son on her own, but I hadn't heard anything about drugs. Where did you get this information?"

"I heard this from a very reliable source. Also, when she comes in sometimes in the morning, her eyes are all blood-shot and tired." Wini wondered whether she had planted the proper seed of mistrust or if she had to spin a little more.

"I don't know if I believe your source. Ivy works very hard and catches on to new procedures quickly. I can't see someone who is on drugs managing to do that. Besides, she looks great in the clothes she wears - a real plus for this area of the store."

"Well, she doesn't get along well with the other members of the staff. They all complain to me about her work."

"Why is it that I haven't heard this from you before?"

"Well, I know that she is trying to raise a child on her own. I want her to hang on to the only job she could probably ever get." Wini was feeling very comforted by the fact that she just submarined Ivy. Certainly the *not getting along* interjection would stop Jana right in her tracks.

"I think that I would like to interview her for the assistant's position anyway. Let's see what she has to say about all of this." Jana walked away in the perky little manner that made Wini sick.

"I don't see her as management material, but you're the boss."

That afternoon an array of young women went in and out of Wini's office. Wini managed to either chase away or discourage the applicants that were a threat to her. She wanted to surround herself with women whom she could control. She already had two trusted minions. Paula and Erica would do anything for her. They weren't very bright and found it easier to play along with Wini's schemes than to try and fight her. Fighting her would just slit their throats. They knew full well her capabilities.

Meanwhile, up in Jana's office, Ivy had just settled into the seat in front of Jana's desk. Jana noticed that Ivy wore a small gold crucifix around her neck. She seemed very at peace with herself and happy.

"Ivy, I have asked you to come into my office for several reasons. The first is to dispel some rumors that are going around about you. Can you explain why you come into work with tired and bloodshot eyes?" Jana felt terrible asking Ivy these questions, but she had to know for herself. She had always believed that Ivy had real potential.

"Why? Have I fallen down in my duties to the store?" Ivy became nervous.

"No, not at all. It's just that I would like to consider you for a promotion and I just need to hear from you that you are not on drugs."

"Drugs! No, oh, my gosh, no! The reason I am tired is that after work, I go to the University and take a night class and then when I get home I have to tend to my son, Gabriel. There was a time, many years ago, that I did take drugs. It turned into a horrific adventure and I have never touched them since. If it would make you feel more comfortable, I will submit to a drug test."

"How do you get along with your coworkers? Do you feel comfortable around them?"

"I usually am so busy that I don't have time to socialize with them. Paula, Erica and Wini seem to always be talking and sharing stories. I just don't ever have the time."

"I see. How would you like to be the assistant department manager of the entire women's clothing area for this store? It would mean a substantial raise in salary."

Ivy was so excited. "Yes, I would love it," was all she could say.

Later that day, Wini found out the news that Ivy had been promoted to assistant manager. The jealousy in her heart exploded. *How
could that stupid Jana do this to me? Didn't she listen to what I was telling
her about this girl? Jana must not have any respect for my opinion. Doesn't
she know the problems this girl will create within my department?* Wini was
losing control. She started to believe the lies she told Jana about Ivy
were true. This was her normal mode of operation. Wini was sick. Her
heart was black with evil. She allowed herself to surrender to every
selfish, immoral manner of living just to make others perceive her to
be better than everyone around her. Contrary to her own belief, it
never got her very far; however, her reward was that she saw herself in
a much better light after the destruction.

It was closing time. Winifred was tired and needed a drink. Heading
straight home was undesirable because she would have to deal with
Danny. In her thirties, Wini did the unthinkable. She fell in love and
got married to the sap and during her two year marriage she became
pregnant and gave birth to a little boy. Danny had just turned eighteen
years old and was a royal nuisance. She never wanted to hate him, but
he grated on her. Motherhood did not become her and this kid was so
needy. Danny was quiet and had true artistic talent. He would sit in
his room for hours working on drawing after drawing. Winifred could
never give him any encouragement. She didn't want to give him a big
head. As a matter of fact, he was displaying his art work at school that
night. *Shit! I promised him that I would be there. Well, there goes the idea
of a drink. I suppose I have to show up at the brat's school, if nothing, just to
make an appearance.* She never wanted Danny's teachers to think ill of
her, so she went.

Wini walked into the gymnasium where all of the Art students had
their work displayed. She saw Danny. He spotted her and walked over
to greet her.

"Hi, Mom."

"Why in the world did you have to wear that pair of pants with that shirt? People know what I do for a living. Don't you take any pride in yourself and in me at all?"

"Mom, I won Best of Show. Do you want to see my work?"

"No. What I really want is for you to look half way decent every now and then."

"Mom, please, you are embarrassing me. Can't you just come over and look at some of the art work on display?"

"Okay. If you don't care, then I don't care either. "

They walked around looking at all of the pictures. There were water colors and oils. Some of the students even exhibited sculptures. Danny's strength was in charcoal sketches.

"Danny, why can't you ever do anything other than sketches? They are so boring and it seems to me that the other kids have one up on you."

"Mom, I just won Best of Show. Can't you at least appreciate that about me?"

"Well, let's see it. Show me."

"Here, come with me. They have it exhibited on the stage."

Wini forced herself to follow Danny to the stage. It enraged her to see his work exposed with such grandeur. It wasn't that great and he was so cocky.

"Here it is. Do you like it?" Danny cringed. He just stood there waiting for the first blow.

"How could you mortify and embarrass me like this? This is an expression of your dirty little mind. Someone should take it and tear it up. Whatever possessed you to draw a picture of a naked woman?" Wini truly thought that it was quite good. The nude that Danny had drawn was exquisite and displayed great detail and was a wonderful example of his remarkable talent. She was so jealous of him. He reminded her of his father and she hated him.

"Mom, it's a nude. It's not pornography. It's artistic expression. Never mind. You never like anything that I do. Just forget it."

"Yes. I think that's exactly what I'm going to do. I'm going to forget it. I'm going home. By the time you get there, I'll be in bed. Don't bother me."

The night was evil. It was corrupted by the hateful, heartless acts of a vain and self-aggrandizing, self-serving woman. Lucifer loved it. This was the kind of evening that encouraged and strengthened him. There was something missing, though. Winifred needed affirmation from one of her own and Satan knew just which one he was going to send to her. The man of her dreams, Geoffrey Myers Downing. What a shame that Geoff and Wini hadn't met while he was still alive. They would have made the perfect pair. A match made in hell.

Wini fell into a deep dark sleep. She felt warm and sexy. Consciousness abandoned, her spirit sensed another in bed with her. He was seductive and charming. His loathsomeness encircled her aura and together they satisfied a quintessential evil. In this dream-like state, her body became aroused and this lustful depravity reached the pinnacle of satisfaction. Geoffrey Downing loved when his master asked him to beguile evil women in their beds. They were so easy to manipulate. This one was so delicious and so hateful and he was looking forward to the opportunity of making her a bride of Satan.

Geoffrey whispered, "Wini, you are the empress of my soul. You bewilder me and I can't help myself when I am near you. Let me encompass you in luscious lust. I will touch you with my mind and excite every part of your feminine nature. Just say that you will let me stay in your bed until I have satisfied every desire."

Wini stirred. She stretched her body across the bed. Her arms fell open at her side, her legs moved apart. This erotic mood had wormed its way into her unconsciousness and was stimulating every part of her body. She wanted more.

Geoffrey eased his essence over her. As he infiltrated her mind with thoughts of passion and eroticism, he also injected a tincture of pure corruption. Just a push, just a push more and he penetrated her spirit with enough foul intentions, enough disgusting acts of degradation that Wini would be hard pressed not to execute them. They were planted in her soul. They were cemented in her essence. They were inescapable traits of cruelty, wickedness, sin, vice and immorality and they would become the core of her future.

Chapter Twenty-six
How Low Can You Go?

Prayer was a major component of the Deathlinks' existence. The very heart of their strength depended on minute by minute prayer for help from the Father. Emily's Deathlinks were of the Christian persuasion, they also tried to heighten their enlightenment of the Holy Scripture, because for them, this was their greatest weapon.

The Deathlinks were aware of one of Lucifer's newest recruits. They shuddered at what she would now be capable of doing, but their main concern centered on her son. A remarkable young man, with a superb artistic talent and kind soul was being tortured by the cruelty of his own mother. They watched him as he was degraded daily without any remorse or shame.

"Danny! Wake up, you little son of a bitch. You need to get your ass to school." Wini awoke that morning with a renewed sense of bitchiness. She couldn't wait to play with her son's mind.

"Mom, I'm up. You don't have to talk to me that way."

"Oh, yes I do. You're worthless. Why did I ever give birth to you? Look at you. You can't even dress yourself and your art work is despicable. I can't believe that they gave you an award for that."

"Well, someone must think it's pretty good. My advisor is going to try to get me a scholarship to college."

"What? They can't do that without my permission. I'm going to call that school and give them a piece of my mind. Don't get your hopes up, Danny. You aren't that good. There are tons of people out there who are much better than you. Their work will sell, yours won't. It's as simple as that."

"Just the same, I would like my advisor to try."

"I won't let her. Besides, you don't have the brains for college. I guess that you're stuck with your job at the grocery store. Ah, well, poor little Danny. Such a supreme failure!"

"What did I ever do to you? Why do you hate me so much?"

"You were born, Danny, you were born. I won't be home tonight. I have a meeting after work. Don't expect me until late." With that, Wini turned and went into the bathroom to get ready for work. At work she had to create even more havoc.

As they were allowed to watch this scene, tears dampened Emily's face. All of the Deathlinks were afraid for Danny. Wini was killing him with her words. Every day there was constant brow beating and Danny bashing. They watched as he sank lower and lower into depression.

"I'm worried that Danny may be forced to do something stupid." Joey was the first to break the miserable silence.

"He will and he is planning it." Andrew shook his head as he talked. "Jason, I have discerned that Danny is yours. You must act fast. I think that we might be able to catch Lucifer and his band off guard. They are so absorbed with what Wini is planning to do to Ivy and they are so consumed with revenge that they have missed the devastation she has planted within her own son. Danny wants to take his own life and Wini has a gun in her apartment. He is thinking about doing this tonight. So, Jason, get ready."

As night fell, the Deathlinks wrapped up their session of prayer. Jason was filled with trepidation. He knew what he had to do and he wanted to assist Danny in any way that he could, however, he was also not as strong as the rest of the Deathlinks. Most of them had already accomplished their missions which made them invincible against evil. He and Marie were the only ones left.

Jason and Marie hovered in Wini's apartment. They waited for Danny to come home. Their mission was to stop him from destroying himself, but they truly didn't know the magnitude of purpose in their final rescue and just how significant this mission would be.

Danny came into the apartment and went over to a desk and opened the drawer. In it was a revolver. He took the revolver out and tucked it into the waistband of his jeans and left. Jason and Marie looked at each other with total bewilderment. This was not going the way that they had speculated. Following him, they ended up in an abandoned warehouse where Danny was met by three other people. There was a teenage girl, and a woman and man that were old enough to be the girl's parents.

"Are you finally ready to do this?" The man asking was perturbed. He acted very nervous and guilty.

The woman chimed in, "Really! We have been waiting here for an hour. Where have you been?"

"Look" said Danny, "This was a big decision. You don't just plan to end your life in a matter of seconds. Besides, I had to stop by the apartment to get Mom's gun."

"Well, you haven't changed your mind have you?" Both the woman and the man began to crowd him. The teenage girl that accompanied the couple began to cry.

"Shut up, will you!" The woman shouted at the girl. The girl appeared to be an unwilling participant in the games that were about to begin.

"Does she want to be here?" asked Danny. "Because if she doesn't you . . ."

"Hey, don't butt in. She wants to be here. Just mind your own business."

Jason and Marie began to sense the unwanted presence of cold-blooded depravity. Icy iniquity and depression filled the atmosphere. The formation of an angry band of spirits, enraged with the forces of sin, appeared before them. They had expected this, but the reality was very intimidating.

"My God in heaven, send help, in the name of Jesus!" Jason was terrified and since prayer was not his forte he fumbled words that he had heard others use before. The angry spirits surrounded the Deathlinks. Marie and Jason were taken by surprise. A large number of angels descended upon them and they bestowed strength. With this Jason was fortified and he said, "For those who are being lost, it is a deadly stench that kills; but for those who are being saved, it is a fragrance that brings life."

After work Ivy, through no physical rationale she could determine, had been compelled to drive down a random street and park. Her heart was pounding. Something of a profound nature was compelling her to rush to rescue someone. Her first thought was that Gabe, her own son, was in trouble. As she rounded the corner and entered the ally, she was framed by white light with two warrior angels attending her on each side and she was filled with fortitude. The man with Danny lunged at Ivy with a knife. An angel flipped the knife out of his hand and the knife flew in the opposite direction and the man fled. Ivy grabbed the girl from the grasp of the woman. The woman held on tight. Ivy, who wasn't very strong, pushed the woman down on the ground. She started to get up to charge at Ivy again, but saw another angel coming towards them and she ran away in fear.

The angels surrounded Jason and Marie until they regained strength. Jason was frightened, but was determined to finish what he started. Hateful demons still infiltrated the atmosphere where the frightened teens remained. Given the intensity of the situation, Jason and Marie were joined by Michael, Rosemary and Grace. They encircled Danny and the girl. Jason's prayer and explanation to the bewildered teens was heartfelt. As Danny and the girl listened in disbelief, Jason shouted words from scripture at the demons, "I am dead in order that I might live for God. I have been put to death with Christ on his cross, so that it is no longer I who live, but it is Christ who lives in me. This life that I live now, I live by faith in the son of God, who loved me and gave his life for me. I refuse to reject the grace of God - forgive them!"

The enraged spirits, whose intentions were to finish off the inexperienced Deathlinks, howled and writhed in pain. The words of God spoken by Jason tormented them and they fought for the strength to endure.

The Deathlinks sensed their weakness. Together they prayed, "Our Father, who art in heaven, hallowed be thy name. . . "

One of the devils shouted, "Oh, please. That old chestnut? It will take more than that to defeat us." Yet, as the words of the Lord's Prayer penetrated the atmosphere, the evil, reluctant to leave, fought the grace that surrounded the Deathlinks and the humans the Deathlinks were given charge to protect. The perversion dissipated and all was calm.

Danny and the abandoned teenage girl remained. Stunned and shocked by what they had just seen, they huddled together still confused and afraid.

"Was it your intention to kill yourselves together?" Jason asked.

"Yes, we thought that if we did this together, no one would chicken out. Hey, are you real or what . . . am I hallucinating?" Danny wasn't sure of their authenticity.

"Do you realize the importance of sticking it out in life, even though it may sometimes seem unbearable and unfair?" Jason was astonished that these kids were willing to just throw away their lives, but worse yet to deepen death's bond, they were going to do it together with two adults.

"What are you?" Danny was still in disbelief.

"I am someone you need to see as an example. I killed myself, not on purpose. It was a stupid accident, but the respect I had for my life was about as equal to the respect you have for yours. When you live and you endure, you prove that you have worth. Everyone has something that they have to put up with. Some kids are beaten; some are abused verbally. It's up to you to find a way to gain the courage to rise above the trash that's dished out to you. That way is to turn to your

Creator, whoever or whatever you perceive Him to be. Ask Him for help and give Him your life. I know that He will forgive so much crap because He forgave me. He will come through for you, even in the worse times."

"You have no idea what I am going through. I would rather be dead." Danny just didn't get it.

"Man, so what if your mother is the biggest bitch on earth? That's her story. You have a different story. God wants you and loves you, even if she doesn't. You are here on earth for a reason. You, Danny, can make the difference in the world out there. You are almost out of school, and you have your own gifts. If you have faith in yourself, you have faith in God and He won't let you down."

Danny was amazed that this teenage spirit knew his name. "Who are you?"

"My father and mother won't leave me alone. They want to sacrifice me to Satan."

"What's your name, honey?" asked Marie

"Venus."

"Venus, there are shelters that can help you. Betrayal is a terrible thing. I know how that feels. I also, accidentally, took my own life. We're here to tell you that you have got to fight for your eternal life and the only way to do that is to start here on earth. This is where it all begins. You think that your life ends when your body dies? Think again. If you want to live in peace and love eternally, you have to skate around a few land mines here on earth. God only wants you to prove your faithfulness to Him. Life can be very hard, but not being able to live in the light eternally is harder, and for most, a second chance is not an option."

"My parents are Satan worshippers. How do I get around that?" Venus was still huddled on the ground with her arms wrapped around her legs.

"Venus, were those two people your parents?" asked Jason. Danny was just as shocked.

"Yes. They wanted to sacrifice me to Satan after this one took his life. They thought that this would help them find favor with the evil one and it would give them great power." Venus was frail and malnourished. It was obvious she had been abused and neglected. "Do you think that God wants to help me?"

"I'm here to tell you that He definitely wants you." Ivy, who remained in the ally amazed by all she had seen, stepped out of the shadows. God's spirit was stirring within her as she followed the call for help. "I was chosen by Satan himself to mother his child. He raped me, terrorized me and I laid in a coma pregnant with his son. God sent his warriors to fight for me and for my child. I am here today, because God loves me, even after all of the horrible things that I did, He still loves me."

Venus, feeling a kinship with Ivy, ran to her and Ivy held her and comforted her. Danny was still shocked by all that happened, but his heart was moved. He never had been taught about God, nor had he given it much thought. But now, both Danny and Venus understood the message and were fortified. Jason and Marie completed their missions. Luminous white light shone around them and they were now considered part of God's army. The Deathlinks praised the Father and once again were astounded by His omniscience. They felt His loving care and prayed that it could be this way for all of His people.

Chapter Twenty-seven
Wini's Brew

Wini arrived at the store early. She had to find a way to discredit Ivy. The schedule was already posted for the week and Wini knew that Ivy made a point of copying her schedule and putting it in her purse. So, she took down the existing schedule and rewrote it to reflect different hours for Ivy.

"This should start the ball rolling." Wini was determined that this little princess was not going to horn in on her turf. Since there were some major responsibilities to be assigned to Ivy, Wini had to sabotage her work. She just had to find out what those responsibilities were. Jana wasn't in her office yet, but she was so unpredictable. Sometimes she would come in at six in the morning. Jana almost caught Wini in the act last month when she was going through the personnel files trying to dig up more information to further her own ambitions.

The wicked essence of two vengeful and hateful souls infiltrated the room where Wini was working. Lucifer and Geoffrey were there to make certain that their trivial disciple carried out her ambitions when it came to that traitorous wench, Ivy Winston. The ruination of this person was the goal here, and they didn't want it botched.

It sickened Lucifer to be reminded of how she and his son were swept away from his servitude by those two discards and the preacher. That preacher had always been a barb to him; going around helping everyone understand the purpose of their existence. Where in the hell did he ever get the idea to do that? Now, there was another such soul being prepared. He thought that the fly ball in the eye was a pretty good touch, but this guy was like the Energizer Bunny. He just kept on going. Unfortunately, that had to be left for another time.

His army took some hits of late. It seemed that they weren't as resourceful as Emily Walker's team and to make matters worse, there were other mediums and other teams from different faiths and religions. They were cropping up all over the place made up of every kind of holy body. There were Christians, Jews, Hindi, Native American Spiritualists and many others. They were just everywhere and he couldn't be everywhere at once, like someone else he knew. God was giving each and every one of them more and more power. As their faith in their Creator increased so did their spiritual strength. Nevertheless, Lucifer was not going to fail in this engagement. He was going to prove that he was greater than Almighty God. That was *his* purpose of existence, wasn't it? If blood had to spill then so be it, but Ivy and Gabe Winston had to be put in their place. Even Winifred B. Thitch didn't know the full details of the party she was planning. Her petty, meaningless stunts were so stupid. They were no more powerful than fleas on a dog's back. Satan's intention, with Geoffrey's help, was to pervert her mind and soul so that she felt no qualms in pursuing the ruination of St. Ivy and her son. Wini would soon be performing deeds the likes of which even she didn't think she was capable. Lucifer could never allow Gabe Winston to become a soldier against him. That would be total disaster.

"Yes, here it is - Jana's list of responsibilities for Ivy. She's giving her the Claiborne line? That hurts. We'll just make sure that the pricing on this inventory is all wrong." Wini quickly made copies of the printouts and returned them to their place in the file cabinet. The store lights were turning on as Wini left the office.

That morning as Ivy attended to her pricing, she found herself thinking more and more about the young girl whose parents were going to sacrifice her in a Satanic ritual. Venus Black was staying at her apartment. Ivy took it upon herself to attempt to save this lost child. She wondered whether it was quite the right thing to do considering she was raising her own son. After all, she didn't know this girl very well and maybe she wasn't as trustworthy as Ivy hoped, or worse, maybe she had a hidden agenda. Still, Gabe was seventeen years old and he and Venus seemed to get along. Also, Gabe's spiritual example was strong. He could move the most zealous agnostic with his gentle but definite trust in God's love and fidelity. She couldn't wait to get off work in order to tend to the teens who were becoming quite good friends.

When she arrived home, she found Gabe and Venus discussing free will and how important it was to pray for direction. Venus questioned how a person was able to recognize their path in life. She, like so many people, expressed doubt in the ability to converse with God directly. How could a person know that the response they heard was God or just their own minds making up its own little script? Indeed, Ivy had felt that way so many times and still did on occasion. It did seem that her skill of actual discernment was becoming easier and more accurate. The dialogue went on into the night until Ivy had to stop the conversation and send the children to bed. It took on a prayerful ambiance, so when Ivy turned in she felt agitated; like something major was going to happen. Her soul grew restless and fearful. What could she be sensing, and who or what should she fear? Throughout the night memories flooded Ivy's unconscious mind. Horrifying acts that victimized her many years ago came back to her. A sense of dread filled her heart once again until she thought of Gabe's sweet innocence and fell into deep repose.

The next morning, Ivy was running behind so she scurried out of her apartment without talking to the children. She ran into the store, up the escalator and as Ivy walked into her department, Erica, Paula and Wini were huddled together whispering. They saw Ivy and stopped. Without a word, they split up into different areas of the department and Jana Blevett was walking towards her.

"Ivy, can I see you upstairs for a moment?"

Ivy followed Jana up to her office. She sensed tension in Jana's voice. Glancing down at her watch she realized that she was on time so Ivy wondered what she could have done to upset her.

"Please, sit down." Jana had a concerned look on her face. "Ivy, the entire line of Liz Claiborne was marked wrong. The tags reflected the wrong department code and the prices were marked way below what was indicated on the printout, not to mention that you have been coming in to work at the wrong times for the last week. What's going on?"

"I don't know. I used the printout that Wini gave me. I assumed that it was the correct one. After all, she is my supervisor. And as far as my schedule, I copy it down as soon as it is posted. Maybe I wrote down the wrong schedule."

"I'll talk to Wini about both of these things. It's just a good thing that I checked your work before the store opened. We would have had to sell these items for the prices marked on the tickets. They have been removed from the floor and are back in the stock room. You will have to stay tonight to retag them. Ivy, I have put a lot of faith in you against the advice of your immediate supervisor. Please, don't prove me wrong. Let's get it fixed."

"Thank you, Jana. I'm very sorry and I can assure you that I will be double checking the printouts from now on."

Ivy's stomach burned with resentment. She knew that Wini didn't like her, but why would she be so low as to put her job in jeopardy? There Wini was, talking as usual to her two favorite gal pals.

"Wini, could I speak with you for a moment, alone?" Ivy's voice was trembling.

"I'm busy. What do you want?" Wini walked over to where Ivy was standing.

"Do you know of any reason why the Claiborne printouts you gave me were incorrect?"

"Because, let's see, your work is inadequate? You have poor concentration? You're dumb? You shouldn't be in the position that you are in." Wini was very good at belittling her subordinates. She ripped many of them apart with her disparaging remarks. As a matter of fact, she was so good at it that she should have been awarded trophies for *Finest Hag* or *Most Lethal Crone*. At any rate, Ivy was enraged and taken by surprise that Wini had the boldness to talk to her this way in a professional environment. But, what was she supposed to do? Run back to Jana and tell on her? Ivy just turned away and went back to work.

Oh, Wini was on a high. She just tore old Ivy to shreds. The more pain and anguish she caused the happier she was. What an opiate. Wini went back to her office to revel in her victory. Geoffrey and Lucifer were present and extended their essences by enclosing her in a film of congratulatory affection. She swooned over her mastery of torment.

Ivy had to call Gabe and let him know that she would be working late. She didn't feel quite right about having to stay, but it was her obligation and she had no other choice.

Sometimes God doesn't let His children know what is about to befall them. He relies on their faith in Him to give them the energy to continue on their journey. What Ivy didn't know was that she was about to face the hardest, most desperate time in her life. She just kept working without a trace of perception. To forgive herself this lack of perception would be the most formidable task of all.

Chapter Twenty-eight
What is Lost is Found

What a harrowing experience. Drew and Elizabeth Black were safely in their house, but their objective had not been accomplished and they were not ready to abandon their plan yet. In the darkness, Elizabeth lit candles. They were everywhere, casting haunting reflections and dismal images on the walls and the furniture. When Drew lit the fireplace the horrific picture was complete. A large portrait of Satan rested above its mantel and loomed over everything in that room. Directly in front of the fireplace where a couch would normally be, a wooden altar had been erected. A pentagram was etched into the face of it and there were blood stains on its table where animal sacrifices were made to their master, but none of those sacrifices would compare to the one that they were still plotting. It was their intent that in one vial, bloody act, they would gain his favor eternally, bringing them everything that they desired. Devoutly, the two knelt down before the altar.

"Oh, supreme master of the underworld, most beautiful dark angel, we worship you and your kingdom. Soon, on this very altar, we will sacrifice to you a virgin." Drew, drone that he was, subjugated himself in devotion to hideous depravity.

"We offer you, dear master, our own virgin daughter, Venus. We bore her and raised her to be our most excellent sacrifice to you." Elizabeth offered her own flesh and blood without even a hint of remorse or pain. When the two of them kept up their idolization of Lucifer, it would end with no results. So, this time, they didn't notice the figure of their master ooze out of the portrait above the mantel. Accompanying him was a coterie of spiritual demons chanting in devotion to the most evil one. Jolted to focus on what was happening around them, Drew and Elizabeth cowered in fear at the reality of it all and in disbelief of what they had actually conjured.

"Faithful servants, I applaud your fervent desire to venerate me with the sacrifice of the virgin, Venus, however I would like for you to augment that sacrifice with one so great that no one has ever equaled its magnitude. There is a boy, his name is Gabriel. Venus has befriended him and is staying at his home. I need for you to bring him here and make him a part of this offering to me. He is also a virgin, but his significance will yield great power to the kingdom of the prince of darkness."

"Master," Drew shook in fear and wonder "we don't know this boy, Gabriel."

"I will lead you to him. He is not a part of my kingdom, he worships another." Lucifer winced in pain at the mere acknowledgement of purity. "You must find a way to bring him with Venus here. You will then offer them in sacrifice to me. If you do this, the world will be at your fingertips. This is my promise to you. If you don't, I will personally rip out your hearts and your spirits will live in the lowest level of hell."

The chanting became louder as if in celebration. There was shrieking and howling. It was deafening. The pack of evil spirits seeped back into the portrait chanting as they departed. All grew quiet. Lucifer's image was nowhere to be found in the picture, leaving Drew and Elizabeth with the impression that he was still near. As they blew out the candles and turned on the lights, they felt the uneasiness of being watched. Drew, by no effort of his own, walked to a telephone book. The book opened to the "W's." A burn mark appeared under the name of I. Winston, as if etched by a smoldering match. Not doubting why that name was underlined, he dutifully called the number.

"Hello," the young voice at the other end answered.

"Yes, I was wondering, is Venus Black there by any chance?"

"Yes, may I ask who is calling?"

"This is Venus's father. I would like very much to talk to her."

Gabe put his hand over the receiver of the phone. "Venus, it's your father. You don't have to talk to him if you don't want to."

"No, I better. He won't leave me alone if I don't." Venus reluctantly took the phone. "Hello, Dad. How did you find me?"

"That doesn't matter. Can we come and get you now? It's time for you to come home."

Venus started to cry. "Dad, I don't want to die. Don't make me come home if you still think that I'm going to take my life because I'm not going to. I've found a different way to live. I want you to meet my new friend, Gabe Winston. He can explain everything to you. I'll only come home if you will promise to meet us at a restaurant or something so that he can talk to you and Mom. I can see us living a better more hopeful life if you just listen to him." Venus seemed to want to change her path. Gabe offered a quick prayer for help in carrying out her wish.

"I know how horrible this has been for you and we understand, honey. Perhaps we were wrong in being so active in the cult. Don't be afraid anymore, Venus. We want you to come home and there will be no more talk of you and sacrifice. How about if we meet you in, let's say, thirty minutes, at *The Door*." As Drew hung up the phone he said, "Well, that certainly was easy. Venus played right into our hands and this Gabe kid is coming with her."

Venus turned to Gabe. He was on his knees in front of a crucifix that his mother hung on the wall in their apartment. Even at the age of seventeen, Gabriel was gifted with innocence and sweetness beyond measure. He prayed for the courage to talk with Venus's parents in the way that God required and his only desire was to carry out God's will for him in this life so that he might live eternally in heaven.

"Gabe, excuse me, but I told my parents we would meet with them soon."

"Alright, I'm ready." Gabriel made a sign of the cross and got up. "I do need to leave a note for my mother. I'll leave it here on the table where she can find it." The two left the apartment, one with hope for the future of others, the other with hope for only her future.

They entered the restaurant to find Drew and Elizabeth Black already there waiting for them. All of the preparations were being made back at their house to desecrate the purity of the teens walking towards them. The Blacks gathered the fellow Satanists in their cult. Tonight was going to be a jubilee, a bacchanal so uproarious; heaven itself wasn't going to know what hit it.

"Mom, Dad, this is Gabriel Winston. Gabe this is my mom and dad."

"Hello, Gabriel. It's very nice to meet you." Elizabeth extended her hand to the unsuspecting soul.

"Gabe. Please, have a seat." Drew gazed into Gabe's eyes. He shuddered. How could someone so young embody so many God-like qualities?

"Mr. and Mrs. Black, Venus wants to strengthen her faith in God. I think that you should let her try."

"Well, Gabe, we are looking to make a change, too. What can you share with us?" Drew lathered his words with charm and interest and Gabe was none the wiser. Venus was pleasantly surprised and filled with hope that her father was serious.

"Well, I guess to start with, I believe that God has prepared a place for those of us who are faithful and remain constant in His love."

"There's too much fear and disappointment. God does not shield His followers from the pain of living. He allows too much suffering." Drew was cold and compassionless

"Even though we go through hardships in our life, we must understand that God allows these things because they are the pathways in our journey that will ultimately bring us to our eternal life with Him. I find rest in Him, and he finds truth in me, because I allow Him to be with me and work through me. I want God to speak through me and I want to hear with His ears and see my fellow humans with His eyes."

"You seem so at peace, Gabe." Elizabeth found it hard not to listen to the young man's message. Drew squirmed in his seat. The truth and the calm with which Gabe delivered his love and loyalty to his Creator bothered him and he worried that Elizabeth was now drawn to Gabe's charismatic demeanor. It was already apparent that Venus was.

"So what you are saying is that if I get beaten and robbed some night, I shouldn't call on God to help me because this was what He wanted?" Drew was trying to blow smoke.

"No, certainly not. God is there to help us through any ordeal, ordained or not. If it is not necessary for us to experience some hardship, then He will definitely remove it from our path, but if it has been placed there for us to endure as a kind of land mark or source of new knowledge in our journey, then I think that we need to trust in God to help us to use the hardship to serve our purpose. It only makes us stronger."

Drew was worried. He and Elizabeth were not getting very far. This boy was not any ordinary teen and his serenity frightened them. To make matters worse, Venus was drawn to his words like a magnet. They would have to make a slight change in their plan to get Gabe and Venus to the house.

"That's all very interesting, but you'll have to excuse me, I have to hit the head." Drew left the table.

"That is an interesting philosophy, Gabe. Heaven must be a wonderful place." Elizabeth knew that Drew was up to something and she also knew that he meant for her to follow his lead. "What do you want to do when you graduate?"

"Oh, well, I already know that I am to become a priest." Gabe smiled with contentment.

Behind them there was a crash. Drew had tripped and fallen into a waitress and was on the floor.

"Dad, are you okay?" Venus and Gabe ran to him.

"Man, I think I sprained my ankle. Can you guys help me up?"

"Drew, how am I going to get you home?" Elizabeth was now on to the program.

"We'll help you." Gabe volunteered. Elizabeth and Drew could only grin with internal satisfaction. The party was about to begin.

Drew and Elizabeth had walked to *The Door*. It was just down the street so Gabe and Venus helped Drew hobble home, one on each side of him. They finally reached their destination where they made it up the porch and to the front door. The house seemed dark, yet there was the flickering of candles in the windows. Immediately, Venus realized what was happening, but as she turned to run, she and Gabe were grabbed from behind. Their mouths were covered and taped shut. Their arms and feet were bound and they were carried around to the back of the house. Four people dressed in black robes carried them through the back door and down to the basement of the house.

"Quickly, take off their clothes." One of the robed males was demanding and gruff.

"Oh, this is so carnal. The incubus is stimulated tonight." A woman who was in charge of disrobing Gabe was weird and sickening. Accompanying her was a strange little man. As they removed Gabe's clothes they would find ways to touch him erotically. By the time they were done the only thing that remained on him was the small crucifix that he wore around his neck. Failure on their part to notice this was a miracle to Gabe. Finally, when he was totally disrobed they covered him in a white robe. They threw him to the floor and slinked around him chanting some satanic mumbo jumbo.

Venus was prepared in a different manner. She had to withstand the molestation of her body by a woman and two men. She screamed and struggled, but the more she struggled the more they restrained her. At last she lay on the floor exhausted. The children were terrified; Venus, more so because she knew what was going to happen. The white robes were draped around their bound bodies and the black robed monsters removed the tape from their mouths, forced lavish kisses on them, and left.

"Gabe, I'm so sorry." Venus was sobbing. "I got you into this. I should have known my parents were deceiving us. I just wanted so badly to believe that they could change. I just wanted them to love me."

"Shhh, Venus, it's all right. Stay calm. I'm frightened too, but God is with us."

"What? How can you believe that? If He were with us, He would prevent this from happening."

"Remember when I said that God allows things because that is part of our faith journey, but that if this is not something we should endure, He would save us? We just have to believe that God knows what He is doing."

Venus became hysterical. "Gabe, you don't get it! We are going to be sacrificed!"

Gabriel fell silent. This was to be the truest of all tests. He was so terrified and yet he wanted to carry out his faith and love of God to the very end, no matter what the end. He was chilled to the bone. The face of his mother flashed in front of him. How would she ever survive this test of faith alone, for that matter, how would he? He began to pray aloud.

"Oh, my Jesus, forgive us our sins. Save us from the fires of hell and lead all souls to heaven especially those in most need of Thy mercy."

A vision of the Holy Mother appeared before them. Gabe cried out, "Help us, Mother!"

Then a devil appeared, just enough to pound panic and fear into their hearts. It lasted for only a brief moment, because the evil vision turned into a snake and was crushed under the foot of the Blessed Virgin. Gabe's heart was uplifted. He drew strength from the age-old Catholic metaphor. It was true and that meant that everything he believed was true. Venus was in awe and she was filled with peace.

"Gabe, will I be allowed to enter heaven?"

"Keep your faith strong, and pray with me. We will enter the light hand in hand."

As they began to pray, the beatific vision that the two beheld was extraordinary. Jesus Christ approached them in His glorified state and sat down between them. Angels surrounded them in blissful grandeur as He rested His hands on their arms to reassure them.

"Children, do not be afraid. My Father's plan is hard to understand. When I was a young man about your age, Gabe, I had glimpses of what was going to befall me as a man. Sometimes the fear would get to me until I put that fear into the hands of the Creator. I asked Him to let me see the truth in the scenes that I was allowed to view and He would. Then I knew that the acts of aggression and hatred were just stepping stones to a greater calling. Suffering took on a whole new meaning to me. When offering it up to my Father for all of the souls that passed away and all of the souls yet to come, I felt the peace of the infinite God and I shared in His complete love for all mankind. He alone is why we live. No man, woman, possession or passion can fulfill the soul of a man, unless it is ordained by his Creator. These things are not the answer. Man craves to see his Creator and the only way for this to happen is to put God above and before everything else in the world. Every breath that a man takes must be for Him. Every action and every feeling of love must be for the omnipotent God, for He is the Alpha and Omega. He is the reason that man exists at all. Children, behold your place in heaven!"

The ceiling of the basement opened up to reveal the majestic setting of an immense spiritual dominion; one of which they were about to become a part, and it was breathtaking in its omnipotence. Their hearts and spirits filled with complete love and awe of the Creator. The children experienced all of the emotions and passions and love that they had ever felt in their young lives together with those that they had never known. They were home and home was with God.

The vision was interrupted. Down the basement stairs the intruders came in their black robes. They were on a mission and nothing was going to stop them. They pulled Gabe and Venus up from the ground and pushed them up the stairs, through the kitchen and into the room where they were to be sacrificed to the evil of the world. They were innocent children led to the slaughter upon an altar of wood. The room was filled with black robed people chanting weird Satanic chants. Behind the altar was the most horrifying sight of all. Lucifer, in hideous splendor was standing there waiting for the two to be brought forth to him. The sick and perverted mob hurled the two children in front of the altar. The savages ripped the white robes from their bodies and made them stand naked in front of their violators.

"Master," one of the men cried out. "Which one of us will you allow the pleasure of taking the girl and then the boy? Our loins cry out for satisfaction, oh, dark one."

The depraved, corrupt and immoral souls that collected for this occasion were disgusting in their appetite for lust. Their groans of desire filled the room. The children were not children anymore. They were only pawns put in place to satisfy the lust and revenge of Satan and his followers.

"Stop!" Lucifer flew over the top of the altar into the face of his son. Everything became silent. "Do you know who I am?"

With great courage and peace Gabe answered. "Yes, you are Lucifer, the fallen angel. You are the destroyer of souls."

"Has your mother not told you who your father is?"

"Yes. My father is the Almighty One who awaits me in heaven."

Agitated with this answer, Lucifer screamed "No, you twit. Has she told you who your biological father is?"

"My mother and I pray for his depraved soul daily. We offer it up through the Eucharist every day at Mass."

Satan and his followers screeched and writhed in torment.

Recovering from the blow, Lucifer grabbed Gabe's throat and with great intensity he looked into the sweet eyes of the innocent and with what he thought would bring him great satisfaction he said, "No, I am your father. I raped your mother again and again until I knew that she was pregnant with you. You are my son." Lucifer loosened his grip, collected himself and put his hands on Gabe's shoulders and with a softened voice said, "You are my son. I will give you everything that you want. All you have to do is say the word and you will reign with me and we will defeat God and you will live here with me on earth, with your real father, and we will be gods of all the heavens and the earth."

"We cannot be God of heaven and earth, for we did not create the heavens and the earth. Only our Creator can be God and I will not turn my back on Him nor will I abandon the love that I have for Him and that He has for me. You and I have no relationship. The only true and real relationship that I have is with the Triune God who waits for me in heaven."

"So be it!" Satan was so enraged he flew into the air and as he came back down he yanked the crucifix from Gabe's throat. It seared his hand and he threw it into the crowd. It exploded as it hit the ground scattering Lucifer's minions. This signaled the demise of the plan. Filled with rage, Satan swooped Venus up and threw her on the altar. "She is mine and as my son I will show you how to take her and you will watch as I show you just how you were conceived. When I am done, you will take her just as I have shown you."

Venus shrieked with fear. She looked into the crowd searching for her parents. *Where are they? How could they allow this?* The chants of the barren, sick souls were deafening. Lucifer became the monster he was and disrobed in order to carry out his revenge.

"A true God is a God of mercy and compassion. You are no God." Gabe in his own nakedness became a mighty warrior filled with passionate words. His voice raised he said, "Jesus, bring our souls close to you. Allow Venus to leave her body and begin her life in heaven before her body is desecrated. Bless all of the poor souls in this room and all those everywhere who do not know you and your Father, but most of all forgive the fallen angel, Lucifer."

All hell broke loose. Fear grappled at the hearts of the evil souls in the room. They all fled the house in panic. Satan, enraged at his son's betrayal and impotent because of the purity of the prayer offered to his enemy, God, grasped the dagger already laid out on the altar and plunged it into Venus's heart. As she lay dying, she whimpered, "Forgive them, Father." With the same fury and uncontrollable storm of wrath, Lucifer turned to Gabe, picked him up, threw him onto the altar and slit his throat. The blood from the two innocents soaked into the wood of the altar. Satan dropped the dagger in horror. What just happened? Instead of a sacrifice to him, this became a sacrifice to the God of heaven. His son was now a pure and sanctified spirit living in the kingdom of God, and Lucifer, god of hell, helped put him there. He was crazed, frenzied and losing control of his plan. Appalled by his defeat, the prince of darkness shrank into despair and retreated back into the fiery depths of hell.

From the kitchen, two penitent souls watched in revulsion at what they had orchestrated. Drew and Elizabeth Black were in shock. Their black hearts pounded with utter loathing for what they did. As they looked into the sacrificial space which once was their living room, they saw angels administering to the sweet, sinless bodies. The white robes were placed over their nakedness and songs of praise, adoration and glory filled the air.

Drew and Elizabeth fell to their knees begging forgiveness. Their journey back to their Creator would be hard, but fulfilled because of His grace and mercy. Their most deplorable sins were forgiven. Venus's last prayer was answered as she and Gabe watched from the peace and glory of their new home.

Chapter Twenty-nine
God! Where Are You?

It was late. Ivy returned home tired and down-hearted. She looked so forward to seeing the face of her son. He was her reason for living. As she walked into the unlit apartment, there was immediate concern that things had taken a sinister turn. She flipped on the lights and she found a note lying on the table. *Dear Mom, I went with Venus to meet her parents. I really think that they are ready to try and understand the meaning of life. Maybe I can bring Jesus into their hearts. I love you. Don't worry, I am with God. Love, Gabe*

Something about the note disturbed Ivy beyond belief. . . *Don't worry, I am with God.*

There came a pounding at the door. Ivy rushed to the door her heart gripped with fear and she was sure something was wrong. The door opened revealing the face of a woman who was ever present in Ivy's visions.

"Hi, Ivy? My name is Emily Walker" An unexpected silence developed between the two women. "My, but this is awkward."

"I know who you are. God has allowed me to see you during prayer - you and many others. Somehow I know that you saved me . . . saved me from a life of damnation and now you are here to tell me what?" Ivy's voice was shaking and distracted. She knew that the war had begun and dreaded the fact that Gabe had a great deal to do with the kick off. Where was her son?

"Ivy, God has sent me to you. He hasn't even revealed to me why yet, but I do know that we are to go to a certain address together to find your son."

The hair on Ivy's neck stood straight up. God brought Emily

Walker, some obscure, off and on vision of hers, to help her find her son? "Where is this place? What address do you have?"

"Well, it appears to be the home of a Drew Black. My son, Andrew, traced it in order to give us a name." Emily noticed the shock on Ivy's face. "Are you all right with this?"

"Yes. I trust you and I trust God. I don't trust the Blacks. Please, let's go. Let's hurry."

The two found themselves holding hands, while Emily hailed a cab. They sat silently as the cab made its way down side streets with all kinds of twists and turns towards their destination. They finally arrived at the Black's house where the front door was wide open. Ivy's face was fraught with anxiety. This was not good. This was not at all good. Her heartbeat thumped in her ears while her mother's intuition screamed something was not right. Ivy's thoughts turned to Gabe as a baby. How sweet he was. After everything that she had been through, her baby was her purification. He was her salvation. He was always an obedient child and never gave her any trouble. When he learned about God, he became even more lovable and his destiny was very clear. Gabriel was one of God's chosen and he prepared himself for the priesthood all on his own. Ivy marveled at the way Gabe submitted to God's will. He would go to their parish priest, Father Chaney, all of the time to learn more about the Church and what it meant to live a celibate life. His knowledge of the Church and his faith was voluminous for his age. But now, Ivy thought Gabe went too far. He allowed himself to be put in harm's way. He was not thinking, and she just had to find out what he was up to in that house.

Emily stayed close behind Ivy, but was overcome with her surroundings. What went on here? As she entered the open door, her mind and body wandered as she sensed the residue of eerie, dark essences. A blood curdling shriek came from another room. Emily had lost track of Ivy, because she was so engulfed in her own investigation of the house. She ran into the living room to find Ivy draped over the dead body of her only son. Emily cried out, "Oh, my God, what have you done?"

Ivy, wrapping her arms around Gabe, cradled him and rocked him as if the rhythm alone by some magnificent miracle would bring him back to life. "Oh, no, God, no. Why? No, this is not what it seems to be. It's all right, baby. Mama's here. Everything is going to be alright. Mama is going to fix this." Ivy stretched her blood soaked hand out and screaming at the top of her lungs, she called out in disbelief. "God? Where are you! God? Help me. Please!" Her broken heart succumbed to tearful grief. "Did you really need the sacrifice of my son? He loved you." A neighbor who was already suspicious of the Blacks called the police and 911 so an ambulance arrived on the scene. The paramedics walked toward Ivy. "Stay away! You stay away from my baby. He's just waiting. God would not do this to him. He will be alright." Gabe's blood covered Ivy's clothes and hands. In shock she murmured, "God would not let this happen to him. Not Gabe. No, not my Gabe." Ivy's grief was inconsolable and her sobs grew into gut wrenching screams. To watch her suffering was to shed in tandem the bitter tears of her loss, to feel the depth of pain that burned in her soul, and to bear the profound ache in her heart. The paramedics and the police were not able to get near her without her screaming at them to leave her alone.

Emily could not stand Ivy's pain. Her thoughts went to her own son when he was that age; the age of painful growth and lingering innocence which no one really understands. But Emily had the comfort of watching her son grow into adulthood, where Ivy would forever grieve the lack of that future with Gabriel. She had no words to console, no gestures to help erase the torture.

The police kept trying to talk Ivy into letting them take Gabe. Venus's poor little body was already taken away and her parents turned themselves in for the murder of both children. In the confusion and grief Emily hadn't noticed the stranger who entered the house. She turned once again to the sorrow filled scene. A man was squatted down talking to Ivy.

"Ivy, can I spend some time with you? You need to have someone with you right now. Can I get you something?"

Ivy looked into the man's face. She had seen him before too, in her prayerful visions. She referred to him as her future, although she didn't know why. "Who are you?"

"I believe God has sent me to you, for whatever help you need. I am here to give it to you."

Ivy released Gabe's body into the arms of a paramedic and reached out towards the man's firm embrace. There she buried her head into his chest and wailed and grieved until she could cry no more. Her life was taken from her. Her very existence was shattered. Her God abandoned her and He ripped away the very person that made her living worthwhile. There was nothing left for her. *Where were you when my son needed you, God?*

Chapter Thirty
Suffering

Suffering, in all of its agony and torment has its purpose in the universe. Is it that through our own suffering we are purified and our path to heaven is made clear? We may not know it now, not during the present anguish that we feel and experience when our hearts and minds are filled with doubt and fear, and not when we question the very existence of God. Not during the time when we wonder why some paths appear to be so easy and others so very hard, but at the end of our life; the end of all confusion. At the end when the light of the earth becomes dim and the brilliance of the Triune God manifests itself on our golden pathway to heaven. Perhaps what we have suffered on earth are jewels; the pearls of purity. Purity in the sense that we have tried our best, even after the hardest of times, to obey God's will and stay steady on our journey back to Him. They are only jewels if we finally bear these trials with the love of God in our hearts and the forgiveness of His spirit in our souls. These jewels are proof of our integrity and resistant to a world of corruption. These jewels are impervious to spiritual failure.

Faith can be a tricky thing. It demands complete stupidity and surrender to something that we only believe. Never can we touch it with our hand, nor is it absolute and science cannot prove its existence. It takes a gigantic heart to allow faith to dwell within it, to nurture it and to keep it strong. This is the miracle of life on earth. This is the game we play with our Creator. One of the cruel rules of this game is that we are not to see the benefits of our suffering. We are just to believe that our God knows and blesses us after every painful sacrifice. Though the reason for our suffering may not be available to see and sometimes it may never be seen while we live, there is a benefit. Somewhere the news of the suffering may affect someone with such profundity that they examine their own state of being and make the decision to change their path. Perhaps the sufferer surrenders to God's purpose and transforms the lives of many others. Maybe God holds the suffering so close to Himself and He blesses it so that the blessing in itself is saved to be used to answer a very special prayer prayed for a very significant and critical time. Suffering is never in vain.

The Deathlinks watched in disbelief as the evil mutilated the body of the pure young soul and his companion. They were rendered helpless to draw near and assist the children in their time of need. It was quite clear that the children were destined to bear this on their own. God in His might and wisdom had a plan and it was carried out, no matter how horrifying. They were happy that they were in a place where they saw the existence of God. If they were still on earth, their very faith would have shattered. But, what of Ivy? What distressing times were awaiting her? She lived her life for Gabriel. He was the reason for her existence. Ivy's strength of faith would be tested, but no one knew the magnitude of God's love for her. Her love for Gabriel would nourish her soul, and her ability to forgive and to alter the future of the world would advance hand in hand.

Emily examined the stranger. She knew him. Could it be him? The compassionate manner in which he handled the situation with Ivy all reminded her of the young minister in her visions. *Was it finally time for him to show up?* She watched him as he gently sat Ivy down into an easy chair. As he caught Emily's eye he walked over to her.

"Hi, are you a friend of Ivy's?"

"Well, yes. My name is Emily Walker and are you . . . ?"

Dumbfounded, he responded, "You have got to be kidding! You're Emily Walker? My name is Fletcher Hodges. I have been trying to locate you. Michael Harrison told me that you were from Alabama, so I naturally assumed that . . ."

"Michael. Oh, my." Emily almost collapsed. "I'm sorry, Fletcher. I have been waiting for you, my dear boy. You have been shown to me in so many visions."

"Listen, we have a great deal to talk about, but first I think we need to get Ivy away from here. This whole thing is sickening. She shouldn't be here any longer than she has to be. Why don't both of you come to the rectory at St. Martin's with me. Father Chaney will be more than happy to accommodate all of us."

"Oh, Fletcher, this poor child. Let's go now, let's get her away."

They gathered Ivy up and escorted her out of the Black's house. St. Martin's was about a block away. As they walked up the stairs to the rectory door, Father Chaney came out to greet them. He took Ivy into his arms. Father hadn't heard anything yet and Fletch knew that he would have to tell him. Gabe was very close to Father and he didn't relish the idea of filling him in on all of the horrific details.

"My child, what is the matter? Please, help me get her inside." Father Chaney was so gentle and kind.

"Father, let's find Ivy a place to rest. This is Emily Walker. She can stay with her. You need to come with me." Fletcher ushered Father Chaney into another room where he told him about what happened to Gabe and Venus. Father's face puckered with the onset of terrible grief. "Father, this kind of evil is never easy to hear about or to understand."

"My son, there is evil everywhere in this world, but I am glad to say that I have never mastered the ability to become numb to its debauchery." Father Chaney steadied himself. "I want to be with Ivy. Her grief is my grief. We raised Gabe together and shared immense love for him. Gabe was like a son to me and I cherished the times that he spent with me; not so much because I felt that I was nurturing him, but that Gabe was offering me sustenance." He was grieving the death of his adopted son. This young man, he thought, was going to do a lot of good in this world and now all of that hope was gone.

Chapter Thirty-two

Dreams

That night, Emily and Fletcher stayed with Ivy in the living room of the rectory. She didn't want to be alone and neither of them wanted to leave her side. The rectory was still. The only movement was wind blowing through the trees outside. Now and then a branch hit the side of the house or banged against a window, making the threesome jump. The mood was solemn and filled with heartache. Sleep was impossible for everyone, but especially for Ivy. She refused a sedative that was prescribed earlier to her by the doctor, and Fletch wished she had listened to the man's advice and taken it, but he was not going to argue with a grieving mother.

As each of them drifted in and out of sleep, a spiritual rhythm rested in the air. Ivy fell deeper and deeper into a sleep that captured her essence. Lucifer seized the opportunity to augment Ivy's misery, as well as tempt her. The beating of his horse's hooves came closer and closer until Ivy could not ignore them any longer. She opened her mind to see Lucifer jump from his black steed and oozing charm approach her. "I am grieving, too, you know. He was not only your son, but he was mine and he was taken from me by your selfish god. Come, Ivy. Let me hold you in my arms. Let us share our grief together. As he sauntered closer he suggested something altogether surreal. "Let's make a new son. We can do this and prove to God that he has not won." Past the dark figure she saw Gabe. He was dressed in a beautiful white robe and was surrounded by celestial beings. They weren't singing, but speaking and comforting her. Gabe came closer. She could see his splendid brown eyes and his face gleamed with love and peace. Behind him were enormous angels dressed as warriors and above him was the light of God. Lucifer, weakened by God's presence, dissipated.

Emily dreamed she saw all of the Deathlinks that were entrusted to her care. They were in fighting formation like soldiers getting ready for battle. In the front of the Deathlinks were Andrew and Joey. All of them maintained the strongest of demeanors blessed with one hundred times their normal strength. Each bore the symbol of eternity on their chests and none of them carried a weapon. They were armed with faith as they marched, marched, marched, marched . . .

Fletcher saw himself at a table dining with Sister Kathy and Michael Harrison. They were eating bread and drinking wine. Another circle of people were standing around them, also waiting to be served the bread and wine. Above them was a light as pure and as beautiful as it could be and it hovered in place. Light shot out of its wings and welcomed all that were present.

Then, the three dreams became one. The threesome was aware of each other's dreams. The atmosphere grew dense with a dark fog. Evil rolled in and the darkness intensified. Out of the gloom Lucifer returned with his army on sleek black horses. The sound of the horses' hooves amplified with every heartbeat and painful shrieking and wailing filled their dreams. Lucifer's horse galloped nearer and nearer and as he drew his sword to strike at them, they awoke. The three looked at each other covered in sweat and chilled to the bone.

"Crimany!" Fletcher stood up to shake off the intensity of the dream.

"What does God want from us?" Ivy thought she already had been through enough and realized there was much more for her to endure. She ran to the nearest bathroom to vomit.

Emily, still shaken, slid off the sofa to her knees. She knew the time had come for all of them to rally. Everyone she envisioned in prayer and meditation was now accounted for and this dream was God's way of letting them know the time was near.

Chapter Thirty-two
And There Are Blessings

Even though God takes people and things from us, He also gives back. Fletcher spent the better part of the year trying to track down Emily Walker. Didn't Michael Harrison say that she was in Alabama? How strange it was to run into her when he did, and he found it odd that he happened upon Ivy the way he did. Fletch had so many dreams about this woman after he lost his eye. Before he became a minister he thought she was just his imagination because her image was always so vivid in his dreams. Yet, he didn't recognize her at first since her face was so stressed with grief and now he couldn't help but wonder what significance this person would have in his life.

"Fletch?"

Fletcher turned to see Ivy standing before him dressed in a dark suit. "Hi, Ivy. You think you'll be okay today?"

"Yeah." Ivy sighed. "It will be awful to say goodbye to Gabe, but he deserves a very special funeral. Will you stand next to me for strength?" Ivy's voice quivered.

"Sure, you know I will. I just hope that Father Chaney is able to conduct this service without falling apart."

"Father Chaney knows that Gabe would have wanted him to celebrate his funeral Mass. I'm sure that he will be just fine."

"Hello, children. Have we all recovered from our dreams?" Emily was still dazed. She knew this was the beginning of an event which she had prepared for almost all of her life and after last night's dream, she was wondering if they were at all ready.

"At least I know that Gabe is with God. I would like to get through today before God decides to throw us into battle with the lord of all evil." Ivy felt bitter. She had been through so much in her life and tried so hard to be close to God. Confusion and distrust were natural reactions to the loss of her son. Emily understood Ivy's feeling of betrayal.

"My dear, God will give us all a break. His love and tenderness will find its way to comfort us."

"Ivy, through the prayers of all of your friends and even Gabe you will survive this. I will be on one side of you and Mrs. Walker will be on the other." Fletch put his arm around Ivy. When she looked up into his eyes, he didn't expect the dramatic connection that occurred. He couldn't pull himself away.

"Well, we better be off. Ivy, I know that this could be too soon to ask, but I believe God wants you to accompany Fletcher and me to Alabama. Do you think . . . "

"Absolutely. As soon as the funeral is over, I will pack my things and the three of us can leave. I know and I have known since last night that we are in this together, whatever it is. I also have known for a very long time I would be joining others in the fight against Satan, so, yes. I may not be emotionally ready, far from it I believe, but God's will be done. Not because I want it, but Gabe would have wanted it that way."

"Good girl!" Emily recognized Ivy's tone was bitter, yet she had no other choice but to keep her focused.

Emily, Ivy, and Fletch found themselves arm in arm walking down the main isle of the church for Gabe's funeral. As they walked, Ivy didn't look up so she didn't see the face of one who had been so cruel to her and who set the stage for Satan's revenge. Winifred B. Thitch had the audacity to attend the funeral of the boy she helped murder. Ivy would need the grace of God to confront this blister on the butt of hell.

Because Gabe would have wanted his funeral Mass to be a celebration, Father Chaney said a high Mass with music. As the music started, the church filled with the full nine choirs of angels, although Emily, Ivy, and Fletch were the only people who could hear and see them.

It was a grand gift. Throughout the Mass, Ivy saw the angels act as servers and they hovered by the Proclaimers while they read the Holy Word. The psalm was sung and the angels lifted up their voices to the Most High. Ivy's spirit was nourished by the sweet presence of these celestial beings. When it was time to receive the body and blood of Jesus, Ivy walked with Jesus beside her and relived the paschal sacrifice the way she never had before. Angels surrounded her, and Gabe walked with her as she received communion with her Lord. In her prayer of solitude, Jesus comforted her and told her she would survive and He was giving her the gift of love once again. She didn't understand this, but her spirit was filled with such perfect love and peace it almost didn't matter.

Ivy stood at the back of the church accompanied by Emily and Fletch. The church was filled with people. Ivy was comforted by Gabe's school friends, teachers, neighbors, and homeless people he befriended at the soup kitchen as well as many priests and sisters. As they all filed out, one by one, Ivy was faced with Winifred B. Thitch. The grace Ivy had received through the Sacrament of the Eucharist gave her an unbelievable amount of integrity. She accepted Wini's condolences without any disdain. Much to Wini's chagrin, Ivy's behavior was loving and kind. Ivy was able to discard Wini without even a second thought. What a waste of time for poor Wini.

Chapter Thirty-three
Let the Fun Begin!

Now it was known that the threesome were all pivotal in the fight for the salvation of the world. Unlike the Christian soldiers you hear about in Sunday school, who act as symbols to free souls from the snares of the devil, these soldiers were going to be fighting the fight of the first Christian martyrs. They were putting their lives at risk to save the whole world from total damnation; living out the apocalypse. It wasn't so much the loss of their lives they feared, but the way in which the angel of darkness might kill them. Torture was not out of the question. They knew it and they were terrified.

Emily and Fletch helped Ivy get together the things that mattered. They all said their goodbyes to Father Chaney, and Ivy once more visited the grave of her beautiful son. While she was there a peace came over her and a power filled her spirit. She felt invincible. As she knelt in prayer, Gabe came into her consciousness. He told her he would be beside her at the most frightening times of the war. He instructed her to receive the Sacraments often and to attend daily Mass whenever she could. She left knowing she possessed the greatest power on earth. The Holy Spirit walked with her and with the Deathlinks, as well as with the mediums who led the way to God's eternal plan.

Fletcher was traveling around in an old station wagon given to him by the congregation that he left with no notice after Sister Kathy died. They loved him, but they were very confused by his sudden fervor to leave and search for this Emily Walker. Jonah King tried to talk him out of it, telling him he just needed some rest and that if he just took some time off he would be back to his old self. Fletcher knew he would never be back to his old self. From the day he witnessed the apparitions of Sister Kathy and Michael Harrison, he was having dreams and visions of people he knew he would someday meet. He dreamed of horrific battles with Satan and he even saw some of the Deathlinks in the dreams. Sometimes, as he did ordinary chores he would see a person beside him or across the room, but then when he looked harder, there was no one there. He knew in his heart these energies did exist and even though he could not touch them, they were with him all the same. He was on his way to Alabama when he was sidetracked by a nagging premonition, which led him to St. Martin's parish in Michigan.

The old wagon was packed, gassed up and ready to go. The three left Gabe's grave site to head off to Alabama where Andrew, Joey, and many others who had been touched by the Deathlinks and their mediums were assembled and waiting for their arrival. They, too, had been motivated by God's gentle, but unmistakable guidance. As the threesome started to pull away, Danny Thitch came running toward the car with a backpack bouncing on his back, sporting a suitcase.

"Stop! Hey, wait! Please, stop!"

"Stop the car. It's my boss's son, Danny." Ivy climbed out of the car and went to him. "What is it Danny? Do you need some help?"

"No, I mean, yes. Ms. Winston. I want to go with you. I had a dream last night and I saw what God wanted the world to be. He told me in this dream that if I went with you I could help make His world a reality. Believe it or not, I was saved in my dream. In my dream, Ms. Winston! God must love me very much to come to me! Jesus's sacrifice was played out right in front of me and I finally get it. Please, Ms. Winston, let me come with you. I have nothing to keep me here. My mother hates me and I can't do God's will with her in my life."

"How old are you Danny?" Ivy's gaze was far away. She knew this was right.

"I'm eighteen. I can go anywhere I want without my mother's consent."

By this time Fletcher and Emily were out of the car listening to the conversation.

"Let him come." Emily was determined. "There will be many converts just like him. Believe me. They may not find their direction from us, but they will find their direction. Let this boy be our first."

The four of them got into the car and drove off. On the outskirts of the graveyard, Wini watched her son's escape. Her look was not one of remorse, but of relief and she resembled a witch who at last joined her coven. She dripped with evil. The sight was chilling and the four pilgrims were only too glad to distance themselves from her decadence.

Emily found her way to that little town in Michigan after the Lord came to her and urged her to pack up and go to Ivy's aid. He didn't let her see what appalling events were going to befall Ivy. Emily just knew it was His will that she be there with her. Now, she met the two people who would tie up the loose ends of the circle of eternity. They found their place within the circle and it all was becoming very clear to Emily just how the force of God would empower the community of Deathlinks and all of His devout followers.

The station wagon rumbled down highway after highway and through city after city. The travelers were tired and in their stomachs they bore the anxious, raw emotions of fear. The fear that antagonized them was the uncertainty of Satan's reach and power. After Gabe and Venus were slaughtered, they saw what he was capable of and knew that God did not want them to battle Lucifer's followers with guns, knives or any other means of physical weaponry. God's heart and spirit was to be their artillery. For Ivy, the Sacraments would be her armor. It all seemed so ambiguous. They knew what He wanted, but was their faith strong enough and would they be able to recall scripture at the moments when they needed it? The stillness was thick in thought and introspection. As they continued their journey, they all heard the faint cries of babies.

"Do you hear that?" Danny was the first to speak up. His newness to this way of life afforded him the luxury of innocence.

"Shhh. Be quiet, Danny. Just be still and listen." Emily put her arm around him. "Fletch, be very careful."

"Don't worry, Em, I . . ." The sound of the cries got louder and more unsettling. It was all around them. Agony filled the little cries. Some were screams and some were mere whimpers. Together they were heart wrenching cries for consolation and love. Loud thumps were heard as if babies were dropped out of the sky and onto the ground. Thumps pounded the car even though there was no evidence of children. Fletch slammed on the brakes in horror. Danny moved closer to Emily, Ivy gasped and Emily screamed in prayer.

"God, show us the reason for this cruel apparition. Please do not let this abomination be real."

An ominous voice pervaded the atmosphere: *These little ones have been yanked from their mothers' wombs. They are also your Deathlinks. There are so many. The work of the fallen angel is everywhere on this earth. The one place where a human being, given the divine gift of life, should find safety and comfort and is sanctified has been assaulted and pillaged. This act just perpetuates lust and defiles the life giving act of love. It illustrates man's selfishness and cruelty. These sins are used as Lucifer's weapons against mankind. He will use your angst against you. You must overcome the pain and anguish that this vision inflicts upon you and know my Word, in whatever Holy Book it avails itself to you. The virtuous use of your free will is your dagger. Your faith is your shield. Use your prayers and knowledge of the holy books as your weapons against the evil one. Pray aloud using my name in reverence. Now, battle this apparition through your hearts and souls and relieve yourselves of man's despicable behavior.*

"Almighty One, I quote Jesus, 'Let the little children come to me, and do not stop them, because the Kingdom of God belongs to such as these. I assure you that whoever does not receive the Kingdom of God like a child will never enter it.'"

The screams continued and increased in intensity. The sky opened up to raining blood. Emily gagged at the sight as she struggled to remember scripture.

Out of the relentless and bloody chaos Ivy raised up her quivering voice. "Amen, I say to you, whatever you bind on earth shall be bound in heaven, and whatever you loose on earth shall be loosed in heaven. Again, I say to you, if two of you agree on earth about anything for which they are to pray, it shall be granted to them by my heavenly Father. For where two or three are gathered together in my name, there am I in the midst of them."

In unison they all held hands and Fletch prayed, "Father, through the Holy name of Jesus, take pity on the parents who endured, for whatever reason, the slaying of their innocent children. Bring the souls of these little ones and their parents to heaven to live with you. We pray."

"Amen!"

The apparitions vanished. Two demons, drawn to the fear and anxiety experienced in the station wagon, peered in at the bewildered group. They chose to close in on the window where Danny sat. Danny vested with his recent conversion and his new exposure to pure faith said with a shaky voice, "Because of my faith in Jesus, Boo!" They vanished.

Everyone, still frozen with fear, just looked at each other and then broke down in laughter for sheer recognition of the incredibility of it all. God wanted them to remember the innocence that is used by evil as weapons on earth when mankind makes selfish and weak choices. He needed to drive this point home. Just as the words of the many holy books in many different faiths and the virtuous free will of man is weaponry for the soldiers of God, so the evils that are done in the world forge the swords and daggers used by Lucifer and his kind against humanity. It was apparent this lesson was taught to every soldier of God. What a bizarre way for the Creator to reveal this teaching.

It was one they would never forget, there was no mistaking that.

All prayers are answered and God's people should be very sure they listen with patience for the answer. Rarely, will God be so blatant, except for in true times of trial. Aborting a living fetus from its mother's womb must be one of man's most abhorrent decisions in God's eyes. It is not the abortion, for however long one lives as a fetus or a fully developed person born into the world, their purpose is God given. What is most offensive is the thoughtless lack of reverence for the sexual intimacy which creates the child and makes the abortion necessary. All the heavens weep for man's ignorance of the life giving flow of God's abiding love.

Chapter Thirty-four
The Return of an Old Fiend

Traveling in the South became more and more disquieting for these disciples. There just was something very eerie about driving through an area with a history of slavery, violence and hatred. Emily realized whenever they encountered a region with an old plantation or historic battlefield her fear increased. It was this way for all of them. A blanket of dread spread itself over them and its fringes wound around their throats choking them with apprehension.

"You know, even though the South has been known for its cruelty, there are other elements that can be looked upon as graceful and beautiful." Emily was trying to break up the emotional constrictions.

Grateful for the disruption, Ivy jumped right in. "Really. What kinds of things are you referring to?"

"Well, the South is very well known for its hospitality and its slow pace; a pace that allows one to enjoy the simple pleasures of life. Take for instance that slow moving river over there. Look at the lovely weeping willow trees that beautify its banks. Doesn't it make you want to stop and drink in the sunshine and the sweet smell of magnolias?"

"Emily, you are right. I think we need a break." Fletcher pulled off the road. Everyone piled out of the car, so happy to be relieved of the tension that was building within the vehicle. Emily and Danny went right down to the river bank. Ivy rummaged through her luggage for a comfortable pair of shoes and Fletcher hung behind in order to spend some time with her. He watched as she talked to herself. There was something so attractive about her. He couldn't tear his gaze away.

"There they are!" Ivy pulled a pair of gym shoes out of her bag. As she looked up, her eyes locked with Fletcher's and for a split second they didn't speak. Fletcher broke the silence.

"Um, I'm glad you found them." He walked over to Ivy and without disrupting the obvious attraction, put his hand out for her to take. He found a place for her to sit and change shoes. "Ivy, how are you doing . . . you know . . . about Gabe?"

"I don't know exactly. I feel his presence around me all of the time, but I still miss him so much. He was such a huge part of my life. I lived for him and now that he is gone, I feel kind of lost." Ivy put her head down. Tears fell from her face and Fletch moved in closer to hold her. They seemed to fit as if two pieces of a puzzle formed a complete picture. They found comfort in each other's arms and it was peaceful and gentle. Fletch kept holding her as she looked up at him and a kiss pulled them together. Their energies breathed life into one another and the kiss became a gift; one that was shared with the creation of the universe; a recipe for the procreation of man. For that moment, only Ivy and Fletch existed. They felt God's blessing upon them and they knew this was His perfect plan. They embraced for a few minutes longer, and then walked hand in hand towards the bank of the river.

Emily and Danny made their way down the river and they came upon an old shack. The hot sun ducked under an overcast sky and the rich smell of the trees and foliage around them increased into an intoxicating level. They sat down on the ground and leaned up against a big rock to rest and soon drifted off into unexpected slumber. Dark shadows surrounded the shack and the trees, and soon covered the sleeping warriors. Emily and Danny awoke in the midst of dusky veils of spectral movement sweeping past them and around and through the entire area. The earthy smell of the river and plants changed into that of polluted sewage and rotting vegetation. Emily was taken off guard and Danny clung to her in abject panic. In front of Emily a familiar image approached. It sauntered over to her, leaned down and whispered, "How are you, Baby Angel. Did you think that I would forget your sweetness?"

"Oh, no! Bentley, get away, get away!" Deep dread and revulsion trickled down Emily's spine.

"You won't escape the wrath of my master this time, sweet girl. He told you he knew your weakness. That seedling of fear was rooted in you many years ago by me." Bentley's evil aura had become much more sophisticated and it oozed his slimy spirit around her. She could feel him touch her. She could smell that same foul breath that gagged her as he raped her so long ago.

Danny, who was torn away from Emily and held tight by two disgusting devils, broke away from their hold and tried to run for help. The demons trapped him and dragged him to the bank of the river.

"Help us! Fletcher, Ivy! Come help us!" Bentley's spirit and many others besieged them. Danny's head was forced down into the water. Fighting the beasts of Satan he struggled. They plunged his head into the water and Danny fought with great strength and conviction. He came up sputtering and spitting water. His whole life he had been held in the clutches of evil, and this seemed no different. Humor, indifference, and cunning were his coping tools, and these tools were going to serve him well. "Since I have not been baptized yet, let this be my baptism in Jesus Christ." The demons were infuriated. They released him for a moment and then tore back after him. During the release, Danny was able to grab onto a tree and he prayed, "Lord, I'm a new Christian. I don't know your Word, but by my new faith in you, help us!"

Emily was thrown down to the ground. Many torrid, determined incubuses delighted in the terror they inflicted. Emily knew she had to dominate the fears that made her a victim to Satan's evil. This was just another weapon used against her. She stiffened and prayed. "Your will has been done. I accept my rape because it became an instrument to be used for your glory. Show me your will again, oh, Lord!"

In the wake of the corrupt confusion came at least twenty warrior angels led by Michael Harrison and Sister Kathy. Grace, Rosemary and many other Deathlinks surrounded the demons in a circle and began to pray. "The Lord is my helper, and I will not be afraid. What can anyone do to me?"

Ivy and Fletch, who were laughing and enjoying each other, had just come upon the disconcerting scene. Fletcher sprang into action and began his own quotation from Scripture. As he spoke, he joined the Deathlinks and circled the band of evil that captured his friends. Surrounded in white light, Sister Kathy stood behind him, giving him confidence, and with the voice of a great orator Fletch said, "Who will bring a charge against God's chosen ones? It is God who acquits us. Who will condemn? It is Christ who died, was raised, who also is at the right hand of God, who intercedes for us. What will separate us from the love of Christ? Will anguish, or distress, or persecution, or famine, or nakedness, or peril, or the sword?" The demons were tormented by the words that Fletcher spoke.

Ivy, seeing the effect Scripture had on the evil that surrounded them, raised her voice in song. She began singing her favorite Psalm remembering the instructions of the Almighty during the apparitions of the babies.

"I will praise you, Lord, with all my heart;
I will declare your wondrous deeds.
I will sing hymns to your name, Most High,
For my enemies turn back;
they stumble and perish before you."

Dark liquid sprang from some of the demons. Others shriveled in agony and pain. The atmosphere blared with prayer, song, and groans and curses against God. Bentley, who loomed over Emily, melted away at her acceptance of her rape as a battle won for God, and in an agonizing shriek disintegrated into ashes. The warrior angels chased the monsters into the ground where they disappeared. Others, exposed to the Word of God, simply exploded into nothingness. Lucifer hovered high above the battle. He watched as one by one his devilish imps were picked off by the courage and holy conviction of God's chosen. The sounds of battle diminished. The demons were gone. The Deathlinks disappeared. Michael and Kathy waved goodbye as they faded away. All that was left were the four travelers, and the god of all evil.

Infuriated, Lucifer swooped down upon them. He held up his sword and screamed, "If you think you are winning this war, think again. I have many out in the world who still forge my swords. Men are selfish animals. They think only of themselves! You, on the other hand, must convince a spoiled world that sacrifice, commitment, and love is the only way to avoid damnation. Lust has taken the place of love in their hearts. I now have them believing that lust is love. Sacrifice is a foreign and very unpopular notion. If the Son of God could not persuade them, how can you possibly hope to achieve this goal? Your God has given you an impossible task. It will be interesting to see just how you intend to accomplish His will." Satan lunged at them swinging his sword, growling and spitting. His rage was terrifying.

The four found one another and held onto each other, but the Spirit divided them. This was the first exercise in one of God's most excruciating lessons. Although vulnerable, each found inner strength of their own and raised their hands up to the heavens. Danny cried out, "Father, I believe!"

Out of nowhere, Andrew and Joey came charging into their midst praying, "We boast in hope of the glory of God. We even boast of our afflictions, knowing that affliction produces endurance, and endurance, proven character, and proven character, hope, and hope does not disappoint, because the love of God has been poured out into our hearts through the Holy Spirit that has been given to us."

Lucifer's sword raged red hot molten metal and dripped down his arm. Disgusted, he howled with contempt and flew off into the sky. Sunshine broke through the gray clouds and the smell of the sweet green trees and bushes returned. Emily ran into the arms of her son and all of them embraced.

"Where on earth did you guys come from?" Emily laughed while breathing a sigh of relief.

"Mother, God is working within our spirits. Last week, all of us began to feel incredible strength of heart and soul. We were embellished with newly found courage because of a glorious victory over evil through the horrific sacrifice of a child. The Lord came to both Joey and me in a dream and told us that we needed to head out of Alabama at His direction and He would lead us to the place where we would receive further instruction."

"Yeah, and get this Emily. Andrew and I were led by like an internal compass. It was so weird. We had no idea where we were headed." Joey was holding Emily in his arms. He was so glad to see her.

"Oh, my God." Ivy reminded of her grief. "Gabriel was killed last week. Fletch, do you think that's what . . ."

"Shhh, Ivy. We have to start thinking differently about living and dying. Gabe only sacrificed his earthly life. He still lives in God's kingdom and I would bet in a very revered position."

"Gabriel! How do you know Gabriel?" Andrew was startled.

"Gabe was my son. Why, what do you know about him?" Ivy was surprised that a stranger knew of her son.

"The Deathlinks appeared to me during meditation. With them came a wonderful young man, dressed in all white. He glowed with the love of God. He told me of the events leading to his death and that he would be with us during the last days. His name was Gabriel. His appearance was so brilliant I thought at first he was the angel Gabriel, but then he told me about his life and told us to call him Gabe."

"Andrew, Joey, I would like to introduce you to Ivy Winston and Fletcher Hodges." Emily smiled at them with whimsy.

"Of course. How could we have been so blind?" Andrew was stunned that he had not made the connection before. He had seen Ivy in visions and he knew about her son.

Joey stepped forward. "Ivy, I'm so sorry for your loss. I know how you feel. I lost my own child not too long ago. Fletcher, it is finally nice to meet the real deal."

"I'm so confused. Will any of this ever make any sense?" Ivy held on to Fletch for comfort.

"The End Times are upon us. We now know how to battle the forces of evil, and we are, at long last, united in order to carry out God's plan. Our next task is to educate others. If we can make them see they have consistently violated the laws of the Creator and have taken the side of evil, perhaps we stand a chance." Emily was excited. This was the first time she really had a glimpse of where God was directing them.

"How are we possibly going to touch all of the lives in this world, and I can't help but believe it is too late." Ivy felt overwhelmed.

"Have trust in the Almighty. He has gotten us this far. We have always practiced the virtues, one of which is patience. Let's take it to a greater level of understanding. If we refuse to try and we are His chosen ones, then the world surely will be lost to Satan. Do you want that?" Emily squeezed Ivy's hand.

"No, and I don't want Gabe's death to be for nothing. Let's go."

The courageous travelers went back to their cars and started to caravan back to Alabama. Each knew the responsibility they bore was tremendous and they also knew the only way to fathom the outcome was to trust in God and His secret plan.

Chapter Thirty-five
God's Plan Unfolds

God's chosen held a keen sense of everything around them. They realized from their last experience by the river that Lucifer could attack at any time. God, also found strange times to allow supernatural occurrences to take them by surprise just to reveal a little more about His plan. Most humans would be close to emotional breakdowns by now, but the Holy Spirit blessed them with a gift of strength like none other. Their spirits were fortified by prayer and fasting.

Everyone also remembered what Gabe told his mother at his gravesite. Her armor would be the graces she received from the Sacraments and attending daily Mass. It was never discussed, yet it was presumed that Ivy was honored in heaven because she was the mother of the young martyr. There were no signs of it now, but they believed in their hearts her spiritual strength, though shaky, would be incomparable. So they were on their way to find the closest Catholic Church. As the odd little station wagon traveled on with Andrew and Joey behind them, they stumbled upon a small town right on the Georgia and Alabama line.

"I don't know. You think this Podunk town is going to have a Catholic church?" Fletcher was weary.

"Did you feel that God led you here?" Emily was irritated.

"Yeah, Em . . . okay." Grumbling under his breath, "God leads, I follow."

"Look, over there. Do you think that something called St. Francis Chapel could possibly be Catholic?" Poor Danny. His ignorance was showing.

"Thank you, God. Fletcher, let's pull over and find out the Mass

schedules and maybe I could even go to reconciliation." Ivy was relieved. Her responsibility was so great and her heart was heavy when
she didn't think she was living up to Gabe's standards.

They walked into the quiet chapel where they discovered a
Franciscan priest straightening up the altar area. Ivy walked over to
him. "Father! Hi, my name is Ivy Winston. We just pulled into your
town and I wanted to attend Mass. Could you tell me when the next
one will be?"

"Ce'tainly. We will be celebratin' the liturgy in about an hour.
What brings you to the South? You obviously are not from here. Your
accent is no'thern." The Franciscan's drawl was soft and enchanting.

"Well, you're right. I'm from Michigan. I guess you might say that
my comrades and I are on a sort of, well, pilgrimage. Do you think that
it would be possible for me to go to confession before Mass, Father?"

"Yes, of course. Do you have time now?"

Ivy motioned to her sidekicks to let them know that she was going into the confessional. They found a pew in the back of the church
to wait. None of them were Catholic, but they all felt the impulse
to use the kneelers and offer up the fears and concerns of their mission. Fletcher remembered using the kneelers at Kathy's church. They
were hard and hurt his knees. She called him a big whiner; how he
missed his friend.

A white light kept sweeping past the confessional and its purity
was moving. Even though it made them anxious, it still filled their
hearts with love and courage and they accepted it as if it were as normal as eating breakfast. Desensitization is a wonderful thing.

"Bless me Father, for I have sinned. My last confession was one
week ago." Ivy blessed herself with the sign of the cross.

"My child, unburden yo'self. It is unusual in this day and time for
someone, especially a traveler, to come to confession within one week
of her last confession. What sin do you bear that weighs you down so?"

"Father, I lost my son one week ago. I feel such hatred. I'm not a hateful person, but the circumstances in which he died were so despicable and he was such a young, faithful, pure soul. Why would God take him from me?" Ivy began to cry.

"Tell me the details, child, so that I might unda'stand bettuh."

Ivy went into explicit detail, explaining the situation that ended her son's life. Telling the story again was agonizing, yet in a strange way, healing and the priest was soothing and calm. When Ivy got to the part where she described the altar and Gabe's mutilated body, Father became silent. He left his section of the confessional, opened the door to Ivy and knelt down before her kissing her hand.

"Father, what are you doing?" Ivy was taken by surprise.

"My child, I have been made privy to this scene ova' and ova' again in my dreams and in meditation. God called me many yea's ago to be one of His prophets durin' the End Times. I witnessed in a dream your brutal rape and the coma that you were thrown into. I have been allowed to share your pain, sorrows and joys all in preparation for the final days. I knew in the very depths of my soul that the end is nea', but last night I asked for a sign to confirm my discernment. You are the ansa' to that prayer. My deah', do you by any chance know Emily Walker?"

"I am here, Father." Emily knelt down next to him. They embraced each other and wept. "You must be Father Don. Praise be to God!"

The light that was hovering around the confessional grew with intensity and filled the church with its brilliance. The rest of the travelers joined Father Don, Emily and Ivy. Every pew in the church was filled with Deathlinks, none of whom Emily knew. Their voices were raised in prayer and song and some were even singing in tongue and in Hebrew. Angels fluttered all about the chapel and it felt as if Heaven descended on a short visit just for them. The atmosphere was charged with perfect holiness. These Deathlinks were all Father Don's and Emily raised her voice in song and adoration for the confirmation that she and Andrew were not the only mediums called into service.

From out of the brightest section of the light came a shape. It came closer and with each step it was apparent it was Gabe. Ivy, numb with disbelief, stood up to greet him.

"Mother, I told you I was with God. You must regain control of your soul and don't allow the evil deeds committed against me to fill you with hatred. Hatred is the fire in which the evil one forges his weapons. Your weapon against him is forgiveness and acceptance of God's will. You must accept it is God's will that I be with Him during the final days. I can do more for His cause in heaven with the full intensity of the Holy Spirit than I could do on earth. God is with you. He has always been with you as you followed His will. He will send His own mother during your times of great distress. Rest in her and you will be fortified with grace." Gabe fell back into the light and the light itself faded away along with the angels and the Deathlinks.

"No wait, Gabe, honey, please stay with me just a little longer." Ivy fell to her knees weeping. The mother of God appeared and wrapped her arms around Ivy. Peace and comfort encompassed them all.

"I absolve you of all your sins, in the name of the Father and the Son and of the Holy Spirit, Amen." Father Don tearful and weak with profound emotion completed Ivy's confession. The church remained silent in deep reverence and awe knowing that God struck once again.

Chapter Thirty-six
Father Don, What a Guy!

In the peaceful silence, Father Don went into the sacristy to prepare his mind and spirit for Mass. He knew this would be one of the first announcements of the coming of the end of the world and here it would be proclaimed, in this tiny, out-of-the-way chapel during a daily Mass. How peculiar is God's will.

The pilgrims accompanied Ivy to Mass. After what they just witnessed, their spirits were enriched with a power so great they realized the only greater experience was the total adoration of their Lord. People started to wander in from outside the chapel. Father Don ministered to, perhaps, twenty worshippers a day during the week, but today, the church pews filled up with person after person. Some were actual parishioners of St. Francis Chapel, but most were travelers who were drawn to this town and this church to attend this Mass.

After the proclamation of the Word the chapel remained quiet and filled with holiness. Father Don stood up and as he took his place at the lectern, he scanned the entire church with sad but determined eyes. The time he had waited for was here and his soul begged God to present him with the proper words worthy of such a weighty announcement.

"As I address you, I am both humbled and honored. The Holy Spirit has taken it upon Himself today to change my homily and I am to embark on the journey assigned to me so very long ago. This, no doubt, will be the beginning of many, very many sermons announcing the second coming of the Son of Man." Some of the parishioners shifted in their seats. Was the good friar going a little bonkers? Father Don's sermon became firm and strong. "I come to you now, not as a Franciscan priest but as an ordained prophet of God. You will be among the first to hear the sounding of the trumpet, the sounding of the call to arms. I've known this time would come and I have watched the world become more and more filled with hate, distrust, deceit, selfishness, lust, murder and the list continues on and on. My message is simple. You, my dea' people, must arm yourselves with the graces given to you by honoring God's will in your life." Father softened his tone as if to console them. "The end is near, the bridegroom is on His way, and you will be expected to ante up and fight for your eternal lives. Some of you may even physically die for your faith. Are you ready to do that if necessary? We have become so involved in our earthly lives that the very commandments of God have just become a cliché." His voice raised and it started to resemble that of a Southern Baptist minister; all fire and brimstone. "The commandments are God's laws! Let me repeat that. The commandments are God's laws and we find it all too easy to break His laws whenever they become inconvenient, which is daily. You know it, and I know it. Mankind is killing itself, literally handing itself over to the fallen angel. We find Lucifer's way of life easier to follow. Do you really think that Lucifer lives in just the mortal sins of the world? No, my friends, he has lured mankind into ruination by the small sins that we dismiss as venial. Sins like *complacency*." Father drew out the word with his southern drawl then slam dunked it into the crowd. "When the world has found it more comfortable to make the beautiful gift of sexuality a mere extra-curricular activity to satisfy lust and we as Christians accepted it, we sinned. Look at where this has brought us. Almost every abhorrent act in this world can be linked to the demoralization of the first gift that God gave mankind. This gift was pure and natural, given in love to all living creations of God." Father's voice intensified. "We don't save this act of creation for a blessed union with one chosen for us. No, we have sex with whomever we want and, oops, we create another human be-ing. Oh, that's all right! We'll just murder this child that was made in the image and likeness of God because it is an inconvenience." Father

Don's speech became pronounced and passionate. The people in the pews became more and more uncomfortable with the truth that was spoken. "Let me ask you all. Since when did being an American become more important than being a follower of the Almighty Creator? When do we start to think and discern for ourselves, people? When do we earnestly in prayer, take responsibility for our own souls? The Supreme Court's job is not to protect your souls. Its job is to protect society and we as a society are made up of many religious and non-religious persuasions. Society is society, but your heart should rest with your Creator. All of God's people should be looking inward for the answers to spiritual questions, not putting that responsibility upon other men. The End Time is upon us and it is too late to go back and correct these sins against life. Your only hope of obtaining everlasting life is through hope, honesty, and pure love. Pray for each other. Pray for the sinful and arm yourselves with the scriptures."

"The degradation of morality and the acceptance of that degradation by us because of our silence, has allowed compounding sins to flourish. Ignoring the simple needs of others, the cruelty of every kind of abuse from child abuse and neglect to abuse and neglect of the elderly, and the neglect of the hungry of the world are all monumental sins in the eyes of our Creator. Judging another because of the color of his skin, his sexual orientation or the way he chooses to worship his Creator is self-righteous and these are unacceptable sins against God. I am here to tell you now, that every time one of these sins is committed, another sword, another dagger is forged in hell. This weaponry will be used against us in the final days." The gentle Franciscan was sweating with passion. He paused for a moment, dabbed his forehead, and then resumed. "Friends, we are living in the End Times. Stay vigilant. Keep alert to the *minor sins* that are committed around you and take steps to correct them. Make silence a thing of the past! You have no time to waste." As he took a few moments to collect himself, he realized the atmosphere in the church was silent and somber.

"As of today, I will be leaving St. Francis. God has summoned me to begin my ministry as a prophet." Gasps and whispers rippled through the crowd. "Most of you know me. You all know that I am a man of peace and I would never take on this kind of task without serious discernment. I am sure of its validity. My prayer for you is that God will touch your lives in a way that will help you to see the truth in my words. Arm yourselves, my friends, with the sacraments, daily Mass and read Holy Scripture in the quiet of your homes. Know scripture so that when the time comes, you will be able to use it against the perils of hell which will seek you out and use the very weapons that you yourselves have forged against you. Knowing scripture is your only hope for protection against the evil that seeks to murder you and take you to hell with it. Jesus Christ is coming back very soon. Please, take this warning seriously, and not just as another sermon on the end of the world. It is real and it is now. God be with you."

As Father Don went back to sit on his chair behind the altar, he was illuminated. Angels came to minister to him, a group encircled him. Through his own humility, he was unaware of the miracle that surrounded him as his head remained bent in prayer. The church gleamed with divine light. Deathlinks appeared everywhere and angels filled the church lifting their radiant voices in song, swooshing through the astonished people. Father Don's southern drawl and passion had indeed pleased God. From outside the church came the sounds of heavenly trumpets; trumpets that were heard at every end of the earth. Just as scripture foretold the first coming of the Messiah, so it was foretelling the second coming of the Son of Man.

Chapter Thirty-seven

The Road to Armageddon

The impact of Father Don's announcement had contrasting effects on the crowd that gathered in the church. Some ran out screaming in fear, others walked deep in thought back to their homes and cars with total calm. Emily and the others wanted to stay and see Father off, but they could feel the urgency to get back to their home base in Alabama, so they all gave him a hug goodbye and wished him courage and love on his mission.

As the concerned soldiers traveled along the highway they listened to the radio. A special news update interrupted the music. "Several reports of angel sightings have been reported to this station in the last hour. We are now live on the scene with one person who claims that she saw immense angels with trumpets flying through the sky. Ma'am, we know that you are not the only one who witnessed these sightings, but could you fill our listeners in on what actually occurred?"

"It was miraculous! They floated over us and sounded their big, golden trumpets and out of their mouths came heavenly singing that announced the end of the world."

"Really! Well, where did the angels go after they did this?"

"They flew back into the heavens and then disappeared."

"Do you think that this could have been a joke or prank on your community?"

"This is no joke." Another person's voice was heard interjecting.

"And what is your name, sir?"

"Reverend Michael Harrison." Fletch slammed on the breaks. He looked at Emily and they each were dumbfounded. "Scripture says that the second coming of Christ will be accompanied by the sounding of trumpets by angels at all ends of the earth and he will raise the faithful dead on the last day. I suggest that you follow up and find out just where else these things have been seen."

"Well, thank you Reverend, I believe that I will. This is WTRS reporting . . ."

The car Andrew and Joey were driving also came to a screeching halt in front of them. Joey ran to their car excitedly. "Emily, did you hear Michael on the news? He is alive and that means that maybe Angela will be alive."

"And Kathy will be alive." Fletch looked at Emily.

"We interrupt this broadcast to bring you further news regarding the sightings of unknown beings in the sky. Along with these sightings, presumed to be angels, we have been informed there are several accounts of self-proclaimed prophets throughout the world who have been preaching to large crowds in major cities. They all have been communicating the same message and that is the end of the world is here and everyone should arm themselves with the quote "word of God" unquote. Chaos and panic has ensued and people are running to stores buying groceries, kerosene lamps and candles."

The atmosphere everywhere on the earth was darkening. The air was thick and breathing was difficult. Gloom and obscurity held the earth captive. Soon the travelers were blinded by the darkness and there was no sun, no moon, and no stars. It grew cold and murky. Both cars came to a halt and their occupants stepped out into the gray, foggy world. An unexplained force wedged itself between each of them and they were pried out and away from the vehicles and each other.

"Joey! Where are you? Andrew?" Emily cried out realizing she was separated from everyone else. She could hear their hushed callings out to each other. It seemed they all were removed from contact with anyone.

Emily prayed, "Lord, what are you doing? We only have each other to depend on. Isn't that why you had us find one another? Now you are allowing us to move about blindly alone."

Similar prayers were offered by the others. No one could hear anyone else. Above, the sky opened up and a brilliant light burst forth. Rumbling filled the earth and the faithful servants were elevated, floating gently on invisible waves of billowing atmosphere.

My children. You are now going to finally understand what being my child is all about. You may have found each other for support for a while, but your sole purpose and the purpose of all of your brethren is to listen to me from within. While you are on earth, I allow you to find what you have all labeled soul mates, but that is only because your journeys can sometimes become challenging so you must be angels to one another. Some become more attached than others. Children are born and the world continues on. Because of free will granted to you, some of you have traveled the earth alone and have felt the empty pain of loneliness. I hear your prayers and I feel your pain and I promise when this war is over, none of you will ever be lonely again. Loneliness will not exist because all of you will share in each other's lives without envy, hatred, greed or lust. Hunger and homelessness will be no more. My spirit will feed your souls and heaven will be your home. Now, the time has come for My Son to come back. All of you will don new earthly bodies and you will share space with each other like you never have before. The old ways will be gone and you will live life the way it was meant to be lived in the garden. Until your last dragons, behemoths and leviathans are defeated and crushed through the purification of your hearts and your souls, you all must find courage within yourselves alone, and will not see each other again until they have been obliterated. You have established a great army filled with your Deathlinks and souls of friends that have already passed. They are alive again, flesh and bone. Do not be disheartened. They will be fighting alongside of you. They have been given glorious bodies, and you will see them when Satan and his demons gather together at the spiritual battle of Armageddon and you all unite in body and soul to defeat the dark angel. Then the Son of Man will return in glory. Go forth and fight for your God. Fight for life the way it was meant to be lived from the time of the first man and woman. You have been given special strength equal to the strength of warrior angels.

Now, go forth and abolish your own personal fears that act as weapons against you. Do not be afraid, I will be with you.

Though separated, the travelers found solid ground. They looked around and found themselves to be totally alone. The sun was shining, the birds were chirping and wind was blowing through the trees, but Emily, Andrew, Joey, Fletch, and Ivy were alone, each by themselves on a road bound for somewhere with no other living human being in sight. Danny, however, was put back down by the abandoned cars. Emptiness and fear filled his heart. *Where did everybody go?* He decided to get into one of the cars and continue on. A map was laid out on the passenger seat of Fletcher's car and Danny followed the directions already plotted out. Perhaps by letting himself follow this map with blind faith he would find his companions. After all, hadn't he discovered this trip was consumed with weird and supernatural occurrences? He just had to keep the faith. As he drove down the road, he saw vehicles abandoned. On the other hand, he found an equal amount of vehicles stopped with people milling about calling out names as if they were trying to locate lost relatives or friends. After passing a couple scenes like this, curiosity got the best of him and he pulled over.

"Excuse me. Who are you calling for?"

A young girl, maybe sixteen years old was crying. She had on too much makeup and seemed to be trying to dress older than she was, but there was no doubt she was in her teens. "My best friend was driving and all of a sudden the car stopped and, pouf, she disappeared right before my eyes."

"You didn't experience anything, like a black out or anything like that?" Danny was trying to make sense of everything which he knew was futile.

"No, and I'm not on anything, even though I wish I was. It sure as hell would explain a few things. Do you think that this could be the rapture? I didn't believe Mary when she would talk about it, but maybe she was right and if she was right then I'm here left on earth to live through God knows what." The girl continued sobbing and Danny wanted her to stop so that he could understand what she meant by this rapture thing.

"What is that? That rapture you just said before?"

"Great! Well, it makes sense that I would be left on earth with someone who hasn't even heard of the fuckin' rapture. Mary told me that a time would come at the end of the world where all of God's faithful would be taken up into heaven bodily and the rest of us would be left here to fend off monsters and demons and straight up evil. Shiiiit! I just thought that when Mary got religion she would grow out of it and get back on track with me and now it turns out that I was the one who was wrong. She was all I had. We had no one on this earth but each other. God! I'm damned! I'm damned to hell!"

"Stop it. No, no you're not. No one's damned. Let's just settle down. What's your name, anyway?"

"Magdalena."

"Hi, I'm Danny. Listen . . . just get into the car with me. The same thing happened to my friends. Let's travel together and maybe we can figure out what to do next." The sun was going down and the air was thick with a muggy, sticky feel to it. Prickles cropped up all over Danny's skin. As Magdalena got into the car with Danny a man startled them from behind.

"Hello, kids." Danny didn't like him. His skin was tan and leathery, like it had been burned by the sun over and over again. His eyes were black and swimming with dark secrets. His voice was deep and raspy. Danny's insides warned him against this man.

"Mister, can you help us?" Magdalena seemed grateful to have an older person around.

"I do believe that those damn preachers were right and the rapture has come and gone and we are out o' luck, kiddos." The man laughed as if it were nothing to be worried about.

"That can't be so. God would have taken me. I love Him and I just recently gave my life to Him. He would not have left me behind." Danny spoke with great conviction.

"Well, son, maybe you just weren't good enough." The man laughed again and then turned to Magdalena. "Look here little lady, I have a place just up this road where you can stay until we find out just what's goin' on." The stranger had his arm around Magdalena's shoulder and was pushing her down the road. He called over his shoulder, "You're welcome to come too, son, if you have a mind to."

"I don't think so. Magdalena, come with me. I'll help you find a safe place and if we can't find a place, you can just keep traveling with me."

Magdalena broke away from the stranger and took Danny aside. "Danny, I'm going with this man. He has a place and I don't want to have to sleep in a car tonight. Besides, he will take care of us."

"Somehow, I don't believe that and I don't trust him. Listen. There are a lot of evil things out there. I know because I have seen them first hand. And now if all of the good people are gone, doesn't it stand to reason that everyone else has a hidden agenda? This guy gives me the creeps. Please, come with me. The car won't be so bad to sleep in."

"What's the matter with you two?" The man came over and took Magdalena's arm. "I have hot soup on the stove and two nice bedrooms with soft beds for you to get a good night's sleep. Come on home with me, girl." Danny didn't like the way that he looked at Magdalena, but she didn't seem to mind.

"No, Danny. I'm going with him. I'll be safer. You go ahead if you want."

Directed by the man's hands on her back, Magdalena went off down the road with what Danny believed to be a black hole. Her choice was made and he had seen enough to know he didn't have the strength to do battle with a demon over someone who just might want to be with a demon. This time he let it go. He had so many other things to worry about, one of which was if this were the rapture then why did God not include him? He had to stay faithful. He had to believe that God had a plan for him. As Danny got in the car and started driving away, he looked into the rear view mirror. He watched Magdalena being ravaged by the stranger who had transformed into a frightening winged demon. The demon watched Danny's car as it was pulling away. It finished its wicked pursuit of death, and then flew after Danny's vehicle. Danny's foot hit the gas pedal. The demon got distracted by another stranded person and his evil chase was detoured.

"ADD is a wonderful thing." Danny sped away, praying non-stop and he didn't look back for hours.

The Road

Emily looked around. Surrounded by a thicket of beautiful trees, the red, dirt road seemed welcoming. Birds were singing and chirping. A few squirrels chased each other around the trees and wild flowers laced the edges of the long and endless road that was her undetermined journey. As she walked, her surroundings seemed familiar, although she couldn't remember it. Sunlight bounced off the leaves of the trees and the smell of sweet honeysuckle filled the air. Perhaps it was the honeysuckle that seemed so familiar. Large rocks could be seen every now and then along the edges as she made her way to a place she could not even imagine.

Filled with heartache and confusion at the thought of being separated from Andrew and Joey, she wanted to question God's reasoning for bringing about the end of the world before she ever had the chance to experience that one wish she prayed for all of her life; the one thing that God never gave her. She only wanted to share both spiritual and physical love with someone that God chose just for her. It never happened. Why did God cheat her out of this one request? Now, she was thrown into an abyss by herself on a road which led where? Resentment quelled within her. Trying to control her feelings, remembering her faithfulness and love of God became impossible. She walked faster and grew angrier and confused. Before she knew it, she found herself walking into a fog. But the fog moved about. It took a shape encircling her at the same time. Straining her neck to see what it was that surrounded her, she heard a deep growl. A sweeping of its tail and a flutter of massive wings led Emily to sense that she was inside a great beast. Slowing her pace, she managed to come to a complete stop. Floating out in front of her stood an immense dragon breathing hot flames fueled by the anger in her heart. Its wings were illusive, fluttering about first seeming real and mighty and then fading away into a soft mist. When her faith in the mission given to her by God strengthened, the wings of the dragon softened like that of angel wings, but when Emily's heart was distressed with selfish feelings of regret and bitterness the beast's wings became heavy and treacherous. At the same time, the dragon breathed out flames of powerful fire when Emily's soul screamed with the deep agony of cold loneliness.

"My God, what is it that you want from me? I give to You and give to You and You still don't answer my prayer. I will have died, burned to death by the breath of this dragon and never experienced that one thing that I have wanted from the time I was a small girl."

It became clear. She was playing a game with God. I will do your will because I know if I do it will manipulate you into giving me what I want. Emily crumbled at the realization of her one great sin. Her decision to do God's will was conditional. God's will is a gift to each of us. The Alpha and Omega chose each and every soul to be a part of his great universe. It all became clear. In eternity all of our prayers are answered. We have eternity to pursue our heart's desires. He only asks that we do His will while we are on earth and it was imperative that she do His will now, whatever the cost might be. Emily shook off the shackles of heartache and disappointment and breathed in the desire to follow God's plan exactly as He laid it out for her. Her dragon dissolved and she reached the end of the road. There before her was her Uncle Zeb's farm. She was home. She was also very confused, but there it was as wonderful and beautiful as the day she lay on the freshly harvested crop - the day that Michael Harrison happened upon her so very long ago.

Enmeshed in uncertainty, Fletch fell to the ground sucking in the red earth of the dirt road that lay before him. Choking from a mouthful of soot, he dragged himself to his feet. The sun was bright and beautiful. Nature was unaffected by the recent events in his life as squirrels and birds pursued their pastimes without a single interruption. A sweet breeze blew through his hair and the air smelled of honeysuckle and greenery. The terrain was rocky at the sides of the road, but Fletch could see a body of water, maybe a river or lake just beyond the next turn. Questions tormented his soul as he walked; the same angry questions that burdened him after Kathy was killed. "Lord, why are you making us all go through this insanity? If you love us and you are the great, omnipotent being that You lead us to believe that You are, then why can't You just love us? Here you did it again. You left Ivy by herself after going through yet another traumatic time in her life, only to face who knows what. Why can't you simply make the world right by killing all of the evil bastards that pollute the human race and work with those of us who truly love you and want to follow you?"

Fletch took aim and kicked a rock with his shoe. It should have landed in the river that was now visible at the turn in the road, but instead it made a loud thud. Fletch, who was pouting with his head down, looked up to see a gigantic monster climbing out of the river and charging his way. "What the hell?" At first he began to run the other direction, but then he realized that God always had a reason for putting him in these preposterous situations. He stopped dead and did an about face on faith just as the beast was upon him. He fell flat. The wet, fleshy skin of the creature smothered him. As Fletch struggled, he took all of his frustrations out by punching and kicking the Leviathan that outweighed him in size by at least ten times. In the heat of his rage, Fletch noticed that he made the beast wince with pain after applying a heavy blow to its massive eye. Although his body was filled with adrenaline, Fletch felt empathy for the beast and he was remorseful for inflicting pain upon another living thing. The Leviathan lifted himself off Fletcher and stood before him swaying in a daze. Stricken with total comprehension of his sin, Fletch prayed, "Dearest Lord, forgive my wrath, and have mercy on your poor servant for not understanding that everything and everyone, good or evil is still your creation and you cherish each and every one. Love thy neighbor as thyself for the love of God. I get it! I finally grasp the concept of being a part of you and I now realize why you are the great energy from whence I come!" With that said Fletch found himself at the end of the road on the edge of a very large area of farmland. No one else was around, but he feared the battle of the End Times was about to begin.

Ivy tumbled out of a dream onto a dirty, red, road where she stood up and fluffed her clothing. Clouds of red dust billowed from her as she beat her body with her hands. Around her there were sounds of every kind of nature. Crickets twittered, while the leaves rustled, as the wind blew through the bushes and tall woody plants, and she could hear a river rushing not too far from her. Streams of sunlight shone down through the trees spotlighting the beauty that surrounded her.

Her heart thumped with fear and anxiety. How could God do this to her? She had just suffered the most horrible loss of her life and now He decided to separate her from the only friends she could count on. Ivy was very tired of playing these games and now she was going to take her life back and put it into her own hands. She had enough and if God thought for one minute she was going to walk down that dirty, dusty road into certain disaster, He could just guess again. She could have been seventeen again. Ivy's hard headedness took over her good sense and she decided to cross the river to somewhere else so she would avoid having to obey God. She found a crossing where there were stepping stones all the way across the river to the other side. *Huh! How convenient is this?* She placed one foot in front of the other balancing herself with care as she picked the most stable rocks to step on. When she made it to the middle of the river she thought she heard a large splash not too far from her. Ivy kept moving from one rock to another when a mammoth head came up out of the water. Startled, she lost her balance and fell into the river. Ivy tried to touch bottom but she could not feel anything. She swam as fast as she could to the other side of the river, keeping an eye out for the enormous head that could take her under at any moment. Her anger and frustration with God burned even greater. Without warning, she was swept up onto a huge thing. She was straddling it between its head and back because there was no neck, and it was thrashing about trying to throw her off. While holding onto its ears, Ivy tried to determine what this hulk of a creature was, but the closest thing that she could compare it to was, well a sort of hippopotamus. "Oh, my . . . ! The Behemoth in the Book of Revelation! Okay! I'm alright! Okay! I am an idiot, Father! I did it again. I will walk down your road and I will stop thinking I know better than you. Just get me out of this predicament, please!"

The Behemoth hunched its back and threw Ivy off of its back. Sopping wet, Ivy found herself in a heap at the end of the dirt road. With red dust and dirt clinging to her soaked clothing, she struggled to her feet grateful to be in one piece and still alive. Beyond her was a beautiful stretch of farmland, but she was the only soul in sight. In her mind all she could think was, *now what?*

Joey woke up from a trance, sitting on a big rock at the edge of a long, gravel, dirt road. He could smell the iron that permeated the air from the rich red earth surrounding him. The sunlight was sweet as it glimmered from one leaf to another and heated the soil so that the essence of nature filled his nostrils. Joey was frightened. Even though he was a big man, he was uncertain of what was to follow and he was alright if he could see what was facing him, but the risk of the unknown terrified him. It was that way with putting himself out there for the sake of love, too. That risk was more sacrifice than he was willing to make. He found it once with his wife, Angela's mother, but losing her was too hard. He did not think he could go through that pain again. He thought of Emily and how happy she made him, but he was much happier just being alone. It was safe and Joey liked safety. An unanticipated sense of loneliness prevailed. This is what he felt when he really wanted Emily around him, but he knew if he pursued her she would respond and he could not allow himself to commit to something more than friendship. So, he convinced himself it was better for her if he just teetered on a cool distance. Joey's heart crumbled with emptiness and sorrow. This was his sacrifice of love for Emily. As his heart hurt, a mist rose up from the ground and swept past his face. The mist situated itself in front of Joey. He rose to begin his journey down the road and the mist stayed directly in front of him. So internalized was his pain, that Joey simply walked on without noticing the mist taking shape. Heaviness of heart burdened him, and he sighed deep arduous sighs. The weight of this burden pressed against his chest and made it harder and harder for him to breathe. Walking was a chore. Each step was heavier and heavier and with every step the mist transformed into a solid, taking the form of an angel. This angel was not your normal, run of the mill sort. It was stern. It held a sword in one hand while clutching its breast with the other. It released its breast to reveal a heart frozen solid and stretched out its arm to touch Joey on the shoulder. Joey's heart turned into a frozen block of ice and his body grew hot. The angel transformed into a figure of a weeping woman. The weeping grew into mournful sobs and then into breathless whaling. The angel changed from Joey's wife, to Angela to Emily and the cycle of change continued over and over again and every time the change took place, Joey's heart cracked a little bit more. His body burned with fever. As the angel changed, it pleaded for love and at last, in the depth of discernment, Joey cried out, "I love you, I love you until I die . . . all of you. I was not aware of the torment I caused by denying you my love. Dear God, I thought that by keeping my distance from Emily and by ignoring my grief over Angela and my wife, I was staying strong and that way I wouldn't hurt anyone. But, I was wrong, so wrong. No matter how this turns out, I give all three of you my heart and my soul, because God expects no less from me. Love is sacrifice and love is a risk, but without it a man is nothing; nothing, but a block of ice."

His face was hidden behind his hands, so Joey didn't realize he was standing at the edge of a vast farmland or that this was the final battlefield chosen so long ago by the Father.

Andrew awoke to a beautiful blue sky overhead. Lying on his back he had to squint because the rays of the sun were strong and steady. He struggled to sit up. There he saw the magnificent, tall trees of a forest. The road, which he was sitting on, was at the edge of the forest, and it was rusty red and made him homesick for his Great Uncle Zeb's farm. The soil throughout the South was often red. He could smell honeysuckle and he heard a river rushing somewhere close. Queen Ann's lace and clover grew along the side of the road. As Andrew pulled himself to his feet, he found himself being grateful that at least he wasn't in a place like Vietnam; a miserable place seven layers deeper than hell itself. A twang of indignation found its way into his heart. Andrew hated violence brought about by indifference for human life. He hated bullies. He grew up with a father who was a bully. Perhaps that is why he chose to enter the military at such a young age. He wanted to kick some butt. Bitterness grew in his spirit; something he had not felt in a very long time, especially since his experience in the Bad Lands. He remembered times when his father would raise his hand to strike his mother just to watch her flinch in fear. He remembered his father's cruel and thoughtless remarks. Then a charge of emotion flooded his soul with memories of bad times at home and worse times in the jungles of Vietnam. A scene of unspeakable terror, where young women of a village were raped by members of another army unit, cropped up in his mind. Memories of the torture of soldiers and the killing of women and children, and still ever present was the fear of the jungle snakes that came out of nowhere. For whatever reason, Andrew was once again feeling the hatred and bitterness he thought he had under control. He knew God wanted him to forgive all of these injustices, but Andrew found it easier to forget them and he thought he had until now.

Conditioned by the jungle, Andrew spun around at the sound of hissing behind him. A cold sweat broke out on his brow as he faced the biggest snake he had ever seen. It reared itself up and swayed to and fro ready to strike. "So you think you can scare me? I don't think so you slimy piece of crap!" At the utterance of these words, Andrew found himself surrounded by snakes of all types and sizes. The more fearful and embittered he became the more snakes appeared.

Past the sea of snakes he saw his father's face. His father, filled with remorse was asking his forgiveness. The figure transformed and Andrew witnessed his father's bloody nose and the bruises on his body after being beaten as a young child by thugs. He saw his father's shame from the sexual abuse endured from a trusted friend. "Pop, I'm sorry Pop, I didn't know." Andrew's heart was barraged with many different kinds of emotion. He remembered his father playing catch with him in the back yard. He once saw him weep softly after looking at a picture of his mother. Perhaps the man wasn't all that bad.

He remembered small acts of kindness by Vietnamese villagers, especially one mother whose own son was fighting for the South. She took a liking to Andrew and he appreciated it. Although he was suspicious of her motives, it helped ease the loneliness he felt for Emily. As peace eased into his soul, the snakes disappeared, one by one. Andrew fell to his knees and wept. "Wankan Tanka, I beg your forgiveness and I promise you I do forgive those who have injured me and mine. Help me to remember we all have our own journey to walk on this earth and I shall not judge because I do not know your divine will for another. Your will be done."

Andrew raised his head from prayer and discovered that he was at the outskirts of his Great Uncle Zeb's farm. When he stood up, Emily, Ivy, Fletch and Joey came running toward him. They all embraced, crying and talking about each of their adventures. The reunion was cut short by the darkening of the sky and the deafening sound of horse's hooves. Off in the distance, Fletch's old station wagon could be seen rumbling up the red, stony road driven by Danny, the child soldier.

Chapter Thirty-eight
And The Hills Came Tumbling Down

Danny was steady in keeping his course as he traveled down the red road to Armageddon. The sky became overcast and dark. Nothing of great significance happened to him while he tackled this journey on his own; however, fear was a vigilant passenger that accompanied him over every mile.

Ahead, he saw a group of people congregated. With every turn of the tires an increasing malevolence crept into the car. Danny's heart pounded hard and a certain familiarity followed the malicious force pervading his space. Passing the group he had to slow down because there were so many of them. All dressed in black, they reminded him of the Goths from his high school - freakish, weird, distorted. Without warning, the group descended upon him. Encircling the automobile, Danny came to a complete stop. They were chanting with bared teeth. Their bodies, although moving around in a circle methodically, were deformed and mutated; hideous and frightening. There was a loud thud. Something hit the window closest to Danny. He jumped so high he knocked his head against the car roof. It was so massive that Danny thought the window would crack. There, starring in at him was his mother, Winifred.

"Mother! Oh, my god, Mother!" Chills ran through his body.

"Don't call me your mother, you traitor." Winifred's voice hissed like a snake. Even though Wini wasn't the most beautiful woman in the world she had held certain attractiveness, but this was all gone. Left was the face of a pale, hollowed out being whose eyes reflected nothing but hatred and the vacancy of any form of emotion. "How could you leave your poor mother? You never even let me try to change or love you the way a mother should love a son." Her voice grew syrupy and saccharine.

The group's chanting got louder and as it reached a frightening level, the windows of the car wobbled and the locks on the doors shook. The windows started to open and snake-like fingers made their way into the vehicle. They tormented Danny by grabbing his hair and clothing. Danny prayed out loud. "Holy, heavenly God! What is it you expect of me?" Danny edged himself to the middle of the car as his mother's hand grabbed at his hair. "My heart is torn. You, God, are the one who made me. She, on the other hand gave me life." Out of nowhere, a young man all dressed in white and gleaming with brilliant light was seated next to him.

"Put your foot on the gas, man, and let's go!" Danny, startled by this sudden appearance and trying to decide which was more terrifying, the stranger surrounded by bright light or the devils outside the car, slid back into the driver's seat and pressed his foot so hard against the accelerator that the car tires screeched. Danny screamed in pain as one of the devils struggled to hang on to a handful of his hair. The forward lunge of the car broke the power of the spell and as the car sped away, the force took out a few of the dark infidels, thud . . . thud . . . Danny's body was rigid and stunned. His guts cramped with fear as he felt a putrid relief.

"Who are you?" Danny swallowed hard, ". . . and where . . . how did you get in my car?"

"Calm down, Danny. You need to regain your strength because what you just experienced is a cake walk compared to what lies ahead. Oh, and by the way . . . hi, my name is Gabe Winston."

Danny would have stopped the car but he was too afraid they were being followed by the band of witches. His eyes went from the road to Gabe and his confusion intensified in light of the fact that he was in the presence of a ghost; but he really wasn't a ghost because he had a body. The car was still going as fast as Danny could make it go.

"Listen. You are new to this so you have to catch up to God's infinite abilities to change anything at the drop of a pin, and, uh, you can slow down now. They're gone. When you are in the presence of either one of the Deathlinks or a risen soldier of the Father, you will be safe."

Danny pulled off to the side of the road, stopped the car, took a deep breath and rubbed his hands over his face. Breaking down in hysterical laughter, he calmed down long enough to look at Gabe with new eyes. "You have got to be kidding me. You are Ivy's son? For real? My god, the scriptures were right. The faithful will be raised up on the last day. Whoa . . . man . . . well then . . . that means that *this* is the last day. This is the Apocalypse? I don't know. I don't know if I'm ready for this."

"Well, Danny, you don't have a choice." With that, Gabe gave Danny a slap on the shoulder and disappeared. Danny found himself and the car at the edge of a piece of farmland. Fletch, Ivy, Emily, Joey and Andrew were racing towards him. The sky darkened and off in the distance he could hear a sound like horses running.

"Danny, Danny. We are so glad to see you, darlin'." Emily opened the door of the car and Danny welcomed a true mother's embrace. They all surrounded him so happy to see their youngest recruit alive and well.

"Ivy! I saw Gabe. He was in the car with me just a second ago."

Ivy grabbed Danny. "Gabe, you saw him? Is he all right?"

"He is more than all right, Ivy. He is a saint. He is magic."

Hail poured down from the sky. It once again grew dark as night. The stars fell like fireworks from the heavens and again the moon receded into the cosmos. The sound of horse's hooves pounding the ground got louder. In reminiscence of a terrible dream, Ivy, Fletcher and Emily all joined hands and formed a circle. Ivy held tight to Fletcher's hand. She didn't know how strong she could be anymore.

She would go forward with God's plan, but her body pulsated with fear. They all lifted their souls to heaven and prayed.

Out of the hearts of these few individuals came a prayer to save the earth from certain evil and complete destruction. At their conception they were no greater or blessed than any other man or woman, but they chose the path God laid before them. Somewhere in their lives, perhaps during or after tremendous tragedy, these common souls became uncommon by the sheer will to serve their Creator. It did not make them wealthy, nor did it come easy. They suffered for their faith, but here they were, enduring the most immense task of all; the survival of goodness in all its ordinary ways in the manner only man could perceive it, submerged in the splendor of purity the way God ordained it. The power was theirs to use.

An enormous rumbling came from beneath them. The earth cracked and began to mound. Seven small hills formed within the circle each spreading towards its own target in the group, except for one which remained in the middle. The sound of horses' hooves surrounded them, but they could not see anything. It was dark and deafening. Between the vibrations and the quaking and mounding of the earth beneath them, the faithful group felt each other's grasp loosen. They were separated once again. Their hearts clenched with fear; they only had time to respond to their immediate, individual situations. Neither Deathlinks, nor warrior angels, nor the faithful that had been raised from the dead were anywhere to be found. Even in this most critical time, God had his own clock.

Of course evil plays by no fair rules, so the first mound grew quickest under Danny. Danny was tossed around in the dirt as it increased in size. The small hill became a very large hill with Danny on its peak. He was bound and wrapped by a thin, wispy spirit. As it spoke, the volume of the spirit's voice resounded throughout the seven hills.

"You are with me because you envy others for what they have. I am the god of envy. I have planted myself in your heart and you have felt malice for others because you wanted to be better than them. In your art, Danny, yes in your art and you wanted their families, didn't you Danny? You wanted to escape the life you had with the Princess Winifred. The only reason you became a follower of God was to think yourself better than everyone else. Isn't that right, Danny?"

Danny twisted and turned in the clutches of the frail specter. Every movement Danny made tightened the strands of curious, indistinct string. He heard the others screaming in horrible pain. This distracted him and made him lose his concentration. Winifred's spirit oozed out of the ethereal prison that disabled him.

"Danny, my dearest son, come over to my side. Listen to the pain that the others are feeling. Where is your precious God now? He will not save you. He is a god of lies. He allows suffering, hunger, home-lessness. These are all of the things that you despise, so why join a god that shows no mercy?" Winifred was face to face with Danny. She grew close to kiss him when he heard Ivy scream.

"Danny, remember God's word! Never abandon hope; always do everything out of love and you must have faith!"

Words of wisdom came spewing from Danny's mouth. "But if in your heart you are jealous, bitter, selfish, don't sin against the truth by boasting of your wisdom. Such wisdom does not come down from heaven, it belongs to the world, and it is unspiritual and demonic. Where there is jealousy and selfishness, there is also disorder and every kind of evil. Because God loves me, I love you, Mother." Winifred screeched with horror and vanished. The binding grip of the spirit loosened.

Making her way up the hill was Marie, one of Emily's beloved Deathlinks. This was her chance to be the mother she had not been because of her act of selfishness. As she struggled to free Danny from the vicious hold of envy, she prayed out loud, "Parents, do not treat your children in such a way as to make them angry. Instead, raise them with Christian discipline and instruction." The hill of evil collapsed and the phantoms dissipated into tiny particles, leaving Marie and Danny to face the fighting that had commenced on the ground.

Emily's Deathlinks banded together in small groups of seven or eight. Holding hands they either sang the Psalms or recited scripture in unison. Every time a demon came too close to a Deathlink the demon was destroyed. Marie, who completed her final mission as a Deathlink, glowed with a beautiful white light. Demons tried to attack them, but exploded on impact. As promised, the word of God was their armor and their strength. Danny and Marie took their place in one of the circles.

The risen faithful were everywhere. There were hundreds of them standing by themselves radiating the white light of the heavens and filled with the graces of the Holy Spirit. Demonic forces tried to stab them with daggers or swords, but nothing could touch them. Instead of piercing them with the blade, as soon as the blade touched the light, the devil exploded, or melted or dissolved into ash.

It was clear the heaviest battles were being fought on the hills where Satan's band of horsemen swarmed around waiting for their chance for just one weakness to permit them to bring down the reign of God. Emily, Fletch, Ivy, Joey and Andrew remained under deep spiritual and emotional attack. Soulful agony belabored their every breath. Little did they know that with them lay the most important battles for the kingdom.

Once again a booming voice came down from one of the hills. "Hear yourself, preacher! *Why did you die? Why did you go through all of that torture and pain? We still have the same bastards on earth as you did centuries ago!* Hear your anger with the God Almighty. You are no better than what I, the god of anger, want you to be. Don't trick yourself into believing that you are one of God's faithful. You are nothing but a hypocritical, weak and shattered soul. You question Him all of the time. Guess what, my dear Fletcher. You are right!"

Fletcher realized his guilt reminded by the words spoken to him.

He recollected countless times when he was angry with God. The demon was right. He questioned the Lord all of the time. As Fletch questioned his faith, he started to hallucinate. The demon's strength clutched harder around his body. Memories inundated his consciousness and he remembered his rages, most of them aimed at God. When he saw innumerable injustices while he was a pastor it distressed him and he blamed God. When Kathy died, he blamed God. When little Annie was abused by her own father, he blamed God. Perhaps the demon was right. Maybe he was no better than the evil that bound him now. So immersed in self-doubt, Fletch didn't see the soldiers climbing up the hill. Sister Kathy and Michael Harrison were singing Psalms as they climbed. The demon hill kept trying to plow them under, but with every word of truth came a sure step closer to Fletch's rescue.

"Fletcher, don't give up. Here I am. I am alive because God has raised me from the dead just as he said he would. Where is your heart, Fletch? Dig down deep and pull out your courage. Use your anger for something useful like getting us out of this."

Fletch yelled at the top of his lungs, "I know that my God loves me, and His will is my will." The demon Anger groaned and the hill stopped churning. Fletch turned to see his friends.

Kathy reached the top of the hill followed by Michael. They put their arms around Fletcher and began to pray. "Never take revenge, my friends, but instead let God's anger do it. For the scripture says, 'I will take revenge, I will pay back, says the Lord.'" The demon shrieked with disdain. The earth crumbled beneath them and they fell into a tremendous heap of dirt. Fletch, still in a daze, turned to Kathy and Michael.

"So you want to tell me what took you so long?"

"Get up, and find a circle." Kathy admonished Fletch while pushing him towards a group of Deathlinks. A demon swooped down swiping Fletch on the shoulder with a dagger, drawing blood.

"Ouch, crap. All right, already. Dearest Lord, give us the strength."

"We still have a lot of work to do. And don't get out of the circle of prayer. That is your only defense." Kathy went off with Michael as they dodged several hideous creatures trying to grab at their legs, but were burned by the white light that surrounded the faithful soldiers.

Fletcher yelled at Kathy, "Yeah, well, I wish I had that special glow about me."

"Shut up and pray, or you might just get your wish."

He looked up to see the rumbling of yet another hill. This one while eerie also carried a stench with it. On its very needle point top, Ivy clung to a tiny strand that had no apparent substance. It was all illusion. Ivy hallucinated with acid flash backs. She thought she had them licked, but here they were again, back to haunt her. As she dangled by her wrists from the peak of this slimy, rank pile of rocks and dirt, music surrounded her; lifeless music that rattled her insides with the memory of the sins of lust and deceit she committed long ago.

Everyone on the ground heard the swaggering voice as it taunted Ivy. "Welcome to my party, you sexy thing you." Lucifer decided to join the god of lust in his torment. His pomposity hovered around her still sitting on his black horse. Ivy screamed at the sight of the being that raped her and impregnated her with Gabe. But then she remembered Gabe, and his relentless love for God and she was strengthened.

"You have no power over me. You had no power over my son and you will certainly fail at your feeble attempt to overthrow the Creator of the universe."

"Quiet, slut! You know, I forgot just how much you loved to be visited by the offspring of my incubus." With this, Lucifer snapped his fingers and snakes crawled out from the rocks. The music intensified. The snakes wrapped themselves around Ivy's legs, and slithered up her skirt. Ivy screamed with disgust and fear. Lucifer continued, "You should really examine your conscience thoroughly. Are you sure you didn't like all of those things that I did to you? Come on, let's do it. Let's make another little devil. You were a pretty active party girl if I remember correctly. Relax. Let your body feel the excitement in their movement."

The god of lust stroked Ivy's face and hair with long, grisly fingers. Ivy shrieked with fear as she fell under a spell. Supernatural power imprisoned her thinking. Maybe she was just a slut. Maybe for all those years she just hid her real self from the world for her son's sake. Then Ivy saw Gabe's sweet face. She heard him whisper, "Pray for help, Mother. God will bring you angels."

Ivy took a deep breath, ". . . let the Spirit direct your lives, and you will not satisfy the desires of human nature. For what our human nature wants is opposed to what the Spirit wants, and what the Spirit wants is opposed to what our human nature wants. Holy God, help me. Deliver me from the hands of this evil. Send your angels through the name of your Son, Jesus."

Angels filled the air. The sounds of the baneful music ceased and celestial music rejoiced as Michael the Archangel galloped out of the mist surrounding the hill and charged at Lucifer. The hill disintegrated leaving Ivy resting on the ground protected by an angelic legion. High in the sky the battle continued with the angel Michael lunging at Lucifer again and again, until the Prince of Darkness retreated into an abyss which shielded him until the next battle.

All around Ivy, there were countless dead. These were the bodies of people who had not shielded themselves with God's goodness. Selfishness was their habit and when it came time to exude spiritual goodness and integrity, they did not know how. The angels left her by herself and she saw there was much fighting still going on. Besieged with fear, her soul only wanted to please God, but her body could not stop shaking. She wondered what Gabe was doing in this time of horror. Ivy sat down on the ground. A beautiful white light came toward her and out of the light stepped her son. Ivy jumped up and ran to him. His arms were wide open and as he caught her, Ivy realized that God was indeed merciful. "Gabe. Oh, my beautiful son. Is it really you? I was afraid that I would never see you again." Tears flowed down Ivy's face from gladness. He was beautiful because he was filled with the grace of God, but Ivy was just happy to see her son again.

"Mother, you did it. Now you have to stay in a circle with the Deathlinks and pray until this war is finally over. Come with me, I have just the right place for you." Gabe took Ivy to the circle where Fletcher was praying and there they stayed until the final battle.

Four hills remained. Upon three of them were mystified and frightened soldiers. Andrew always prided himself on the fact that he didn't need anyone in his life. His home life taught him that. Perhaps this is why he was such an accomplished soldier. During his reflection of his very capable skills he wandered the mountain. There were no constraints to hold him and he questioned the reason for being there. Deep down, he felt they would need his help on the battlefield and maybe that's why Satan had him isolated on this mountain. While he was patting himself on the back for being such a good man, a man of God, and a good son, something seized him and pinned him up against a canyon wall. Scenes of his life paraded before him.

"What the . . ." Andrew was in complete amazement for there before him was Aneliese. As he watched, his heart burned. Aneliese was the one woman in his life that he loved and who had loved him without reservation. She waited for him for five years. She supported him in everything that he wanted to do, but when the time came for him to surrender his pride and give himself to her in marriage, he backed away. Aneliese went her own way and he ignored his loneliness ever since. Pride replaced any need for companionship. He convinced himself God wanted him to remain alone because life had better plans for Andrew Walker than that of a mere mortal. God wanted him to walk with saints.

The walls of the mountain groaned. "You will stay here for eternity. You will have your wish and you will be alone, but not with your God. Prideful men fall heavily among sinful men. If you cannot love another human being on a human level, then you will never love mankind on God's level. You, Andrew Walker, belong to us."

Andrew fell to his knees. Prayer was not going to save his soul from damnation. Repentance was his only choice. "Father, I now see the many gifts of love you have sent my way and that I have spurned because of my arrogance. How could I believe you loved me more than you loved any other person? My service to you was only elevated in my eyes not in yours. I'm sorry because I refused your gifts of human love and I have avoided emotional involvements that would bring me closer to you by helping me live the life of a human, not a god. 'I know that you ask of me; only this, to act justly, to love tenderly, and to walk humbly with you, my God.' Almighty warrior, forgive my arrogance and let me fight for the right to live as a man in your holy sight."

Andrew felt a rumbling and then a swift rush of air. The demonic presence disappeared. As he looked up from his position of prayer, a man approached him. He had long dark hair with a beard. He was dressed in army garb, but carried no weapon. The stranger smiled at Andrew and offered him a hand. "Andrew. Why do you ask the Creator for forgiveness?"

"Only my God can forgive me, and where did you come from?"

"This mountain is where I am supposed to be in order to fulfill the legend."

"Have you been taken prisoner, too?"

"No, nor have you."

"Yeah, well, I think that weird creature has a different opinion."

"Look around you. Do you see any malevolent forces or demonic strangers?"

"Only you."

The stranger ignored Andrew's insult and turned to climb back up the mountain path. "Andrew, I need you to help me get to the top of the last mountain. You need to have my back on this one. Are you willing to do that?"

"That depends on who you are exactly." The man turned toward Andrew. His eyes pierced Andrew's disbelief.

Andrew gasped as the gaze touched his soul and he fell to his knees. "Oh my, God. The Son of Wankan Tanka. I get it."

Putting his hands on Andrew's head, he said, "I told you before, you have been groomed to walk along side me during this final battle. The last hill has no one to pray from within. It represents all of the small sins created by mankind which grew into much greater and harmful desecrations against the Creator. These sins have been ignored." Jesus helped Andrew to his feet and they began to climb.

"Lord, to what sins are you referring?"

"The ones perpetuated by those who call themselves "Christian", but who have no better idea of how to represent my teachings than those who never had a scripture to follow in the first place. One grievous sin is judging others because they think that as Christians they have the right to do so - this simply because they have rewritten scripture to suit their lives. Another is speaking unkindly of those who do not share the same religion and then damning them to hell on their own authority. How dare these so called Christians assume that the Creator will only recognize them at the gates of heaven?" Jesus started to scale the side of the mountain with greater purpose and Andrew struggled to keep up. "The Father is omnipotent in every respect and that includes His abundant love for all who strive to be close to Him. There are those who see only Him, serve only Him and do not know me, but this does not mean that eternal life in heaven will be denied them. Oh, yes, there is one more sin which is my personal favorite; casting fellow believers out of churches because the judgmental faction of that flock believes that their brethren have sinned. What is the purpose of having a place to commemorate my teachings if the sinners are not welcomed and forgiven? All of these are sins that fight against the collective consciousness of goodness and purity which is the universal and almighty Creator."

Andrew was in awe of this man and now he was to stand beside Him during the final battle. "My Lord, I am not worthy, but I am here for you."

Jesus stopped and turned to look at Andrew. "I don't know why you all say that. You are all worthy of God's love."

"Wow. O - okay."

Jesus and Andrew made it to the top of the hill and Jesus took Andrew by the hand and the hill that they were on crashed to the earth. As it hit the ground, there was a demon launching a frontal attack. Upon recognition of the presence before it, the demon shrieked in terror and exploded.

"Guess he's having a pretty bad day." Andrew smirked, and in admiration he ran behind Jesus to the unmanned hill.

Upon the fifth hill, Joey Cercione found himself tied to a boulder. His head was unable to move from side to side. The god of gluttony kept forcing food into Joey's mouth. Joey tried to blow it out, but the devil kept shoveling more and more into his face. The demon stopped and said, "Mr. Joseph Cercione; the big vegetable gardener; the great Italian cook. You like to eat, right? You like to garden, right? You do everything in excess in order to forget your wife and daughter. You build things, but you don't stop to build relationships. And now you have this obsession with God. Everything is an obsession with you, everything except the things that matter most; which is very good, because that is why you belong here with me. You see, we need at least one hill remaining in order for us to win this war with Him and my bet is on you."

"You're full of it. I know what really matters. I love Emily and I know that she loves me."

"You think? Don't be so sure that you know what's what. Besides, she may not make it through the rest of this war. We have a special surprise cooked up for her; something that she would never expect. Now, let's get back to you. How about you just surrender and we'll get together and . . ."

"Ahhhhh! I will not allow you to hurt her." Joey struggled against the restraints that held him to the rock. He finally centered himself and meditated on scripture. *Get rid of your old self, which made you live as you used to - the old self that was being destroyed by its deceitful desires.*

The spirit swirled around Joey trying to tighten the constraints that bound him, but Joey kept his focus. *Oh, Lord, You are my strength. Without You I can do nothing. Please, bring me closer to you by allowing me the privilege of loving Emily.*

Joey was released from bondage. He rode the hill down to the ground. The hill was leveled out and there he was face down in the dirt. He noticed a gleaming white light. He turned and rose to his knees to be standing face to face with none other than Angela. "Angela! Angie, it's true. God has raised the faithful. Where is your mother?"

"Mama stayed behind in heaven. She is happy there, Daddy. She did not want to come back with me. Can you understand that?"

"Yeah, sure, I guess. But look at you. Look how beautiful you are." Out of the sky came a flying demon who tried to strike at Joey. Angela put her arm up to protect him and the demon immediately disintegrated.

"Daddy, you need to find a circle of prayer with the Deathlinks. They need the strength of many to overcome the evil that holds the earth captive. I'll take you to one." Angela took Joey's big hand in her little one and led him to a prayer circle. Then she walked off in a fog of serenity, fielding devil attacks with the ease of an angel.

In the middle of the field there were only two hills left. Joey looked on, wondering which one held captive his beloved Emily. Emily was the only soldier left. There were two hills remaining and one had no one to pray from within. Victory still seemed too hard to predict.

Emily stood hopeless and frightened midway up the hill. What did the master of deception have planned for her next? Above her floated a light mist that kept moving up and down and around her body. She did not feel any hostility from it, yet she knew never to trust anything supernatural until it showed itself. It took shape. Instead of the white mist that seemed to offer no threat, a great dark figure loomed over her. "Did you ever stop to think, Emily, that you wanted sex? First, the rape and then the nasty, loveless relationship you had with your husband?"

What was this apparition talking about? Her life was innocent and pure before Bentley came to steal it from her. As for James, she did not see him coming. She tried to be the best wife she could, even though James fought love and emotion throughout their marriage. But maybe she wasn't the pure sweet woman she perceived herself to be. She often wondered how her sex life with James could have been so satisfying, when she had lost any worthwhile romantic love for him early into the marriage. Perhaps there was more to her than she was willing to acknowledge.

She tried to walk down the hill, but every time she did malice filled the air building an impenetrable barrier leaving no other alternative but to climb higher up the mountain. Each step was more and more arduous. Her stomach churned. Her forehead moistened with every step. Her dress was damp under the stress of the climb. Her shoulders began to droop under a terrific weight, and as she climbed, her left ankle began to hurt. It did this off and on for the last five years, but she just attributed it to varicose veins. But now, the pain was pounding like a hammer. James, it was James. She felt him grab her and throw her down on the floor. He was kicking her again and again. He kept kicking her in the ankle over and over even though his rage prevented him from seeing where he was inflicting the blows. She fell to the ground under the weight of the memory. Heaving gulps retched in her stomach and as she retched, abominable, tormented spirits spilled out of her mouth, shrieking and groaning. Emily lay on the ground exhausted from the release of such a horrible memory; one that she had hidden even from herself. Still, the trip up the hill was not over.

Once again the dark evil surrounded her, pulling her to her feet. She tripped up the hill, drained from endless memories that inundated her mind causing pain and distress. Her back and upper arms grew tender to the touch. The hateful evil tracking her journey kept poking her with long, frightful fingers. Again, her mind revealed a past beating from James that she had wiped from her memory. He was hitting her over and over again on her back and her arms with his fists. Clenched in his fists were his own agonizing recollections of indignities and molestations. He was unmerciful with each blow and each blow was filled with his own personal pain, which Emily took from him in the form of physical and emotional abuse. James passed on the evil essences that pervaded his own soul and they were quite content to settle within Emily and unaware of their existence, she did nothing to purge them. She only remembered she had shielded Andrew from his father's rage by enfolding him in her arms to protect him, so she bore the brunt of each impact with her back and arms. She needed to keep Andrew safe. After the memory ceased, Emily fell to the ground and the retching in her stomach began again. Out of her mouth spewed miserable, screaming spirits that drenched the ground with black, stagnant bile. She lay there, with labored breathing, trying to regain some dignity.

The great and dark apparition floated over Emily's weary body and once more dragged her to her feet. This time the horrible pain of arthritis swelled in her hands. Arthritis plagued her hands for many years now, but it seemed to come and go. Rubbing her hands together, as she always did to make the pain subside; she made the tedious climb, putting one foot in front of the other. When Bentley raped her, he took away choices. Those choices could have made a big difference in future decisions. After James died, she was obsessed with filling the void left by the pain he inflicted. In doing this, her need for a relationship became paramount. She would do God's work, but there was always that underlying emptiness and loneliness. This emptiness was just another thing out of her control. With each hour spent alone out of helplessness, her hands ached, just as they did now. Only now the pain throbbed in every joint of every finger. Her wrists were inflamed with intermittent spasms and when she tried to make a fist, they were stiff and did not move.

Enduring great pain, Emily reached the top of the hill. Down below, the war was raging. Deathlinks and all manner of faithful were in prayer circles, singing and praying and quoting sacred scriptures. Catholics were reciting the rosary. Quotes were flying from not only the Christian Bible but from the Qur'an and the Alkitab Alaqdas, the Tripitaka and Bhagavad-Gita, while Native Americans chanted traditional spiritual prayer and Jewish faithful prayed through the Torah. They split these circles into two great ones, each encircling the two remaining hills. Angels on white horses filled the sky doing battle with the dark soldiers of Satan. God's faithful that had passed were on the ground surrounded by blinding white light. Every time a demon became overconfident in their power, they would try to attack one of these and the demon exploded upon contact. With the demise of every demon a loud crack of thunder shook the earth and a flash of lightening lit up the sky. The feeble and impure souls of the unfaithful had no armor to protect them. Some of them tried to speak words of God, but they did not understand them because they never afforded themselves the time to learn goodness. Dark demons preyed on them first for they were easy. They terrorized them and then slaughtered them. One after another they were murdered saturating the ground with their blood.

Emily, her arms outstretched amid the thunder and lightning, the wails of defeated devils, the screaming of the unarmed children of God, and the endless explosions of demons, cried, "My God, where are you? The evil in my life has concealed itself deep within my heart. I thought too well of myself and in doing so refused your healing grace. Emotional pain and mental torment have manifested themselves in my body. They cannot, Almighty God, be hidden from you, the Creator of the universe. Heal my body, Lord. Heal my soul!"

From the base of the final hill, Andrew heard his mother's voice and felt her loneliness and pain. He looked at Jesus whose eyes filled with tears as He identified with the same pain felt by a son for his mother. Jesus lifted his hands up and a great light pierced the sky. Billowing clouds rolled through the atmosphere and as the light traveled through the heavens, many of the demons met their demise. Magnificent bursts of light surrounded each as they exploded filling the air with smoke. Emily's hill fell to the ground. She found her way to Joey who was already running towards her and they joined the Deathlinks and all of the faithful in looking to the final hill. During the mayhem, Jesus and Andrew began the climb up the last hill.

The hill groaned. Demons flew around it, guarding it. When any of the demons flew close to the areas where Jesus climbed, they lost altitude and balance and fell to the ground. Lucifer sat upon his black steed at the top of the hill. He called out to his son. "Gabriel! You still have a chance to reign over the universe with your father. You may bring your mother with you if you wish."

Fletch had to hold Ivy back. On a winged white horse, Gabe, without pause, rushed to the hill. "For the last time you are not my father. The Alpha and the Omega caused my existence and after we take this last hill filled with injustice and conceit, the universe will live in the Creator's pure collective consciousness, which does not include you and your evil."

Gabe was surrounded by flying demons. Lucifer swooped down to meet him. He swung his sword nicking the bright light that encircled Gabe. Lucifer's wings were singed by a fierce fire that sprung out of the light. He dropped down, hissing and then regained stability. The accompanying demons hissed and growled, but their ferocious demeanor was lessened by fear.

Meanwhile, Andrew and Jesus climbed the backside of the hill. The pure presence of Jesus was felt by both Gabe and Lucifer; strengthening

Gabe and distracting Lucifer. This was an odd entrance for the Son of God to make on this long awaited day of existence, but effective.

Lucifer addressed Gabe, "You know that your people cannot fight me with anything but mere words. Now that we are face to face, what do you have to say for yourself, son?"

"The word of God is weapon enough. You are the one who should be worried. Your way has not succeeded. Look around you. There are very few of your evil sycophants left to help you defeat God, and have you forgotten that you still must face Jesus? This is what I have to say to you before you are obliterated. Your arrogance and perversions are merely evil. They don't frighten the pure of heart and they don't carry great authority. The simplest and meekest soul carries its own source of power if it is pure. Now, you, get ready to meet your maker."

Lucifer's attention to Gabe was diverted and he groaned a great, heaving groan from the depths of his black soul. "Where is He? I feel His presence, but why does the Son of Man hide from me?"

"I am here." Jesus stepped up to the top of the hill. Brilliant light surrounded Him and all bowed to His majesty. The remaining devils exploded sending their final screams into the atmosphere. Deafening booms were heard throughout the world for the demise of each remaining demon.

Gabriel, because his part in the Almighty's plan was completed, flew his winged horse down to be with Ivy. He held her hand and she held Fletcher's. Next to him Sister Kathy stood with Michael, Claire, Aaron and Jacob Harrison, and, of course, Grace. Rosemary, who had a little cherub hovering over her, stood with Jason and Marie. They all huddled together accompanied by Danny and Venus. Uncle Zeb's corn field was filled with people; dead, alive again, saints once sinners, always saints and some who were recycled through the efforts of good and godly hearts.

Andrew, who knelt behind Jesus, raised his voice and said, "We who are strong in purity ought to help the weak to carry their burdens.

We should not please ourselves. Instead, we should all please other believers for their own good, in order to build them up. For Christ did not please himself." With that, the final hill fell to the ground leaving Jesus floating high in the sky above the massive destruction below.

From far away, the sound of trumpets could be heard. The horned proclamations intensified, until they reached such magnificent proportions that the world stopped and all focused on one single being. The Son of Man still clothed in army camouflage and very much human, hovered overhead with His arms stretched forward to the faithful in victory over evil. But Lucifer, who had eluded extinction thus far and filled with conceit, charged at Jesus. In one ludicrous gesture, Lucifer committed the final act of suicide in heaven and on earth as he ran headlong into the brilliant light of Jesu Christe. The earth shook with the colossal blast. Smoke hung thick in the air and everyone on the ground searched through the lingering smog for any sign of the Son of God. Jesus, transformed into His radiant and glorious spirit, emerged unscathed. Cheers of relief and adoration filled the atmosphere above the humble Alabama farmland, and the deserts of Egypt, the streets of Europe, the plains of Africa, and the whole world watched in wonder while a flawless white cloud floated beneath the Son of Man and carried him high above the crowd. The sacred prophecy was fulfilled. He took his rightful place as ruler of heaven and earth where hell no longer existed and the universe, because of the pure collective consciousness of all followers of its Creator would at last and forever be at peace. Evil no longer exists where purity is power.

"*Then afterward I will pour out*
my spirit upon all mankind.
Your sons and daughters shall prophesy,
your old men shall   dream -dreams,
your young men shall see visions;
Even upon the servants and the handmaids,
in those days, I will pour out my Spirit.

And I will work wonders in the heavens
and on the earth, blood, fire, and columns of smoke;
The sun will be turned to darkness,
and the moon to blood, at the coming of the
day of the Lord, the great and terrible day.

Then everyone shall be rescued who calls on
the name of the Lord; For on Mount Zion there
shall be a remnant, as the Lord has said,
And in Jerusalem survivors whom the Lord shall call."

Joel 3:1

References

Living Waters: The New Testament in Today's English Version. 1993. American Bible Society, New York, NY.

Saint Joseph Edition of *The New American Bible*. 1991. Catholic Book Publishing Co. New York, NY

Taylor, Terry Lynn and Mary Beth Crain. *Angel Wisdom*. 1994. Harper, San Francisco, CA

CPSIA information can be obtained at www.ICGtesting.com
Printed in the USA
BVOW06s2246230815

414597BV00016B/180/P